ALSO [

KATYA NOSKOV'S LAST SHOT

DANA GOLDSTEIN

Publisher's Note: This book is a work of fiction. Names, characters, places and incidents either are a product of the author's imagination or are use fictitiously, and any resemblance to actual persons living or dead, events, or locales is entirely coincidental.

ISBN 9781778147166 (softcover) | ISBN 9781778147173 (EPUB)

Cover art and design by Julie Boake, Awedity Creative

To all women of a certain age:
I see you.

ONE

S tanding over the body, Kat forced a short breath out of her nose. When she breathed in again, the smell of chemicals and bodily fluids flooded her nostrils. Blood was everywhere in the pool house, splattered on the wooden planks of the ceiling, peppered over the kayaks mounted on the walls, and staining the rubber tiles on the floor.

What a complete fuck-up.

This kill was not supposed to go so wrong. She'd watched the mark for weeks, as she usually did. She took note of his habits, his schedule, the kind of food he ate on business lunches and whether they made him sluggish or energetic. He went places she should have known well but didn't, despite having chosen Portland as her base more than thirty years ago.

Three weeks ago, Kat had waited at the Palm Court Bar in downtown's Benson Hotel lobby, sipping a tall shot of Beluga Noble vodka as she watched him flirt with, then escort, the most attractive woman in the bar into the elevator. She wondered, for a moment, if his wife knew he was cheating. Kat didn't care one way or another. All men either dipped or thought about dipping their wick into some random stranger.

And in her experience, women were not much different. They were just slightly more discerning about who they spread their legs for.

The next day, she followed her mark to the gym, waiting in her car until he came back out so she could assess how he moved before and after exertion. She watched him eyeball a group of four schoolgirls pass him on the sidewalk. Her stomach turned when he licked his lips, ogling these children from behind. This would be a satisfying kill.

This job had come via the dark web, as most did. It was a brief request, with only a name, an address, and simple instructions: *Make it look like suicide. And not inside the house, please.* Kat was sure it came from a woman. Men were always more callous with their murderous requests and did not care about the mess.

She had all the pieces in place for this kill, except for one nagging detail: She hadn't been able to clearly identify the wife. She pushed her concern aside; this was a simple job, and the mark was a despicable human being. Only once over her month-long surveillance had she seen the wife outside the house. From three houses down and across the street, Kat watched her emerge from the passenger side of her husband's custom pearl-painted white 2023 BMW X3. The woman's face was obscured by a hoodie and dark sunglasses, but the way her shoulders slumped and torso curled over itself as she shuffled to the house were sure signs of an abused woman.

I'm doing you a favor, friend.

She wasn't concerned about the wife. Abused women were never an issue in the after. It did not matter to Kat precisely how the woman's life would play out; it would inevitably be much improved by the removal of her vile husband.

What *was* her concern now was the mess in the pool house. There was nothing left of the top half of the mark's head. The angles of his jaw slackened, as they do after a natural death, but also after the cheek muscles holding them in place have been blown away.

What the fuck happened?

Kat played it all over in her mind again. She'd crouched behind the row of full-grown Japanese maples edging the ravine at the end of the property. Her legs were warm in her hiking pants, her boots barely muddy despite the March rains. She had a clear view across the hundred-foot lawn to the rear of the two-story house. The entire back side was made up of windows to take advantage of the vast landscape. The wife moved slowly through the kitchen, keeping the island between her and her husband, head down to avoid any confrontation. Kat winced and ignored her own rage when he grabbed her hair and backhanded her, spitting on her as she fell unconscious to the floor.

Her mark emerged from the back of the house, striding with purpose past the covered pool. When he slid open the glass doors of the pool house and walked inside, she made her move. She kicked through the debris of mushy leaves and pushed past the trees. Without waiting, she took aim. As she put pressure on the trigger, her scope went out of focus. Her shot went low, and instead of puncturing the flesh on the side of his head and lodging into his brain, it took off the top of his left ear. He screamed, and she reacted, sprinting up the lawn.

Now inside the pool house, she pushed him against the back wall, jammed the gun inside his mouth, and pulled the trigger again. His body jerked and blood and flesh sprayed everywhere, but at least the missing part of the ear—evidence of her failure—was obliterated. She let gravity pull him down to a natural position.

Satisfied the kill looked like a suicide, Kat wrapped his still-flexible fingers loosely around the grip of the gun. She scanned the pool house, finding the stray bullet lodged in a kickboard, the Styrofoam melted from the heat. Tucking the board under her arm, Kat casually walked back to the tree line, disappearing into the ravine. She pushed through the ferns and weeds until she found the creek she'd noticed earlier.

"Damn it," she hissed, noticing the blood splatter on her brand-new boots and down the front of her pants. Blood and brains flecked her fleece jacket, but she was going to burn that ugly thing, along with the kickboard. She peeled off her latex gloves and crouched down, her knees cracking and popping, then brought her hands to her face, washing the remains of the mark from her skin.

Touching the downy fuzz along the edges of her cheeks, Kat felt wet flecks—maybe blood, maybe something else—stuck there. She rubbed roughly, cursing the postmenopausal facial hair she suddenly woke up with one morning. She looked at the back of her hands as she plunged them into the creek, wishing the lines she saw were caused by the ripples of the water but knowing full well they weren't. If she could turn the clock back twenty years to her forties, she would have moisturized more.

She pulled the auburn wig off as she climbed up the other side of the ravine, shaking it to disperse the pink bits clinging to the hair. Her car was still the only one at the trailhead. She unzipped the fleece and threw it into a black garbage bag in the back, along with the wig and kickboard. She sat on the lip of the open hatch, her legs stretched out in front of her.

What happened back there?

On the eight-mile drive from Southwest Hills to her bungalow in southeast Portland, she again replayed everything in her mind. Her hands were steady, and the mark had been barely moving. It was an easy target, but her shot went wild. The scope had gone fuzzy at the last second. *Must be something wrong with the gun*, she told herself sternly.

Kat stripped down in the shower, using her foot to push her clothes to the corner. She let the hot water wash over her head and face, the steam opening her pores. She picked up the luxurious new exfoliating scrub she'd treated herself to a few days ago, turning the pot to read the instructions. The words were so tiny. She moved closer to the shower's glass door where the light spilled in. She extended her arm, but the words barely came into focus. And then it hit her.

There was nothing wrong with the gun.

TWO

A trip to the eye doctor confirmed what she suspected. After a lifetime of twenty-twenty vision, age had caught up with her.

The optometrist had been glib about Kat getting to her sixties without her eyesight degrading, but all she could think about was how much her life was going to change.

"You've been lucky," he remarked, handing her a prescription for reading glasses. "For most people, presbyopia starts in their forties. You must have good genes."

"Can I get laser surgery to fix this?"

He shook his head. "You can, but there are risks. Your ability to judge how close or far away things are may get worse, or you may suddenly have trouble seeing things that are farther away. Reading glasses are your best and safest bet."

At a garbage can outside the optometry clinic, Kat crumpled the prescription. She violently flung it at the rim, and missed. She picked it up, crushing the paper into a tight ball, tossing it again. It bounced off the edge and landed at her feet with a silent plop. Kat sighed, smoothed out the prescription, and squinted at the scrawled numbers. Maybe she would hang on to this, just in case.

As she slid behind the wheel of her sporty Lexus, anger flooded her veins. The enormity of this change hit her hard. When you have to pause for a moment to get your glasses, not only is it humiliating, but your career as an assassin is over. She would no longer be able to make split-second decisions. If she could not rely on clear vision, she could wind up missing a mark who could turn on her. She was lucky that the last job was just an abusive asshole and not a high-ranking gang member. She'd be dead if he'd been armed himself.

Kat headed out of downtown, hitting the highway that would take her to the rural roads. She needed to drive without distraction and think about her next move. Her heart started pounding when she saw the blue and red lights flashing behind her. She glanced at her speedometer, confirming she was flying at 130 miles per hour. Kat considered flexing her foot heavily onto the gas pedal and trying to outrun the police. She would lose, but it would be fun to try. She opened the sunroof, gave the pedal a bit more pressure, and drove for another half mile, enjoying the chase.

The sirens screamed behind her, drowning out her own laughter. When she finally decided to pull over, the police car pulled in behind her, lights still flashing. Kat kept her hands on the steering wheel, flexing and relaxing, her skin smoothing, then wrinkling with the motion. In her rearview mirror, she watched the officer get out of the cruiser, hike up her duty belt, and adjust it over her slim hips.

Kat rolled down her window, license and registration already in hand. The quiet burst of adrenaline peaked and flooded her veins. Her heart hammered beneath her breastbone.

"Good afternoon, ma'am. Do you know why I pulled you over today?"

Kat turned to look at the officer standing by her open window, close enough so she could see inside the car, but far enough away in case Kat pulled a weapon. She looked like she was barely old enough to have finished high school, but to Kat's sixty-three-year-old eyes, everyone looked like a baby.

"I have a bit of a lead foot." She grinned. "I know I was speeding. I'm not going to play stupid."

"Fifty over the speed limit," the officer said, not returning the smile. "License and registration, please." Kat handed her the documents. "What's the rush?"

Kat shrugged. "No rush. Just open road and some great music. I have no excuse, officer."

As Kat watched the officer walk back to her cruiser, her high dissipated. Nothing incriminating would turn up on the officer's search. Every speeding ticket, every late fee at the video store, every plane ticket ever purchased were all purged from her identity. All the officer would see was the same address for the last thirty years and two vehicle registrations.

"Katya Noskov ... from Russia?" the officer asked when she came back to Kat's car.

"Uzbekistan, actually," Kat corrected. "People say we all sound alike." She made no effort to keep the sarcasm out of her voice, but the officer didn't take the bait.

"Where you headed?"

"Book club," Kat lied.

"Must be some book," the officer said, a smile tugging at the corner of her lips.

"It was garbage, actually."

"What was the book?"

Now it was Kat's turn to smirk. "*How to Murder Your Husband*. True crime."

The officer threw her head back and laughed, but Kat saw her eyes flick down, checking for a ring on her left hand.

"It wouldn't happen to be an instruction manual, would it?"

Kat shrugged. "Well, she got caught, so ..."

The officer held Kat's gaze for a moment. Then she looked up over the roof of the car before turning her face to the empty road ahead. Kat watched the tight edge of her jaw soften.

"I should really make more time to read," the officer said, locking eyes with Kat. "Take it easy out there," she scolded, handing Kat her identification, "and have fun at your book club." She knocked twice on the roof and walked to her cruiser.

Kat cautiously pulled back onto the highway, swallowing the hurt of defeat. She had wanted a ticket, craved one, actually. She ran her hand through her recently shortened brown hair. When the sun caught the strands of gray, Kat considered stopping for some box dye before she went home. Perhaps after a lifetime of wearing wigs and continually changing her look, she could be fine with letting her natural colors come through.

With nothing but road ahead, Kat turned up the music as loud as her eardrums could handle and sang along. She pushed the pedal to the floor, feeling the surge of speed traveling from her toes to her hands.

THREE

K at's phone started vibrating as soon as she pulled into her garage. She answered, listened to the offer, and turned down the job.

Sitting on her couch with her laptop on her knees, she booked an all-inclusive vacation in Costa Rica, then canceled it forty minutes later. She searched for other means of escape, but there were too many places in the world where cartels, mafias, or other crime syndicates had a target on her back.

Instead, she booked a two-hour session at the firing range. From the very first shot, she knew the eye doctor had been right. Her vision was no longer what it used to be. Kat channeled her rage through the barrel, emptying two boxes of ammunition. The clerk behind the counter didn't even blink when she bought another two boxes. By then, she wasn't even trying to aim anymore.

Defeated and frustrated, Kat went home and chased two sleeping pills with a shot of vodka. She took off her clothes and crawled into bed in her bra and panties, burying her head under the sheets. Within a half hour, the world went black.

Kat woke almost thirteen hours later, groggy and still

pissed off. When an assassin retires, there is no party, no cake, no mass email to send out. No one would congratulate her for her contribution to the world. There would be no speech complimenting Katya for her high productivity and success rate.

She had no clue what the rest of her life would look like. For the remainder of the day, she roamed the house. She stood at the front window, watching the movement of cars and people on her street in a neighborhood that was foreign to her because she had spent the last three decades on the move.

What the hell do I do now?

With forty years of an assassin's income in various bank accounts, she could go anywhere and do anything. So that's what she did for the next year. She signed up for solo skydiving, arguing with the instructor who forced her into a tandem dive when she couldn't produce a license. Of course she couldn't tell them she had eighty-two jumps under her belt, sixty-five of those a KGB requirement.

She went to Las Vegas, spending a few thousand dollars driving exotic race cars around a track. She tried a Ferrari, a Lamborghini, a Maserati, and was asked to leave when she pushed the McLaren to its maximum of 200 miles per hour.

Kat flew to Bordeaux, France, to indulge in a zero-gravity flight on an Airbus 310. She giggled like a schoolgirl when she went from sitting on the floor to slowly lifting up and floating. She pushed off the plane walls, soaring effortlessly wherever she wanted to go. It was a magical experience until one of the other passengers threw up and half-digested kale went wherever it wanted to go too.

Her next adventure took her to the ocean for cage diving with sharks. The water was murky and freezing cold, and even the chumming did not bring out the sharks. She was already contemplating how to ask for a refund when a great white emerged from the darkness, swimming right up to the cage.

Kat couldn't tear her eyes away, taking in the triangular teeth and battle-scarred skin.

When she wasn't in the sky or underwater, Kat struggled to find things to keep her busy. She worked on puzzles at her dining room table until the pieces for ten thousand happy little trees made her want to set the thing on fire. She tried her hand at gardening and killed everything she touched. Bingo and cooking classes made her want to put a bullet into her own head. At the lowest point of her desperation, Kat considered singing karaoke or zip-lining on a cruise ship. Retirement was slowly killing her. She really needed to find another way to infuse some excitement back into her life.

Faced with absolutely nothing to do, Kat's anger and resentment dammed up inside her. She searched for an outlet for her restlessness by exploring her creative side but found herself in a pottery studio, throwing clay at the overcurious, patchouli-smelling woman next to her who chattered on like a nervous mark. Kat tried again, signing up for an evening of guided painting at an art supply store, but her efforts at small talk were interrupted by the enthusiastic instructor who sang a medley of Broadway tunes to fill the silence.

Kat pivoted away from people, volunteering at a small animal rescue. She happily took on the assignment of dog walker, but the animals tested her patience with their incessant wandering and compulsive need to smell *everything*. She transferred to the cat side of the shelter but soon discovered she was allergic to their dander. Kat quit, then made an anonymous donation that would cover the shelter's costs for five years.

The community newsletter that arrived in her mailbox monthly was filled with new things Kat felt obligated to try. Yoga made her uncomfortable. She spent more time clamping down her desire to choke the flexible flake on the mat beside her than breathing deeply. After three classes, and some disturbing dreams about losing a knife fight over the last box of Thin Mints being sold by some Girl Scouts in front of a grocery store, she quit. Kat didn't need that kind of negativity in her life.

She attended a seminar about running an e-commerce business, quickly figuring out it was a multi-level marketing scam. Kat stayed for the full three hours, oddly enjoying the bullshit. The lying, thievery, dishonesty, diversion, and deception were traits familiar to her. It was like her whole life, but with top performers earning a free cruise.

"I noticed you have some age spots on your face," a woman she met while mall-walking told her. "Would you like a sample of a cream that would reduce the discoloration?"

"Did you go to school to be an aesthetician?" Kat asked.

"No, but I've watched all the training videos the company provides," the lady answered proudly.

"Do you have evidence this cream works?"

"It's been scientifically proven to reduce the appearance of age spots."

"Probably by the same group who says ejaculate is loaded with vitamin E," Kat said, "but I won't be rubbing my lover's load all over my face."

The lady clutched her hands to her chest, her mouth hanging open in shock.

"Go away," Kat snapped, "before I do something that will leave you with PTSD for the rest of your life. There's no cream for that."

A week later, accepting that maybe she wasn't meant to make friends, a flyer pinned to a bulletin board at the grocery store caught her eye.

Are you looking to add someone special to your life? Do you need to build new relationships with people in your age

group? Come to our monthly 50+ Speed
Dating Nite. Third Tuesday of every
month at Fireside Restaurant.

Pushing aside her distaste for Courier font, Kat decided it was worth a shot.

FOUR

The event hadn't even started, and Kat was already in a bad mood. She circled the parking lot four times, looking for a spot. She had a visual showdown with a man attempting to steal the space she was waiting for. Her signal had been blinking when he swooped around the corner, turning on his own signal like she wasn't sitting there. She glared and stewed, looking for a fight. She would have glee-fully taken a tire iron to his dusty black Tesla and made it a convertible. When he noticed her and cruised by, she felt a twinge of disappointment.

Kat sat in her car for a few moments, practicing her smile in her visor mirror until it became genuine. Genuine enough, anyway. Subterfuge came naturally, but being vulnerable was foreign. She could get through this. She *needed* to get through this. She wasn't looking for love, but a one-night stand with a Viagra-vitalized man could be enough for now.

As Kat moved to climb out of her car, she felt the familiar tug of her knife holster secured to her left thigh. Realizing she'd put it on out of habit, Kat pulled up the hem of her dress and unbuckled the leather strap. She caressed the smooth steel on the hilt, then stuffed the knife and holster into her glove compartment.

Determined to make the best of it, Kat wove her way through the full parking lot. She passed a woman sitting in a car who pushed her hijab off her head, then pulled it back on again. A steady stream of people got out of cars and headed to the restaurant.

Kat smoothed the front of her dress. She had always been lithe and athletic, but age and inactivity were filling her in. Truthfully, she enjoyed having a hint of a curve at her waist and hips. Her body was still strong, her regimen of at-home hand weights maintaining her muscle mass. She lifted her chin, pulled her shoulders back, and readied herself for a challenge.

Kat nodded but did not smile at the man who held the door open for her. The place was already packed with clusters of people. She beelined for the bar, settling for a second-rate American vodka. She threw back the shot, turning her head away from the bar as she grimaced.

"What do you have for red wine?" she asked.

"We have a pretty good selection. A house merlot too."

Kat eyed the two shelves of alcohol behind the bartender. Judging from the assortment of low-cost liquors, she did not have high expectations for the wine.

"Can I see the wine menu?"

The bartender snorted. He reached to his right, pulling bottles from under the bar. "Here's the merlot, a cab sav, a malbec, and a pinot noir. That's the menu."

"Exactly what I expected." Kat picked up the malbec, running her thumb over the peeling front label. "Penfoids? If you're going to sell a counterfeit, you should know that *Penfolds* doesn't produce malbec," she sneered.

The bartender shrugged. "Look around you. Do you think anyone here knows or cares? We're a notch above a dive bar. But if I were drinking, I would stick with the vodka." He leaned closer to Kat, lowering his voice. "I can't even remember when these bottles were opened."

Kat raised her eyebrows. "Good tip. I will have vodka with a splash of cranberry."

Drink in hand, Kat turned her attention to the people in the room. She watched the interactions, studying the cues she'd been trained to notice. A silver-haired woman nodded as the man standing next to her talked, but her eyes scanned the room, looking for a way out. A balding man stood with his hands behind his back and his hips pushed forward, shuffling to close the space between him and the woman next to him. Kat saw a flicker of regret on his face as the woman leaned back, avoiding contact. At the far end of the bar, a woman crossed her legs toward the gentleman sitting next to her with his legs spread wide. He was claiming his space; she was showing interest.

Those two will be at it before the night is over, she thought.

The continuous opening and closing of the front door brought in a welcome gust of fresh air and cleared the cloying mix of perfume and cologne. Kat watched two women come in together, removing their coats at the rolling racks placed to the right of the door. The blond was wearing a sleeveless Gucci wrap dress that outlined her subtle curves and clung to her generous breasts, a brave choice for the beginning of April. Her mousy-haired companion wore a shapeless blue dress with buttons down the front, which made the frock look more like a housecoat than something that should be worn to a speed-dating event.

How these two are friends must be a great story.

"Ladies and gentlemen," a female voice announced, "welcome to the senior edition of speed dating. We will be starting promptly at seven o'clock …"

"So we can be in bed by nine-thirty!" A male voice from the crowd interrupted, causing several people to laugh.

"If you're lucky!" another woman shot back.

"Please take the next thirty minutes to get a drink and have some food."

Buffets were always a fascinating place to study human behavior. Like hungry pigs to the trough, people beelined for the buffet table. Kat ordered another drink while she watched plates being filled. A salt-and-pepper-haired man selected one of everything, not pausing to make careful choices, while the short-haired brunette behind him assessed every platter down the line ahead of her before putting anything on her plate. A woman with curly gray hair loaded up with crudités, clearly favoring cauliflower, while bypassing all the non-vegetarian foods without a glance. A balding man whose shirt buttons strained also chose vegetables, but at the last minute forked up some cheese and salami from the charcuterie board. Kat smiled to herself. He was trying to eat better, but the call of sodium was strong. As someone who considered pickles and olives a food group, Kat understood.

Once the line had thinned, Kat approached the table, balancing her drink on a plate.

"Not much left, is there?" a female voice said behind her. "Makes choosing much easier."

Without turning her head, Kat nodded. "I only wanted tempura, anyway." She chose four pieces of shrimp, then dipped them in the sauce, stirring up the dark brown liquid.

"Do you know what's in that?" the woman asked.

Kat added a pair of egg rolls to her plate and spooned plum sauce over them. "It's *tentsuyu*," she answered, still assessing the other choices on the table. "A mix of soy sauce, sugar, mirin, and dashi."

The woman laughed. "I don't even know what those last two things are. I'm Annalise, by the way."

Kat placed two carrots and two celery sticks on her plate. She turned to look at the woman who would not stop talking. It was the blond in the tight Gucci dress. "Katya," she said, turning her attention back to the buffet.

Annalise leaned forward, invading the space in front of Kat's face. She smiled, revealing perfectly straight, bright white teeth. Her skin glowed with an expensive tinted cream, her pores invisible.

I should ask her about her skin care routine, Kat thought. *I'd probably make a killing investing in the stock.*

"Nice to meet you, Kat." Annalise bent over the table, bringing her perfectly straight nose close to a mostly full platter. She sniffed, then grimaced. "Why is there always quiche and why do they always have onions? Not a great choice for a dating night, don't you think?"

Kat let her eyes linger on the muted yellow triangles in the chafing dish. "It's easy to make and holds up well after it's frozen," she said, choosing to ignore the second question.

Annalise put one hand on her hip and assessed the remaining food. She placed three hamburger sliders, an egg roll, and two jalapeño poppers on her plate. Kat raised her eyebrows, impressed with the choices and quantity.

"Would you like to sit with me and my friend?" Annalise asked.

Kat shook her head. "I prefer to stand."

"I would too, if I looked as fab in a von Fürstenberg silk wrap as you do. It perfectly complements your complexion."

Kat kept her face impassive before she remembered she was here to socialize, not surveil. She should not be surprised that a woman wearing a couture dress herself would recognize labels. Kat twitched, trying to shake off her unease like it was an unreachable itch.

"Thank you," Kat said. She knew she should offer a compliment in return, but Annalise was scanning the crowd, having already lost interest in this conversation.

Kat was bringing a shrimp to her mouth when Annalise grabbed her wrist.

"Oh, I see Millie!" she exclaimed. "She's standing at a high top. Let's go!"

Before Kat could understand what was happening, Annalise yanked her away from the buffet.

"Wha …" She gasped, lurching forward. Kat was trying to keep her shrimp from flying off the plate. Her muscles tensed in the arm Annalise held, but Kat forced herself to relax, allowing the woman to pull her across the bar.

"Millicent, this is Katya. Katya, Millie." Annalise had let go of Kat's wrist, but now she snaked their arms together, like schoolgirls about to skip across a playground.

Millie, the brunette in the shapeless blue dress who had come in with Annalise, glanced up, giving Kat a glimpse of hazel eyes. Despite the slightly crooked nose and limp hair, Kat noted, this woman was a little pretty.

"Nice to meet you, Katya."

"Thanks for getting me the wine," Annalise said. She picked up the glass, taking a short sip. "If you're going to eat, you better go now," Annalise advised her. "There's almost nothing left."

"I'm not hungry." She shrugged. "I'm too nervous to eat." Next to her friend, the woman looked tired and pale. *Shiny penny versus tarnished penny.*

Annalise reached across the table and gave Millie's hand a squeeze. Even their hands were in sharp contrast. Annalise's was smooth, only a hint of wrinkling; Millie's was landscaped with ridges, folds, and dark blue veins.

"That's okay," Annalise assured her friend. "But I can tell you everyone else here is nervous too. Right, Katya?"

Kat frowned. "I do not know what everyone else feels."

Annalise tilted her head. "Um, okay, let me try again. Are you nervous?"

"No."

"You're going to have to up your conversation game if you want to meet a man tonight," Annalise said, taking a bite of a slider. "Then again, men aren't always the greatest conversationalists," she corrected.

"Unless they are actively trying to sleep with you," Millie added.

"Oh my god, yes!" Annalise exclaimed, oblivious to the weariness in her friend's tone. "Then they won't shut up."

"Like dogs begging for scraps at the dinner table," Kat added with a wry smile. "Whining until they get their way."

Annalise raised her glass to Kat.

"Folks, we will be starting in ten minutes," the event host announced. "Gentlemen, please select a seat at any table. Ladies, I invite you all to meet me at the bar to receive your instructions."

Kat drained her vodka, tamping down the flutter of nerves in her chest. As she followed Annalise and Millie to the bar, she slid into the persona she thought would be perfect for the night. "Mia" was fun and flirty, a woman who batted her eyelashes and asked insipid questions. Mia was a coquette who only had eyes for her mark, who led him to feel like he was the most important person in her world before she drove her custom-made push dagger into his liver and watched him bleed to death. Tonight, she decided, she could be Mia, without the bloodshed. Get in, make an impression, exchange some words, get laid.

After ordering sex on the beach, Mia's cocktail of choice, Kat relaxed her facial muscles, ready for play.

FIVE

T he event host, a gray-haired woman whose name tag identified her as Reena, rang a bell.

"Ladies, you have five minutes for each date. When you hear this bell, it will be time to move on to the table to your right."

Reena talked as she walked through the collected women, handing out blank name tag stickers and cue cards. Kat squinted at her card, refusing to extend her arm to bring the lines into focus.

"Grab a marker from the bar and write only your first name on the tag. I also have pens for the cue cards. Please write your name at the top right of the card," Reena explained. "On the lines, you'll indicate which gentleman you'd like to see again. If your name matches that of a gentleman who selected you, you will be introduced again through email. What happens after that is up to you."

Reena rang her bell again.

"Time to start, ladies," she announced. "Please proceed to a table occupied by a gentleman. Have fun!"

Like meerkats newly emerged from their burrows, the women turned in unison, surveying the men sitting alone at the tables. Kat scanned the room, not knowing who or what she was looking for. The bell rang again, and Kat was knocked aside as women pushed past her, choosing their first dates.

"It's like a sale, but instead of TVs, we're being offered men at a discount."

Kat looked over her shoulder at the source of the husky and accented voice. A woman about her age, with long, dark brown hair, stood with her hands clasped in front of her. Kat, at five foot six, stood a head taller than her. The slender woman was spectacularly dressed in dark gray denim with a matching jacket. Kat admired the cut of her white blouse— fitted, but not tight, with a scalloped hem that came just below the edge of her jacket.

"Do you want the one with his face in his phone or the one wearing the backward baseball cap?"

Kat snorted. "Pick of the litter, yes?"

The woman threw her head back and laughed. "Serves us right for bringing up the rear of the pack. I guess we better do what we came here to do …"

The man with the phone looked up, surprised that no one was yet sitting with him. He flicked his eyes from Kat to the woman next to her, then back to Kat. He licked his lips, then waved her over.

"Shit," she muttered. "I made eye contact with phone guy." She worked her face into a smile. "Good luck with the overgrown child."

Kat kept her smile in place as she approached the table. The man—his name tag said Louis—put his phone down on the table, face up. Louis was stuck in his past: what was left of his hair was permed, his cable-knit sweater yellow with age, and he smelled like he'd been using the same bottle of Drakkar Noir for forty years. Kat shuddered when he took a ChapStick out from the inside pocket of his bomber jacket and smeared it on his lips, mashing them together.

"Hello, beautiful." He smirked. "Today might be your lucky day."

"For what?"

"To meet the man of your dreams."

Kat turned in her seat, looking around the restaurant. "Is Tom Selleck here?" She smiled demurely.

"Oh, you are one of those clever ones"—he peered at her name tag stuck below her left shoulder—"Kat. I'm Louis."

"Hello, Louis. Are you clever as well?"

He grinned. "I like to think so." His phone buzzed on the table. Louis glanced at it, and Kat followed his eyes to the text notification.

"I have to answer this. Sorry," he said, picking it up as he slid off the bench.

Kat leaned back in her seat, crossing her arms in front of her, pushing her lips into a pout. While she waited, she used her peripheral vision to watch the women on either side of her. The woman to her left was rubbing her neck in an effort to soothe her nerves. The woman on the right had her hands clasped on the table, a sure sign, Kat knew, that she was struggling with some anxiety.

"Sorry about that," Louis said when he returned less than a minute later. "My sister has dementia. That was her caretaker."

"I'm sorry to hear that. I had a brother with mental health issues," she lied. "I understand how hard it is."

Louis let his eyes travel from her lips to her neck, then down to her chest. *Men never change,* she thought.

"You're the first woman who did not make me feel bad about that."

"Do you come to a lot of these? I can't imagine how such a handsome man is still single."

His face reddened. "This is my third time. Maybe I need to accept that I'm a consummate bachelor."

Kat smiled and tilted her head. "You say that like it's a bad thing. I think it takes a high degree of skill and flair to be a bachelor for so long."

He chuckled. "Most women don't see it that way."

Kat leaned forward, closing the distance. "Most women don't swallow either. But I am not most women."

The bell rang, and before Louis could say anything, Kat was up and out of her chair.

The next date, Bill, asked Kat questions about why she was there, if she had been before, and would she come again.

"I'm here to meet people," she answered honestly. "It's my first time and you're only my second date." She tilted her head. "It's too soon to decide if I'll be back."

"Maybe you'll meet the right person and you won't need to come back."

As Kat moved from table to table, her scalp started to sweat. The competing smells of perfume, cologne, fried foods, and beer, coupled with body heat and a mild hot flash, were making her uncomfortable. She knew she was getting cranky, but she needed to keep a lid on that. She smiled politely and practiced her small talk.

Kat was instantly attracted to Seth. His wavy salt-and-pepper hair was layered on top and clipped at the sides. The lines at the corners of his eyes crinkled when he smiled. His beard and mustache, neatly trimmed, matched his hair. He made his fetish known the minute Kat sat across from him.

"Do you prefer a back rub or a foot massage?"

Kat squinted at him, trying to determine if he was being serious. Seth stared back at her, waiting. His leg jiggled under the table.

"Foot massage," she smiled. A little kink was always fun.

"That's good." Seth peered under the table. "How hard would it be for you to take those boots off right now?"

Kat kicked up her right leg, resting her heel on his thigh. His leg stopped moving. She ran her hand over the black leather running up to below her knee.

"It would take more than the five minutes we have now."
She winked.

Seth took a short breath, which encouraged her to play some more. She bent forward from her waist, pushing her extended leg farther up his left thigh.

"May I?" he asked, raising his hand over the boot.

Kat held his gaze. His eyebrows were raised. His brown eyes darkened with desire. She had all the control here.

"Wipe your hands first," she ordered, tilting her chin toward the napkin next to his plate.

Without tearing his eyes away, Seth unfolded the napkin, wiping each finger on his left hand carefully. He did the same with his right. When he dropped the crumpled napkin onto the table, Kat nodded her assent.

Seth reached under, resting his open right hand at the top of the boot. He tucked his pointer and middle fingers under the lip, awakening a flutter of desire in Kat.

"This is not cheap leather," he said, moving his hand down her shin. He closed his hand around her ankle, using his thumb to caress the top of her leather-clad foot. He moaned at the exact same time as the bell rang.

Kat pulled her leg back, dragging her heel slowly down his thigh. "Nice to meet you, Seth."

"You too, Kat. I'll be … in touch." He smiled and winked.

After Seth, the men became dull, lecherous, or boring. By the time she sat across from her ninth date, Kat was ready to leave, but she was only at the halfway mark. She dashed to the bar at the break, switching from the fruity cocktail to vodka on the rocks. As the next few dates droned on, her mind kept drifting back to Lorenzo, her last romp in Mexico. He had been unacceptably young, insanely flexible, and shockingly attentive to her needs. *Was that already two years ago?*

Before him, there was Stefan in Poland, and two days before him, Darcy in Toronto. She missed the anonymity of a night of uncomplicated sex. Her career had been too unpredictable for any kind of long-term relationship, but she'd never felt the need, until retirement gave her time to be lonely.

"So Nick," she said to date number twelve, "tell me about the one thing you did that you are most proud of."

Nick rubbed his hand over his tight, black curls. "Leading my first team. For the longest time, I was the only Black man in the company—at any company I worked for." He paused. "Do you really want to hear this?"

Kat nodded.

"This one time, a member of a client's executive team walked into the conference room for a scheduled meeting and addressed the white man sitting at the head of the table. He assumed he was the team lead. My team member pointed to me and let the exec know that I was the one to be answering their questions. It was a victory."

"Racism will never die." Kat sighed.

"I don't think he was being overtly racist. There's just not a lot of Black leaders in the software industry."

"It's a white realm, for sure." She laughed. "In some boardrooms, it's not much better for women."

"I may be overstepping here, but I sense you've had to hide your intelligence. Did you ever try to fit yourself into someone else's prejudice?"

Kat took a long sip of her vodka, looking at Nick over the rim of her glass, trying to determine if he was being patronizing or genuine.

"All the time," she answered. *If you only knew how many versions of me there are.*

"Yeah, me too," he said. "It's lonely, right? You can't get close to people when you have to hide everything about who you really are, when the skin you're in is the first thing they see."

She was silent, absorbing his words. She didn't know how to respond. He raised his eyebrows, then took a sip of his own drink. She could smell the whisky.

"It's been nice chatting with you, Nick." She smiled when the bell rang.

Kat stifled a yawn as she proceeded to the next date. She paused in front of a man, Del, whose bored face reflected her own. *Why did I even come?*

She saw Annalise, a few tables away, leaning forward. The man across from her was looking at her cleavage. Kat smiled as Annalise leaned forward even more, giving her date a deeper view. *She knows exactly what she's doing.*

At the next date, Kat mimicked Annalise, trying to give the man a visual treat. His eyes had been everywhere but on her. When the bell rang, she glanced down at her chest, seeing only wrinkled, deflated balloons.

For the last few dates, Kat sat ramrod straight, answering questions without revealing anything, defaulting into quiet observation. Kat let the men fill the void with their own voices, not one of them noticing she had barely said a word. She spent more time eavesdropping on conversations than participating in them. Playing Mia had lost its gloss, especially without the satisfying payoff of a job well done. The release she had grown accustomed to from a completed kill never came.

SIX

K at was completely depleted when the final bell rang and Reena called for everyone to hand in their cards. The noise diminished as people filed out of the restaurant.

Kat had only two names on her card—Nick and Seth. She was confident Seth had put her name down on his, and if Nick didn't, by his own admission, a Black man in IT leadership was a rarity. Finding him would be child's play for her.

She heard snippets of conversation as she made her way to the coat rack. Women were comparing notes, while men were shaking hands with a quick "Nice to meet you." A few people had coupled up at the bar, name tags still on, engaged in conversation.

Kat was slipping on her coat when Annalise, followed by Millie, sidled up to her. "So how many names did you put down on your ballot?" Annalise asked.

"I didn't even think to count," Millie admitted. "Was I supposed to count?"

For a moment, Kat wondered if she had done something wrong. Perhaps she had been too harsh with some of the men she met, dismissing them too easily. She had always been picky, but maybe Millie wasn't so discerning.

"I think it's actually better not to keep track," Annalise said, moving toward the doors at the front of the restaurant. "It would drive me crazy if I chose ten people and only four chose me."

"I'll be happy with one." Millie sighed. "I'm not sure I was any good at this."

"It's your first time. You aren't supposed to be good at it. No one is. It's all awkward fumbling." Annalise winked.

Kat smirked, laughing quietly to herself. She appreciated a quick wit. Annalise had a confidence Kat rarely saw in women, even those who had been surgically altered, as she suspected Annalise had been. Many times.

"I guess … oh … OH!" Millie exclaimed, red creeping from the collar of her jacket up to her face.

"There were a lot of quality men tonight. Some seriously hot sixty-year-olds out there," Annalise gushed.

"And some very disturbed ones too," Kat added.

"Sadly, we can't get away from the creeps. It's Katya, right?" Millie asked.

"Kat, yes," she answered.

"Okay, I need to know if anyone else was asked about foot and back rubs," Millie wondered.

"Aiyee, that man was creepy," a voice said. Kat looked up and smiled at the woman with the brown hair she had met earlier. "So many red flags there." The woman raised an eyebrow. "Unless you like that kind of thing."

Kat wanted to slink into the shadows. She had enjoyed teasing Seth.

Annalise threw her head back and laughed. "Right? He was staring at my chest, licking his lips."

"I imagine you get that a lot, though," Kat said.

"I can barely take *my* eyes off them," Millie joked.

"Millie!" Annalise gasped. "Are *you* making a sexual reference?"

"I guess you're rubbing off on me." Millie blushed.

"Did you ladies all come together?"

"Oh, no. I mean, Millie and I came together, but we just met Kat. I'm Annalise."

"I'm Farzana. Call me Farzi. Nice to meet you."

Kat stared at Farzana. Her eyes were dark brown, with streaks of gold radiating out from the pupils, and topped with thick brows. Her jaw was slightly widened, a common change for women of her age.

"You're not from here," Kat blurted. She noticed tension rise into Farzana's shoulders. She thought she heard one of the other women inhale sharply.

"That wasn't a microaggression," Kat said. "Merely an observation. You're from Afghanistan." It wasn't a question.

"Yes, I am." Farzi blinked in surprise. "You're the only person who ever got that on the first try. Most people assume I'm an Arab. You must travel a lot."

"I've been to a few places." She shrugged.

"I'm not ready to go home just yet," Annalise said. "Can I interest anyone in some late-night pub grub?" She turned to Millie. "If you want to go home, that's okay too. You're my ride."

Millie looked at her watch. "No, I'm game, if that's what you want to do."

"I think some curly fries and gravy would be great," Farzana said. "How about you, Kat?"

"Not me, no. If I eat this late, I will suffer a night of heartburn, insomnia, and restless legs."

"Come on," Annalise implored. "Three is such an odd number. And let's be honest. You're going to experience those things regardless. I really need to talk about these men tonight, and my husband won't be as much fun as you ladies."

"You're *married?*" Farzi exclaimed.

That's why she's so self-assured, Kat thought. *She has no real skin in this game.*

"She came with me," Millie explained, "because I was too nervous to come by myself. She is a gift from god."

"Jesus may be at the wheel," Annalise joked, "but it takes a woman to do the driving. I won't beg, but when was the last time you stayed out past 10:00 p.m.? We've got less time ahead of us than behind. I'm going to eat fattening food tonight. Screw the inflammation."

"You're right," agreed Farzi. "I'm in."

"Kat, are you coming?" Millie asked.

Kat followed Annalise, Millie, and Farzi into the parking lot, reaching into her purse. She stood apart from the others, clutched her keys, and started to shake her head. Once again, Annalise snaked her arm through Kat's.

"Yes, she's coming," Annalise announced.

Kat frowned and pulled herself out of Annalise's grasp. She had no desire to go anywhere with these women she didn't know, and she resented the assumption that she would. Socializing with twenty men had been enough.

"I think I'm going home," Kat said, "but thank you for the invitation."

They stood in the haloed glow of the parking lot lights. The temperature had dropped. Curling up in her living room with a warm shot of brandy and a fuzzy blanket sounded really good.

"Do I have to kidnap you?"

Kat looked at Annalise. Despite her curated and perfect body, her blond hair and big breasts, Kat could see this was a smart woman who never heard the word *no*. Kat stared at her, and Annalise held her gaze. The woman was determined to go to a pub, and Kat's resistance was fading. Her curiosity was piqued.

"People have been underestimating you your whole life, haven't they?" Kat asked.

"Every damn day."

Millie's car keys jingled in her hand. Farzi stood silently, waiting for someone to make a decision.

"Okay. We can go. But I'm driving," Kat said.

"Sure," Annalise said, bouncing on her two-inch heels. "I know just the place."

SEVEN

Kat was energized by the mix of people at Lulu Bar. The women walked with the confidence of queens; the men skated around them like they were dancing on ice. The place smelled of bourbon and fried pickles. It would have made her mouth water if not for the pervasive note of old sweat hanging in the air. Chaos in public always comforted her. She could do what she needed to and never stand out.

"Will we even find a table?" Kat asked.

"It's still early," Annalise said. "I bet you there's some in the back."

They followed Annalise deeper into the restaurant. So many people were congregated at the bar, some sitting on stools, others clustered around. Kat watched as people leaned close to one another or touched each other, their body language loose and lustful. Three bartenders hustled behind the bar, their speed and movement an unchoreographed dance. She scanned the bar from left to right, unconsciously looking for her mark.

There is no one, she reminded herself. *You can relax. If you remember how.*

They found a table on a raised area on the far side. Kat slid onto the blue leather bench, feeling more comfortable with a full view of the entire place. Millie and Farzi sat in the rounded-back chairs flanking the table. Annalise plopped down on the bench next to Kat, flicking her hair over her shoulders.

The waiter brought menus. "I know you're not going to drink," Annalise said to Millie, "but are you going to have something to eat?"

"I'm not really hungry," Millie protested.

"But you hardly ate at speed dating," Annalise pressed.

"I'm still a bit rattled," Millie admitted, shrugging. "I've never done anything like that." She shifted in her chair, peeling off her jacket and adjusting her dress so it bloused more than it clung.

"I wish my appetite worked like that." Farzi sighed. "I get so hungry when I'm nervous, but I can't eat or I'll throw up."

"Has that really happened?" Kat consciously inflected the question to appear curious and not skeptical.

Farzi nodded. "When I was a little girl, my mother used to say the magpies would follow me when I left for school, hoping I would leave my breakfast on the dirt."

A laugh burst out from Annalise. Farzi and Millie joined in. Kat relaxed her jaw, forcing out her own laughter.

"Looks like you ladies are already having a good time," the waiter said when he returned. "What can I get you tonight?"

While the others ordered specialty cocktails, Kat opted for an iced tea. She had already foolishly gotten behind the wheel of a vehicle after having a few drinks. While her alcohol tolerance was high, she would still blow above the limit if pulled over.

"I never know what to order," Farzi said. "I can't even remember the last time I went to a bar."

Kat glanced at the blurred words on the menu and let Annalise take charge of ordering a variety of appetizers for the table to share. She leaned against the back of the booth, content to watch and wait to see what would happen next.

Farzi closed her menu. She turned in her seat, looking around. "Does anyone else feel like we are the oldest people here?" she asked.

"We are." Annalise smiled. "But I like being in a young crowd."

"Don't you feel out of place?" Millie asked.

"We are invisible to these … children." Kat shrugged. "They are not even seeing us."

"We've gone from being hip to needing a new hip," Annalise laughed.

Millie also turned in her seat. There were some very drunk people trying to play darts. A man closed the space between him and the woman he was speaking to, trapping her against the wall. Kat noticed Millie rubbing her thumb and forefinger together in her lap, as if she were praying on an invisible rosary.

"I wonder what Jesus would say if he returned and found me in a place like this," she said, shaking her head.

"Jesus ate with sinners," Kat pointed out. "All the time."

Millie whipped around in her chair. "Pardon me?"

"Jesus went where others thought it was disgraceful for him to go." Kat shrugged. "He wanted to connect with people where they felt most comfortable to show he did not judge them. Forgiveness above all. He'd be okay with you being here."

"Ooh, Millie," Annalise teased. "Kat has got you one hundred percent figured out."

"I am a proud Christian, and not embarrassed about it," Millie said, her cheeks reddening. "I'm just uncomfortable with all this … this debauchery. I should have stayed home."

"What part of the Bible says you can't go to a bar?" Farzi asked. "There is nothing sinful about enjoying time with your friends."

"I know that," Millie agreed. "It's just … I don't go to bars. Our pastor was always warning us about the things that happen to drunkards."

"Terrible things happen to people who don't drink too," Kat said. "I'm sure your pastor has a nip or two now and then."

Millie squirmed in her seat. "Please don't say those kinds of things. I have my beliefs and my faith," she continued, examining her cuticles. "Please respect that."

Kat held up her hands, palms facing Millie. "I don't mean to be rude. I am sorry. I will refrain from now on."

"'A good word is like a good tree,'" Farzi added. "My father repeated that from the Qur'an often. You have to mean what you say."

Millie snapped her head up to look at Farzi. "We have a saying like that in the Bible. In Matthew. 'If the tree is good, the fruit will be too.'"

"Are you religious, Kat?" Annalise asked.

No, I'm not interested in that delusional horseshit.

"Not really," she answered. "My parents didn't care much for that."

"Same," Annalise agreed. "My dad always said religion was a business. I mean, we all grew up in the era of the evangelical billionaire, didn't we? Every Sunday, all day on TV. Inspiring millions to part with their money."

The waiter appeared carrying a tray filled with their appetizers. Kat's stomach rumbled in response. Despite the promise of bloating later, she aped Annalise and dug in, piling her plate with truffle fries, salt-and-pepper pork belly, edamame, chicken satay skewers, and the house specialty, fire-grilled carrots.

"This is a lot of food," Millie said.

"When I'm hungry, I order with my eyes instead of my stomach," said Annalise. "Trust me, this all goes down easy, especially after a night of social interaction. Flirting makes me hungry."

"The constant talking depleted all my energy," Kat complained, helping herself to a skewer. "I am grateful you ordered all this." *Who cares if I'm up all night digesting? I have nothing to do tomorrow.*

"Agreed." Farzi nodded, filling her own plate. She took a bite of a honey-charred carrot. "Waa! These are amazing! This makes me miss my mother's carrot jam."

"That sounds interesting. Is it like strawberry jam?" Millie asked.

"It's more of a chutney. We used to eat it at breakfast on toast. But I would sneak into the kitchen at night for a snack and spoon it onto crackers."

"That sounds delicious," Annalise said, chewing a bite of fries.

"It's really easy to make," Farzi continued. "I can bring you some, if you like."

"Oh, I like the assumption that there will be a second date." Annalise laughed. "I'm in."

"I like my odds better with you ladies than I do with any of the men I met." Kat sighed.

"What did you think of Carlos?" Annalise asked.

"Was that the software guy?" Millie wondered, nibbling a tiny piece of carrot.

"No, that was the bedding guy," Kat answered. "The one who asked how often I change my sheets and then gave a discourse on Egyptian cotton and thread count."

"That guy was awful." Farzi laughed. "I gave him a piece of my mind about listening instead of talking."

"I did too! I kept calling him Stu, though," Annalise confessed, dropping her chin to her chest to hide her smile. "I honestly didn't even feel bad about it."

Kat spent the next hour listening more than talking. Conversation came easily for the others. Her head swiveled like she was at a tennis match, watching as Annalise, Farzi, and Millie compared notes about their dates and talked about their favorite pub foods and the restaurants in Portland they'd always wanted to try.

"Why don't we start a dinner club?" Annalise ventured. "We could try a different place once a month."

"I love that idea," Farzi gushed. "I want to try new things, but I'm always too timid."

"It's now or never," Annalise said. "I don't want to spend the rest of my life bored and afraid."

"I find it's harder to take risks now that I'm over fifty," said Millie. "More bones to break."

"You've always had the same number of bones in your body," Kat pointed out. "What you said doesn't make any sense."

Millie's face reddened. Her fingers were twitching again. "I … I meant they can break easier."

"Do you always take things so literally?" Annalise was staring at her, her lips pressed together.

Kat pulled a cold edamame shell slowly out of her mouth. She met Annalise's eyes while chewing the beans. There was a bond between those two women that she had missed. She tamped down a spark of irritation.

"Only when the information is wrong. Children have more bones to break. We're born with three hundred and by the time we are twenty-five, they've fused down into two hundred and six."

"You must be fun at trivia night." Farzi smirked. "But I think I'd like you on my team."

Kat used her fingernail to split open another cold bean. "I like facts. Details matter." She brought the pod to her mouth, using her tongue to scoop out the soybeans. "Did you know that happy hour in Japan is not complete without edamame as a drinking snack?"

"Did you live in Japan?" Annalise asked. "You must have."

She leaned forward, speaking to Millie and Farzi. "At speed dating, she knew the ingredients in the tempura dipping sauce."

"I've never lived in Japan. I've never even been there. I don't know." Kat shrugged. "I just like gathering information." *And it's necessary when your mark is yakuza running his mafia through Hawaii and you need to know what flavors mask poison.* "I'd love to go there one day." *Assuming I'm not on a hit list.*

"You know what I'd love to do?" Annalise said. "A walking food tour. Have any of you done that?"

"Who wants to walk around the city with their food?" Kat scoffed. "That sounds complicated."

"Holy shit! Again?" Annalise huffed.

Farzi let out a throaty laugh. "That's not what it is, Kat. A guide takes you to different restaurants to try a drink and a small plate. It gives you a wide experience of many restaurants for what it would cost to go to just one."

"So, how many restaurants would we visit in an evening?" Millie asked Annalise. Kat looked at Millie's plate, which still held the same carrot she put there two hours ago.

"Usually five or six," Annalise answered. "A couple of hours walking a couple of miles. I did one in New York way back."

"I'm in," Farzi announced, pulling her phone out of her purse. "Let's exchange numbers and then pick a date. Want to go on a weekday or weekend?"

EIGHT

K at swiped through the screens on her phone, squinting at the tiny images and print. Never having had to use the app, she had no idea what color the contacts icon was. She placed her phone on the table and leaned back on the bench, the distance making things clearer. One by one, they swapped names and numbers. Annalise Onofrio. Farzi Noor. Millie Collins. Kat watched the others' thumbs fly over their phones as they inputted the information while she struggled to focus her vision.

"You are all so fast," she said.

"Here"—Annalise reached out—"give me your phone and I'll put my info in for you. Want me to do the others too?"

"Sure. I'll let the expert handle it." Kat shook her head. "I was so bad at regular typing, it doesn't surprise me that I can't manage this tiny keyboard."

"Like anything, you get better with practice," said Farzi.

"I never knew my thumbs were so clumsy until I had to use them to send an email," said Millie, finally cracking a smile.

"All done," Annalise said, handing Kat's phone back.

"Thank you." She looked at the screen until it blanked

out, then put it back in her purse. "How do you and Millie know each other?"

"We live across the street from each other," Millie answered.

"Have you been friends long?" Farzi asked.

Millie glanced at Annalise, who was still looking at her phone. "Not long, no."

Kat watched Annalise drag her thumb on her phone, scrolling her calendar. Farzi and Millie were doing the same. She wasn't sure if the invitation for the walking tour extended to her. She had been mostly silent for the last couple of hours, listening to the women chatter about topics with which she had little or no experience. She did what she did best—watching others without being noticed herself.

"Kat, aren't you going to look at your calendar?" Annalise stared at her, gesturing with her own phone.

"I don't need to," Kat answered coolly. "I have it all in my head." *There's not a single thing on my calendar.*

"Oh, poop." Annalise pouted, showing her phone screen to the others. "Walking food tours don't start until June."

"Why don't we just go somewhere for dinner?" Farzi suggested. "Somewhere completely different. Is there a place anyone wants to try?"

"I'm curious about Sultan's Tent," Millie said, suddenly coming to life. "I've always wanted to try Moroccan food."

Kat glanced at Millie's lone and untouched carrot, wondering if she had read the woman wrong. Maybe she truly just didn't want to eat late.

"I would *love* that," exclaimed Farzi. "Is it a genuine Moroccan restaurant?"

"What do you mean?" Annalise asked.

"She's wondering if you eat with your hands," Kat answered.

"Wait a minute," Annalise balked. "Like, there's no cutlery

at all? I'm not sure I can do that." Annalise looked down at her long, perfectly manicured nails.

"It … it could be fun," faltered Millie. "It's fine if no one else is interested."

"I'll go with you, Millie," Farzi said, reaching across the table to squeeze Millie's hand. "I'm used to eating with my fingers."

"So am I," Kat added. "I spent some time in Marrakesh. The most divine *bastilla* I ever had. I can still taste the savory meat and that sweet pastry." She closed her eyes, remembering the good things about her time in Morocco.

"How long were you in Morocco?" Annalise asked.

Kat opened her eyes. She looked down at the glossy tabletop, suddenly missing the opulence and color of the Marrakesh markets.

"Only three days."

"That's a long way to go for a few days," Millie pointed out.

"It was a business trip."

"What kind of work did you … do you do?" Farzi asked.

"I'm retired." Kat smiled thinly. "I was a consultant. Independent contractor. Foreign affairs."

"Ooh, that sounds intriguing." Annalise moaned. "I've always wanted to travel for work."

"I thought you did," said Millie.

Annalise laughed. "I meant outside the US."

"Did you work for the government?"

Kat shrugged. "I did mostly trade relations. Some national security advising. Nothing I can—or want to—talk about."

The job in Marrakech had been particularly brutal and complicated. The heat and the dusty streets made her uncomfortable, and tracking her mark in a sea of people was an exhausting challenge. The Souk Semmarine overloaded her senses with sounds, colors, and smells, but the market provided the perfect diversion for a killing. She moved so fast through the market, not even a pickpocket had time to lift anything from her body.

"So mysterious," Annalise quipped. "I'll get the details one day. I'm good at that."

Kat raised her eyebrows. *You might be,* she thought, *but I'm so much better.*

"How about one more shot for the road?" Farzi proposed. "Strawberry shortcake to end the night?" She rose and walked to the bar to place the order, then brought four red and white shots back to the table.

"What's in this?" Annalise asked, sniffing the glass.

"Vanilla vodka, strawberry liqueur, amaretto, and cream," explained Farzi.

"Cheers to new friends!" Annalise raised her glass and licked the liquid spilling down the side.

"Cheers to a great night!" Farzi answered.

"I'll cheer to that." Millie smiled, bringing the shot glass to her mouth for a sip.

"*Oldik,*" Kat toasted.

"And maybe some new dick too." Annalise laughed.

Kat brought her drink to her lips and gulped the entire thing. She raised her eyebrows, surprised it wasn't sickeningly sweet. She wished she hadn't driven and could have one more. She was going to need the liquid courage.

NINE

Annalise almost smacked her head on the frame as she bent herself into the front seat of Kat's car.

"I don't care if this is the alcohol talking," she slurred, "but I had an amazing time tonight. I think I love you ladies. Thanks for inviting me, Millie."

"I'm glad I asked you," Millie said from her seat behind Annalise. "I would not have gone speed dating on my own."

"A good friend supports all your … um … questionable choices." Farzi chuckled.

Annalise craned her neck to look at Kat. "What about you? Did you have fun tonight? It's hard to tell with you."

"It was amusing." Kat busied herself with checking her mirrors as she started the car.

"I'm going to hurt tomorrow." Annalise burped.

Kat kept her eyes on the road, her vision wavering for a moment. The idea of driving glasses crossed her mind, but the burning in her stomach was her more immediate concern. The inflammation in her joints and the bloating would hurt more than any hangover. Alcohol, salty food, and menopause were a vicious mix.

"Matteo is going to be so pissed if I start puking," said Annalise.

"Matteo? Your husband?" Farzi asked.

Annalise nodded. "Husband number four. I met him at a plastic surgery clinic."

Kat glanced in her rearview mirror. Millie was looking out the window, her lips pressed together. Farzi's mouth was open to ask a question. Kat really didn't want to hear any stories about broken and bad marriages.

"Was he the surgeon?" she asked.

"Nope." Annalise grinned and her eyes sparkled when she turned to look at Kat. "He was a patient. Penis enlargement."

"Oh Lord," Millie said, crossing herself.

"What were you having done?" Farzi boldly asked.

"Botox." Annalise pointed to the barely there lines on her forehead, then ran her fingers on either side of her mouth.

"So was his surgery a success?" Kat wondered aloud.

"Oh, yes. There was not a single scar. Juvéderm injections, same stuff I get in my lips." She pushed her lips out in a fat pucker.

Kat flicked her eyes over, wondering what in Annalise was genuine, original parts.

"You never know what life will bring you around the corner, where you will meet the next person to be part of your story," Farzi mused. "What's the oddest thing that ever happened to you? The most unbelievable coincidence?"

"I missed a flight once and it saved my life," Millie volunteered. "I was touring universities in New York and Michigan, and my next leg was to go to Phoenix to visit Arizona State University, but I didn't make it on to the plane. That plane crashed three minutes after takeoff. Everyone died, except for one little girl."

There was silence in the car.

"Holy shit," Annalise whispered.

Kat again looked at Millie in the rearview. "Why didn't you get on that plane?" she asked with genuine curiosity.

"I couldn't find my ticket."

"Holy shit," echoed Farzi.

"I thought it was divine intervention," Millie explained. "I searched my carry-on, my purse … I tore apart my backpack, shaking out every college brochure and handbook, searching for my ticket. God saved me."

"You must have freaked out when you heard about the crash," Annalise said.

"I didn't know about it until I got to ASU the next day. I was so panicked, I could only focus on buying a new ticket and rescheduling my tour. And anyway, I was seventeen and never paid attention to the news.

"I found the ticket when I got home the day after, tucked inside the course catalog from the University of Oregon, which I brought to compare programs. I had shaken that one *and* I flipped though pages on the rebooked flight to Phoenix. It wasn't there."

"That gives me goose-bumps." Annalise rubbed her arms.

"Me too," added Farzi.

"You were just lucky," Kat stated. "It's that simple."

"I choose to believe god's hand was involved. His ways are mysterious."

Kat snorted but otherwise remained silent.

Annalise turned to Kat. "What's your story?"

Kat stared out the windshield, keeping her face in the neutral zone. She couldn't recall a memorable moment that didn't involve bloodshed. She'd have to come up with something fast.

"I made friends with an octopus," she blurted out. It was the first thing that came to mind, remnants of a childhood dream to become a marine biologist.

In the rearview mirror, Millie looked at her. "Like, as a pet?" she asked.

"No, in the wild. I used to scuba dive off Vancouver Island. When I was in my late twenties. I went every weekend."

"Okay, I have to know how this happened," Farzi pressed.

Without a moment's hesitation, Kat spun the story. "One day, shortly after I went out offshore of Campbell River, I noticed something moving in the kelp fields. I swam over and came face-to-face with the mantle of a giant Pacific octopus."

"Weren't you scared?" Annalise asked.

"Not at all." Kat shrugged. "They are not aggressive. Just curious. We stared at each other for a few moments and then it reached out its tentacles and began tasting me. I could feel the suckers through my suit. We were eye to eye. It pushed off, then returned, wrapping its arms around my whole head. Through my mask, I could see all the tentacles and got a peek at its beak. I blindly reached up, intending to try to pull it away, but I pet it instead. I could feel it moving its tentacles around my upper body, pressing on my tank, investigating me. This lasted for about three or four minutes and then it swam off.

"Every weekend for that summer, I went back out both Saturday and Sunday. And every weekend, I met with that same octopus. It pushed sand at me through its siphon, swam circles around me. I took off my gloves and let it pinch my skin with its suckers."

"How did you know it was the same octopus?" Farzi asked.

"I never thought to question that it wasn't."

"I read that they are highly intelligent creatures," Millie said. "More so than we could ever imagine."

"I would have shit my pants," squeaked Annalise. "I mean, how big was that thing?"

"Its mantle went from the top of my head to my waist. So, giant, I guess?"

Millie, Annalise, and Farzi all burst out laughing. Something loosened inside Kat's chest. When her brain caught up, she grinned. It felt a hell of a lot better making people laugh than to hear them plead for their lives. She could get used to this.

"A little more than a year later," she continued, weaving the lie tighter, "I was at the Vancouver Aquarium for a company luncheon. The backdrop of the space was a tank that ran the length of the room. I was sitting at a table in the middle, happily eating a salad, when I heard a loud bang from the aquarium. Everyone turned to look. A giant Pacific octopus was throwing two of its tentacles against the glass, full force, its double row of suckers pulsing. Looking right at me."

"There's no way it was the same octopus." Annalise gasped.

"It was." Kat nodded.

"How did you know?" Millie asked.

"The octopus waved at me. All eight arms flapping and pointing. It started spinning and bouncing in the tank like an excited toddler."

"That is like the experience of a lifetime," Farzi said. "I don't know how to follow that with my own story. It'll sound boring now."

"We're here," Kat announced, pulling into the parking lot at Fireside. "Maybe next time you tell your story."

"No one gets out of this car until Farzi tells us her story," ordered Annalise. "So, go!"

Kat unbuckled, then shifted in her seat, resettling her hips into a more comfortable position. She turned to look back at Farzi, blinking away the blur in her eyes. She was tired, but intrigued. This whole night had been filled with new experiences, and even though she no longer had the stamina of her youth, a fresh energy crept up on her.

"Umm … let me see …," Farzi faltered.

"No pressure," teased Annalise, "but I'm going to have to pee soon."

"You can go over there." Kat pointed at the cluster of bushes at the far corner of the parking lot.

"She can't squat in the bushes," Millie protested. "Someone could see her."

Farzi chuckled. "Who? There is no one but us here. If you have to go, go."

"I'm not dropping my panties and crouching in that laurel in Gucci," Annalise protested. "Farzi, stop stalling and spit it out so I don't have to risk ruining my dress."

Kat watched Annalise bouncing in her seat. Beauty and brains and no bullshit. Annalise really was the whole package.

Farzi looked down at her hands in her lap and smiled. "I visited America for the first time when I was twenty-six, on a three-month Islamic missionary trip. It was the only way my parents would let me go abroad without a family chaperone. We visited the Metropolitan Correctional Center in Chicago to meet with Islamic women prisoners and to bring them a bit of comfort. We also held workshops for anyone interested in the Islamic faith. Some prisoners were forced into the workshop to open their minds to exploring other religions—"

"I can guess how that went," Kat interrupted. "You can't force someone out of their racism."

"No, you can't," Farzi agreed. "We went every week for six weeks. Over time, they came to appreciate some of the similarities between religions."

"Weren't you scared to be in the prison with murderers and violent criminals?" Millie asked.

"Yes. But there were always guards in the meeting room with us. The women were calm. They had nothing to gain by attacking us. It was a very rewarding experience in the end. I was free from the scrutiny of my parents, I was part of a group doing good work, and I was securing my place in paradise."

Kat bit the inside of her bottom lip to stop herself from

scoffing. The notion of an afterlife where everything is perfect with no pain or problems sounded excruciatingly boring.

Annalise twisted around to pat Farzi's knee. "That's a nice thing, Farzi."

Farzi nodded. "One weekend, four of us rented a car to go to the outlet mall outside of Chicago. We set the GPS and off we went. We were making our way out of the city and had been driving for less than ten minutes when we knew we had made a wrong turn. We were deep in the projects."

"You must have been freaking out," Annalise said.

"We were. At a stoplight, two men came up to the car. One tapped on the driver's window with a crowbar. The other yelled at us to get out. We froze. We said prayers. The man with the crowbar raised his arm, and just before he brought it down to smash the window, a hand grabbed his forearm. I was sitting in the passenger seat. I peered past my friend's teary face and saw a vaguely familiar one next to the car. The person who saved us from a carjacking and who knows what else was one of the prisoners from the workshop. She had been released two weeks prior."

"Close call," Millie murmured.

"Yes. This was in the early days of GPS, and the car's navigation took us on the easiest route, not the safest."

"One wrong turn can change your whole life." Kat sighed.

"Yeah," Millie agreed.

There was quiet in the car for a moment, each of them lost in their own thoughts.

"I really need to pee." Annalise broke the silence. She climbed out of the car, wobbling in her heels. She grasped the car door, hanging on. "Mil … can you help? I'm a bit drunk."

Millie sighed quietly. "That was fun tonight," she said. "I hope we can do it again." She got out of the car and draped Annalise's arm over her shoulders.

"I had a great time," Farzi said. "Thank you for driving, Kat."

Kat nodded and watched Millie and Annalise hobble to Millie's car. She waited until Farzi was in her car, the engine running.

Kat pulled out of the parking lot, pleased with herself for taking the first steps into a new world. She knew this satisfaction, having felt it every time she tracked a mark with prowess and finesse. As she pulled into her garage, Kat was confidently imagining another night out with the women.

TEN

Kat was not ready to go to bed when she got home. She was exhausted, but invigorated. Her first instinct was to fire up her laptop and Google the women. She swiped her thumb on her phone and tapped on the contacts. Staring at the newly added names, Kat wondered what she would find on the internet. *Why do you care? That was your old life. If you want to live differently, you have to commit.*

Kat dropped her phone back into her purse. She unzipped her boots, smiling at the memory of Seth's hand resting on her ankle. In her walk-in closet, she loosened the sash of her dress and let it fall to the floor. She slipped on yoga pants, a fitted tank top, and a hoodie. Kat leaned forward into the full-length mirror mounted on the back wall, swiping away the mascara that had collected under her eyes.

She poured herself a couple of fingers of brandy, the smell reminding her of her mother, all warmth and spice, until cancer leached her away. Kat curled up on her couch, looking out the curved bow window to the dimly lit street. The houses directly across from her were dark, not even an exterior light to cut the blackness.

Kat had owned this house for almost three decades, yet

she didn't know any of her neighbors. It was only since she'd retired that she caught glimpses of the others who lived on the street. In the early days of her retirement, she lurked at the front window, watching the comings and goings of the people in her neighborhood. She knew who left their houses early in the morning, presumably going to work, but that was the extent of her familiarity.

Unlike a mark, whom she carefully tracked and observed, these people were strangers. She fought the urge to creep the streets at night, poking into recycling bins and trash cans, to learn which of her neighbors might be cheating on their spouse, or suffering from addiction, or embezzling funds. She had to remind herself she was no longer working, and there was no benefit to getting to know her neighbors by their vices and imperfections.

Kat took a gentle sip of her brandy, closing her eyes as the alcohol soothed her. Again, she thought of her mother, who sipped a finger or two of brandy almost every night after dinner. "It pulls me away from the day, my *shirinim*," her mother explained, gently caressing young Katya's cheek.

Kat touched her cheek in remembrance, but instead of feeling the soft skin of her youth, her fingers met with fine hair. She didn't need a mirror to confirm her face was more lined than it was a year ago. The effects of boredom and age converged on her skin, drying out her face, arms, and legs, sculpting a new roadmap on her hands and neck. Her work had invigorated her and kept her young, she believed.

Despite the late hour, she felt an unfamiliar energy flow into every part of her body. Again, she smiled to herself, replaying parts of the night in her mind. As the brandy worked into her bloodstream, Kat thought about each of the women and built their profiles based on what she observed. Annalise was confident, but she hadn't always been that way. Her multiple surgeries were proof of that. Millie was shy, her low self-esteem the result of a lifetime of diets and restraint.

Farzi was adventurous, now able to live free from the oppressive rules of Islam.

Kat wondered briefly what they thought of her and was surprised she cared. She had never once given thought to anyone's opinion of her, nor had she cared, as long as they paid on time.

She stared into her empty glass, contemplating a refill. Her stomach gurgled, still full of fried and decadent foods. In the kitchen, as she poured more brandy, Kat realized they had never made an official plan for another outing.

Maybe "Let's have dinner" is one of those empty platitudes like, "Next time you're in town, let me know."

Kat dug her phone out of her purse again. She tapped the screen to wake it, feeling deflated when there were no texts. She should not be surprised, having only just met these women.

Staring at the four names filling two inches on her contacts screen, Kat considered starting a text conversation. She changed her mind after glancing at the clock on the stove, the blue numbers glowing 1:18 a.m.

She was still holding her phone when she got to the bottom of her second glass of brandy. The screen was blurred and in her sleepy, barely drunk state, Kat didn't care if it was her eyes or the booze. She left her phone on the kitchen island and fell contentedly into bed. A deep and cozy sleep took over, leaving her oblivious to the chime of a notification.

ELEVEN

K at huddled inside her fleece-lined rain jacket, in awe of the show the sunrise had put on. As the sun made its ascent from behind the mountains on the other side of the Columbia River Gorge, the sky was painted with jewel tones of pink, purple, and orange. Just as the edge of the sun peeked over the ridge, the clouds moved in, and with them, a light drizzle. She reached under her camping chair for her umbrella, its whoosh upon opening the only sound.

She knew there wouldn't be anyone else at Vista House that early in the morning. It had rained hard all night, and the forecast called for more throughout the day. As she drove twenty-five miles east out of Portland in the dark, there was minimal traffic in front of her and some early-morning commuters heading in the opposite direction.

She was tired, her short, deep sleep truncated by insomnia, along with mild indigestion. She had plodded into the kitchen to swallow pink antacid medicine, then sat up in bed reading while waiting for it to work. By five in the morning, her stomach had settled, but sleep was elusive. This was a curse of retirement; her change from an exciting and active life to an excruciatingly boring one often robbed her of a good night's rest. She chuckled at the irony of never losing sleep when she was actively killing people.

Kat stayed under her umbrella until the sky turned blue and the clouds moved on. Maybe the rain was done for the day. In the silence, she found herself thinking about last night.

The women chatted and laughed with such ease while Kat struggled to join the conversation. She had never had trouble engaging with a mark, slipping into their world. Of course, she had spent weeks studying what they liked, what they did, and where they went, gathering all the information she needed to start a conversation and get close enough to complete the job. Every word that came out of her mouth was practiced and deliberate.

But sitting at the table at Lulu Bar, she was lost. These women were strangers, and without time to observe and prepare, Kat had no idea what to say. She had contributed little to the conversation, instead answering questions efficiently and without elaboration. She watched their faces, nodded and laughed when the others did, even when she didn't understand what was funny. Being a master of deception and fabrication, she easily masked her uncertainty. How could she be any different?

After folding up her chair and closing her umbrella, Kat stared out over the valley to the mountains. She inhaled deeply, closing her eyes, trying to calm the restless twitch inside her. For almost thirty years, Kat had been coming to witness the Vista House sunrise to reset and remind herself that there was still plenty of good in the world.

By the time she got home, Kat had decided she would text the women and commit to another night out. *Treat this new thing like the early stages of a new job. Play a role. Learn what you need to know.*

Her phone sat face down on the kitchen counter, where she had abandoned it last night.

"*Cyka blyat*," she swore at the dead screen. She had never let her phone die, not once in her professional life.

She connected the charger, then started a bath. Some time in her jetted tub would take the chill of the morning out of her bones. With the water still running, she sank into the heat with a sigh. She laid back, watching the steam rise around her. As she reached to turn on the jets, she heard a ping from her phone, followed by more pings in quick succession.

"Fucking shit," she swore again, this time in English.

Kat padded into the living room, stark naked and leaving wet footprints on the hardwood. Text message notifications lit up her phone screen. Kat blinked, not quite believing what she was reading. Annalise had already put the wheels in motion while Kat watched the dawn of a new day. The time stamp on the first message was more than four hours ago. She scrolled through, catching up on the conversation she'd missed.

ANNALISE

Some dates to consider for our Moroccan dinner. Pick one or two and the majority rules. May 10 or 21?

FARZI

Can we do the 10th? I don't want to wait too long to hang out with you ladies again. Is it okay to say that?

ANNALISE

Yup.

FARZI

What about Millie and Kat?

ANNALISE

I'm with Millie right now. She says the 10th is good.

ANNALISE

Kat?

FARZI

Kaaaat?

KAT

I'm here. I was out for a hike. The 10th is fine.

Kat watched the screen, waiting for the incoming response dots. Nothing happened. Maybe they decided she wasn't interested and moved on. She pushed aside the twinge of disappointment. It's not like they were friends.

Kat waited another minute. She was heading back to the bathroom when her phone pinged.

Annalise had responded.

Hiking in this weather? Girl, ur crazy.

Kat took a moment to craft her answer.

Not the first time I've heard that.

ANNALISE

'm sure. I'll make a reservation for 6:30. See you on the 10th.

Back in the tub with hot water bubbling around her, Kat added the event to her phone's calendar. Twelve more days. The tension in her shoulders eased, and the pressure in her chest evaporated. She had passed muster and made it to the next level.

TWELVE

From the outside, Sultan's Tent looked like an ordinary restaurant, but as soon as Kat opened the wooden door, she was transported. Swaths of canvas draped from the ceiling and the walls were covered with tapestries and rugs. The patterns cut into the brass pendant lamps diffused the light into artistic shadows. The soft twang of tambourines, lutes, and other stringed instruments played quietly through speakers hidden in the dark corners of the ceiling.

She was surprised to see Millie already seated in a corner booth, nestled among the cushions set around the low table.

"You're here early," Kat noted.

Millie shrugged. "I've never been very good with timing, but I'm never late."

Kat saw an involuntary flinch lift Millie's right shoulder. *Someone else didn't like her to be late,* she thought.

"This place is really something," Kat said, swiveling her head to take in the booth.

"I feel like I've walked into a nomad's tent," Millie said, craning her own head to look at the light on the canvas.

A waitress appeared, asking if they would like something to drink. When Millie told her they were waiting for two more, the waitress poured four glasses of water and left menus on the table. Kat and Millie were silent for a moment, each taking a sip of water.

"Of all the places you've been, which one is your favorite?" Millie wiped condensation off her glass, avoiding eye contact.

"I never really had time to visit most places. It was work. I was mostly in and out. I saw more of the airports than any city," Kat explained.

"Will you start traveling now that you're retired?"

"I might …" Kat let the words die on her tongue. Her work had taken her to eighty-one countries, places she wouldn't and couldn't revisit. And now that she was retired, the thought of planning a trip to a place she might be safe felt like a burden.

"Good evening, ladies!" Farzi announced as she slid into the booth. "This place is beautiful!"

"I hope the food is just as authentic," Kat said.

"Where's Annalise?" Farzi asked Millie. "You didn't come together?"

"She is coming straight from work," Millie answered.

"Oh? What does she do?"

"She runs lash boutiques—"

"Yoo-hoo!" They heard Annalise sing as she walked toward them. "This place is like being inside a jewel! The colors are amazing." Annalise dropped down onto a large gold and red silk pillow. "Oooh, this is nice and squishy." She rocked from side to side.

"These colors should clash," Farzi said, "but somehow they all work together."

"It's an overload of the senses," Kat added. "A risky choice for a restaurant."

"What? Why?" Millie asked. "I like this bohemian feel."

"Overstimulating one sense dulls another," Kat explained, "and our brains are wired to pick the one that will help us survive. The noise of all this distraction will confuse the brain. The food might taste bland because of that."

"Actually, no," argued Annalise. "If you really look around, you'll see more red and orange than anything else. Red enhances the appetite, while orange stimulates appetite and conversation, encouraging us to eat, talk, and spend more money. These were deliberate, money-making choices."

Farzi sucked in her breath. Kat's eyes narrowed. Annalise raised her eyebrows. Millie threw her head back and howled with laughter.

"I'm … I'm … sorry," she sputtered, "but Kat, I think Annalise just firmly put you in your place."

Kat manipulated her face into a smile, while under the table she squeezed her hands into fists. Her fingernails cut into her palms, her irritation easing slightly.

Annalise picked up one of the menus sitting on the table and opened it in front of her face. "I didn't mean to sound bitchy," she apologized. "I'm sorry if I offended you."

Kat uncurled the fingers of her right hand, letting it drop to the side of her thigh. A fleeting panic seized her when she didn't feel the dagger usually concealed there.

"Not at all." Kat smiled, then switched to flattery. "I learned something new. How do you know this about colors?"

"I took a course in interior design a long time ago …"

Before she could continue, the waitress came back to the table to take their drink orders.

"Let me know if you have any questions about the menu," she said before turning away.

"Actually," Annalise called after her, "we've never been here and we don't know what to order."

"Or how the whole eating without cutlery thing works," Millie added.

The waitress opened a menu and held it up like a teacher reading a book to a kindergarten class. "I would recommend the Sultan's Feast. You pay per person, but you get an assortment of things to try and share." She ran through their options for appetizers, entrées, and dessert. "All the meals come with *khobz* bread. You rip the bread and use it as a scoop. The piece should be as big as your mouth. If you have a small mouth, you have a small bite. You use your thumb to push food onto the bread."

"We'll try the feast," Millie decided, gathering menus from the table and handing them to the waitress.

Kat was about to protest but remembered it was Millie's choice to come here. Or perhaps it was a power play, and she had misjudged the woman. Kat shrugged off her irritation. There wasn't anything on the menu she wouldn't eat, anyway.

"Millie said you run a lash boutique, but are you an interior decorator?" Farzi asked Annalise.

"Oh no. That was just one of many things I investigated while I was trying to figure out what I wanted to do when I grew up. I own several lash bars. Two hundred and six locations of Blink across the country."

"Wow, that's amazing," Farzi gushed. "I always wanted to get my lashes done, but you hear so many horror stories …"

"I don't understand. How is it possible to make money with eyelashes?"

Annalise looked at Kat, a smile spreading across her face.

"It's not just lashes. We also do eyebrow tints, waxing, threading, microblading … and …" She leaned forward, reducing her voice to a whisper, "We just signed a contract with a national brand to offer teeth whitening and tooth gems. Not official yet, so …" Annalise mimed zipping her lips shut.

"I'd like to come one day." Farzi smiled. "Get these thick eyebrows under control."

"Oh my god, YES!" bubbled Annalise, glancing at Farzi's eyebrows. "I mean … sorry … I get excited when this topic comes up. Your brows are lush, by the way. But you should come and I'll treat you. You know what? You should all come. We'll make a day of it. My treat."

"Ooh, I'm in!" Farzi clapped her hands like an eager child.

"I wouldn't even know what to choose." Millie chuckled. "There are so many options."

"Do you do anything with … you know … down there?" Farzi tipped her chin down to her lap.

"Nope. But I can send you to a great sugar shop. Best vagacials in the city."

"Va-what?" Kat furrowed a brow.

"A vagina facial. It's a spa treatment for your vulva. They clean up the bikini line and all the strays. It's good for treating ingrown hairs, removing dead skin cells, smoothing the bumps … you know … to keep your vag healthy and hydrated."

"Women really do that?" Millie gasped.

"All the time." Annalise smiled.

"I've been a woman my whole life and did not even know you could do more than wax," Farzi said.

"Trust me." Annalise patted Farzi's hand. "Once you see how nice your vulva looks and feels, you won't stop."

Millie waved her hands in front of her face. "Can we stop? I don't want to talk about this when we are about to eat."

"It makes you uncomfortable?" Kat questioned. "Why? We all have vaginas here."

"Some things are meant to be private," Millie muttered.

"We have to talk about these things," Annalise said. "We are not our mothers. Kat's right. Why isn't it okay for us to talk about vulvas? Vaginal health is important, and we have to take charge of that," she urged. "It's a clinical treatment. It's no different from going to the optometrist."

"Except nobody tries to poke anything in your eye," Kat deadpanned.

The waitress approached with a large silver kettle sitting in a matching silver basin. Her lips were pressed in a tight smile and Kat wondered how much she overheard.

"What is that?" Annalise asked.

"It's for washing. Hold your hands over the basin," she explained, placing it on the table in front of Annalise. The waitress poured water from the kettle over Annalise's outstretched hands.

Kat could smell the oranges infused in the water. The waitress repeated the process for each of them, handing them fresh linen napkins to dry their hands.

The waitress took the kettle and basin away, returning almost immediately with a plate of stewed white beans and tomatoes.

"Your first dish," she said. "*Loubia.*"

THIRTEEN

As soon as the waitress walked away, Annalise burst out laughing, as did Millie and Farzi. Kat smiled, pulled in by their joy, and found her own laughter bubbling up. Her cheeks flushed and her whole body loosened.

"Did we know what this dish was called when we ordered?" Farzi asked, breathless from laughter.

"I–I–don't remember," Annalise sputtered through giggles, "but ... it's ... perfect."

Kat leaned back into the cushions behind her, holding her arms across her stomach. Spending decades as an assassin had removed laughter from her life. She had forgotten how a genuine laugh could spread through her body, relaxing and nourishing her. Now, she could not wipe the smile from her face.

Kat leaned forward, tore off a hunk of bread, and dragged it through the stew, picking up beans, tomatoes, and sauce.

"This is like velvet in my mouth," she moaned after the first bite. "How do they make butter beans taste so ... creamy?"

Annalise burst out laughing again.

"What's so funny? What did I say that is funny?"

"*Butter bean* is a nickname for clitoris," Annalise explained.

"English is so bizarre," Farzi said. "No matter how fluent I think I am …"

"It doesn't bother me," Kat interrupted. "I mastered all the English I needed before I finished primary school. My parents demanded I take lessons three days a week."

"I can't imagine *clitoris* coming up in any kindergarten conversational practices." Annalise grinned. "I didn't even know about my own clitoris until I was almost twenty."

Kat stole a glance at Millie, who kept her eyes down on the beans on her plate.

Is this how women friends always talk? she wondered.

"Lucky you," Farzi said. " I didn't discover mine until my mid-forties."

"Oof. Self-directed, or …?" Annalise prodded.

Farzi's cheeks darkened. "First lesbian lover."

"What about you, Millie? When did you find your—"

"No." Millie cut Annalise off. "I am not talking about this. I claim my space as the resident prude."

"Farzi, do you still do missionary work?" Kat glanced at Millie again. The woman nodded at Kat, her gratitude for the topic change written on her face.

"No. It was a one-time thing."

"So what do you do now, if you don't mind my asking?" Kat dipped her bread in the nearly empty stew, soaking up sauce.

"I pass my time with art. Painting, mostly. Do you work, Millie?"

Millie shook her head. "I was a stay-at-home mom and a housewife. I find myself thinking about finding a part-time job now, but who would hire a woman who hasn't worked in thirty years?"

"I'm sure you can find something," Annalise assured her. "I can reach out to some people, see who's hiring."

"That's so nice." Millie smiled. "I may take you up on that."

"How many children do you have?" Farzi asked.

"Just one. A daughter." Kat noticed Millie drop her eyes to the table for a moment before she lifted her chin and looked past Annalise's shoulder. "Oh, here comes the food."

When the fluted lids of the tagines the waitress placed on the table were removed, Kat's mouth watered. Inside were heaps of meat—chicken with chopped olives on a bed of rice and lamb stewed with plums—filling the booth with aromas that brought her back to her brief stay in Morocco. This restaurant was the real deal. Unlike the last time she had Moroccan food, Sultan's Tent was not tainted with memories of subterfuge and deceit.

She watched Millie rip off a small piece of bread and dip it into the lamb. She hesitated, unsure of what to do.

"Here, watch me," Farzi said. Using her thumb, she pushed a succulent plum and a chunk of lamb onto the bread she cradled with her index and middle fingers.

Millie copied the motion, closing her eyes after the first chew.

"Forgive me, Jesus, but this is heavenly." She sighed around the food in her mouth.

"Annalise, why aren't you eating?" Kat asked as she pushed chicken and olives onto her own bread.

"I'm not sure I can do this," Annalise croaked. "I think I'll ask for a fork."

"Nonsense," Kat snapped. "It's not hard. You stick your fingers in and eat. Like you did when you were a toddler. Why did you come here if not to try something new?"

"Kat, let her be. This was my idea." Millie looked over at Annalise. "I'm sorry if this made you uncomfortable."

"Ach," Kat snorted. "You can talk about a facial for your vagina, but you can't pick up a piece of chicken with your fingers?"

The table fell silent. Kat looked up from the tagine she was dragging her bread through, but only Annalise returned her gaze.

"What is your thing, Kat? What is the one thing you can't do, no matter what?"

Without tearing her eyes from Annalise, Kat pushed the lamb into her mouth. She chewed slowly, trying to come up with an answer. Despite her lacking experience with friend-ships, even she knew *killing a child* was not an appropriate response.

"I can't let a doctor see my underwear," she blurted out. "Even when I go to the gynecologist, I have to hide my under-wear under my pile of clothes."

Annalise tilted her head and lifted her perfectly shaped eyebrows. Her shoulders were shaking, and it took Kat a moment to realize she was laughing.

"I DO THAT TOO!" she shouted.

"Me too," Millie and Farzi added in unison.

"Why are we like that?" Kat could feel the eyes of the other patrons shifting to their table, but she didn't care.

"I hide my bra, too, when I go for a physical." Farzi chuckled.

"Or a mammogram." Millie rolled her eyes.

"I buy the prettiest bras and pay a fortune for them," Annalise mused, "so why do I fold them under my ugly cargo pants?"

"I doubt anything you own is ugly," said Farzi. "I wish I knew how to put an outfit together as well as you do."

"You looked great at speed dating," Millie said. "You made denim sexy. I need to learn how to dress."

"It's not hard. I can show you."

"Once you know what works for your body, you can look good in anything," Kat declared. "My mother taught me that."

"I've always wanted leather pants," Millie said. Kat heard

the sadness in her voice. "But I never had the money. Now that I do, I don't have the body for it."

"Nonsense," Farzi huffed. "We should go shopping and get you some."

"I'm all in for that," said Annalise. "But forget about leather, Millie. Synthetic leather is so much better. It's lighter and made with the greatest invention ever—Lycra!"

"And faux leather can go in the washing machine," Farzi added.

"Millie"—Annalise took hold of the hand Millie was not using for scooping—"I think you will be gorgeous in some faux leather pants and a flowing blouse." She closed her eyes. "I can picture it."

Millie shook her head. "I'd look like a beach ball. I can't do it."

"You won't know until you see it like I do," said Annalise. "Trust me, it will become your favorite outfit. You have to get out of your own head, Millie."

Millie shrugged, wincing like she was in pain. Kat watched her shoulders drop, noticing one was a little higher than the other, possibly from an old injury.

"It's not so simple." Millie looked down at the tablecloth, smoothing out a crease. "I've been hiding my body my whole life. It's hard to change the internal conversation."

Annalise squeezed Millie's hand. "I understand, I do. There are things we do with such habit, we don't even know we are doing them."

"Like eating with your hands," Kat said.

"What are you talking about?" Annalise shot back. "I have never eaten with my hands!"

"How do you eat pizza?" Kat asked. "How about a burger? Any sandwich? With a knife and fork? You've eaten with your hands before."

"She's got you there," Farzi said.

Annalise narrowed her eyes at Kat. "Are you going to be the pedantic one in this group?"

Kat could not hold back a smile as she watched Annalise rip off a hunk of bread and defiantly scoop up the last of the bean stew. The woman grimaced when a tomato squished around her thumb, but recovered quickly, closing her mouth around her fingers.

"Was that so bad?" Kat asked, gentling her tone.

"Yes," Annalise replied, "but this food is so good, I think it's worth it."

Millie leaned forward, scooping out a healthy serving of chicken. "Our preacher says when you make yourself uncomfortable, you learn more about who you are."

Annalise smiled. "No need to be uncomfortable. Lycra will change your life, Millie."

FOURTEEN

"This is a work of art," Farzi exclaimed when the waitress placed a couscous dish in the center of the table. The pearls were buried underneath grilled vegetables, with long carrots pinwheeled from the middle to form sections for the eggplant, zucchini, mushrooms, red peppers, and sweet potatoes. "It looks like pie."

"What are those on top?" Millie pointed to glistening orange circles.

"Grilled apricots drizzled with honey," Farzi said. "If you have never had one, be prepared to give up dried apricots forever. My mother made these all the time."

Kat reached in, forgoing the bread, using a chunk of apricot to scoop up couscous. Millie and Annalise did the same, their faces changing as they bit into the food.

"The apricot is so sweet," Annalise said, licking honey from her lips.

"And not tough and stringy like the dried ones," Kat added.

"The grill brings out the sweetness and makes the flesh almost … crispy," said Farzi.

"I think you mean caramelized," Millie pointed out.

"Yes, that too." Farzi nodded.

"What other secrets did you bring from Afghanistan?" Kat asked.

Farzi brought her napkin to her mouth, then swallowed, hard. The question was intentional. Kat knew everyone had something to hide, but for a fleeting moment, she regretted putting Farzi on the spot.

"I meant about food," she clarified.

Farzi relaxed. "There are rules to follow when you eat with your hands. Using one finger means you are selfish," she explained eagerly. "Two fingers shows you are caring, and if you eat with three, you are generous. And you should only eat with your right hand."

Annalise pulled her left hand back from the couscous. "Why not the left hand?"

"It's considered unclean, because it's typically one used for, uh, personal hygiene," Farzi explained.

"First we talk about vaginas and now we talk about assholes?" snarked Kat.

"We did that already," Millie joked, "at Lulu, after speed dating."

"I swear, Millie." Annalise laughed. "How did I not know you were so clever? Have any of you gone on any dates yet?"

"I had two dates." Farzi nodded. "And neither will go beyond that. One was just coffee and the second took me to a vegan restaurant. The food was good, but he spent the whole meal talking about the evils of meat and dairy."

"I had two matches," Kat answered. "One uninteresting date and the second appears to only want to talk on the phone."

"I had three dates." Millie blushed, hiding her smile behind her hand. "They were fun, but only one man reached out for a second date. I might go … we'll see."

The waitress approached, a plate of pastry triangles in hand.

"Your dessert is *braewat*," she explained. "Almond paste wrapped in phyllo and soaked in hot honey. Can I get anyone a coffee or tea?"

"Mint tea for me," Farzi said.

"Same," said Kat. Annalise and Millie both ordered orange herbal tea.

"I miss being able to have coffee late at night," Farzi pined as she chose a pastry.

"I miss being able to stay up past midnight and not wake up feeling like I ran a marathon," Millie said, licking honey from her fingertips.

Kat picked up the plate of gooey triangles and examined it before choosing a piece. "Why is it we sleep less and nap more as we get older?"

"Everything changes," Annalise agreed. "I spend more time getting ready for bed than I ever have. Between the serum for my face, the retinol, the lip mask, and the body moisturizer, it takes forever until I crawl into bed. Matteo is almost always fast asleep by the time I get under the covers."

Farzi helped herself to a second braewat. "It's not any better in the morning." She laughed. "My morning ritual used to be jump out of bed, shower, get dressed, have coffee, smoke a cigarette, then be amazing for the whole day. Now I have to pivot slowly out of bed, praying I don't pull a muscle or throw out my back. There are days when I walk into the kitchen and look at my espresso maker like it's a foreign object."

"Everything takes longer these days," Millie said.

"I am very unprepared for aging," Kat admitted. "I didn't think I'd live past fifty."

"Why not?" Millie asked.

"My mother passed away too young. Cancer." She let the word hang. "I thought the same would happen to me. But here I am, still thriving." *While almost everyone I trained with is dead.*

"Every morning, I do an inventory check of my aches and

pains," added Annalise. "Knees, creaky. Hips, sore. Neck, stiff. Fingers, swollen. Why does aging hurt so much?"

Millie reached for a second pastry but pulled her hand back. "And why are there so many vitamins? I now take collagen, turmeric, magnesium, and a multivitamin."

"I stare in the mirror for way too long," Annalise said. "I try to ignore the wrinkled eyelids and the giant pores, but at least I still have my own teeth."

Kat picked up her teacup and examined the contents. "I spend too much time thinking about bowel movements," she confessed.

Farzi choked on her tea as she tried to hold in her laughter. "I … I … pray for an easy pass," she sputtered. "You know what I mean?"

"I do!" Millie exclaimed. "I worry I'll push too hard and give myself a stroke."

Annalise took another braewat and nodded. "I sometimes feel like my vagina is turning itself inside out."

The waitress, who was approaching the table, stopped, and turned right back around. Farzi let out a snort and the others started laughing again.

"We had better leave a good tip." Annalise chuckled.

"This has been so much fun." Millie was beaming as she picked a pastry off the tray. "Can we do this again?"

"Dinner, or something else?" Kat asked.

Farzi leaned forward, like she had a secret. "Have you ever been to see a medium?"

FIFTEEN

They were all squeezed together in the circular booth, colorful pillows askew. Farzi had placed her phone in the middle of the table, cued up to a video of the medium.

"I found her on Facebook," Farzi explained. "And she's fun to watch. You know how some people just attract you and you don't know why? She is one of those. She makes me cry too."

"I'm on the fence about whether I believe in this," Annalise said. "Do you believe it?"

Farzi waggled her head from side to side. "I don't know. I want to believe, but at the same time, it seems implausible. What about you, Millie?"

Millie shook her head. "The Bible adamantly says we should not turn to mediums. It makes us unclean. We should turn our eyes to god only."

Kat turned away so no one could see her roll her eyes. She pressed her lips together, holding in her sour opinion of organized religion.

Farzi hesitated over the play button. "Would you rather I not play this?"

"It's fine," Millie said. "I think it's fine to watch a video."

"God will not punish you for watching YouTube," Annalise said, patting her hand.

Farzi's screen came to life. The camera followed the medium as she paced the stage, calling out details she said Spirit was showing her. She turned suddenly to the left and pointed to the audience.

"There's a man here, telling me his wife won't take off her wedding ring." The video changed views to a second camera focused on the audience. "He's telling me you work with legal papers ... not a lawyer ... more like a paralegal?"

"Oh, please," Kat muttered to herself.

"What?" Annalise said.

Farzi paused the video. "Are you not a believer?"

"No," Kat said. She did not like how they were all looking at her, waiting to hear what she would say. "There are so many different jobs that handle legal papers. This feels kind of vague. She's just calling out to let the audience come to her. There is probably more than one widow in the room still wearing her ring."

Farzi shook her head. "Office work is vague. The medium specifically said a law office."

"Did she?" Kat was sure she heard the medium only mention legal work. Something inside her head told her to back off. "I must have heard wrong. Please, push play."

The medium went on, searching for the one person who would connect the dots. Kat sipped her now-cold tea, keeping further thoughts to herself. After more prodding, a woman in her early thirties in the audience raised her hand. The camera zoomed in.

"I think that might be my husband," she said, her voice wavering.

The medium nodded. "He wants you to know he is no longer in pain. He's showing me a crushed heart ... is that how he died?"

"Yes." The woman gasped. "He was in a bad car accident."

Oh, for fuck's sake, Kat thought. *Car accident, heart attack, suicide … take your pick of a dead heart.*

"What is with all the sage and incense?" the medium asked.

The woman teared up. "I have it everywhere in my house. I think it welcomes his spirit."

"No." The medium shook her head. "It stinks and he hates it." There was a burst of laughter, including the woman who was just in tears. "Can you lay off that stuff? You're scaring the shit out of him."

Farzi stopped the video again. "So? Want to go?"

It took almost no effort to convince Annalise to go, but Millie and Kat were both reluctant.

"I thought we wanted to try new things," Farzi said.

"I'm in," Annalise said. "I've never seen one and I'm totally curious."

"I don't believe these people can really talk to the dead," Kat huffed, "but I am curious too. I will try to keep an open mind."

"Who would you want to talk to?" Farzi asked after the waitress brought a fresh pot of tea.

"My grandma," Annalise said without hesitation. "I miss her so much. And my aunt Claire. She died when I was a baby and everyone has always told me I'm so much like her. How about you, Millie? Will you come?"

Millie brought her hand to her neck, stroking the skin. "I … I don't know. I'll come if you want me to. It might be a fun night out. I mean, it's not a sin just to be there, right? I don't have to speak up, right?"

"No, you don't. I've watched some videos where no one says anything. The medium just moves on." Farzi looked into her teacup and shrugged. "I'd want to hear from any one of my people who passed."

Kat frowned. The pieces were not fitting together. Farzi brought this idea to the table, so why wasn't she specific about who she wanted the medium to channel? Now Kat had to know.

"I will go too," she said. "I like the circus."

SIXTEEN

"This is so exciting," Farzi said as they walked through the theater's front doors. "Maybe I'll get a message from my grandmother."

"Look around." Kat pointed to the people filling the lobby. "There are at least two hundred people here. It's unlikely your grandma will be heard above all the noise. That old lady there"—she pointed her chin to a hunched-over, white-haired woman—"probably knows more dead people than live ones."

Farzi drew in a short breath. "Kat! That's a horrible thing to say. Old doesn't mean everyone you know is dead."

"Not all, just most," Kat said.

Millie fanned her face. "Is it hot in here or is it just me?"

It *was* hot in the building, Kat noted. The day had been unseasonably warm for early June.

"I'm kind of nervous," Annalise whispered as they took their seats. "Now that I'm here, I'm not sure I want anyone to contact me. I don't think I could handle my mom showing up. Do you think people get nicer once they pass to the other side?"

A disembodied voice blared from the speakers. "Good

evening, everyone! Please welcome Portland's favorite medium, Carina Gray."

Applause burst out all around them. The woman who stepped onstage wore leather—or faux leather—pants with gold scrolls creeping up the outside of each leg. Her crossover fitted tee was the same gold as the scrolls. She looked more like a rock star than a spiritual medium.

"See, Millie," Annalise whispered, "everyone can rock the leather look."

"Welcome, everybody!" the medium called out from center stage. "Thank you so much for coming tonight. Can I get a show of hands ... how many of you have never been to see a medium before?"

Kat, Annalise, and Farzi raised an arm in the air, but Millie kept her arms in her lap.

"If you didn't raise your hand and this is your first time, I'll know." Carina winked. "Spirit is the best tattletale." She smiled as the crowd laughed.

Carina spent a few minutes explaining that she wasn't in control of who showed up. It was the responsibility of everyone in the theater to listen for the specific details relating to their loved ones.

"If you know the person I am channeling, and you don't speak up, I want you to ask yourself why you came here. If Spirit has a message for you and you don't want to hear it, why did you buy a ticket? Spirit is not here to criticize or make you feel bad for your choices. Your loved ones who have passed aren't going to waste their time telling you to buy a reliable car or to remind you to take out the trash. They have more important things to say. My assistant, Layla, will be in the audience with a microphone, so once you are sure that the spirit I am channeling has come for you, please either raise your hand or stand. The best way for you to see how this works is for me to just start. There is a very persistent man pushing through right now."

Carina looked up toward the ceiling. "This man is showing me yellow ... yellow ... yellow. A yellow car, yellow flowers, and the letter *D*. If that resonates with you, please identify yourself. Yellow ... the name is Dave, or Drew, or Dean ..."

"I think that's my grandfather," said a quiet voice from the back. All heads turned to find the source.

While everyone in the theater watched the assistant run from the front of the stage to the back of the auditorium, Kat kept her eyes on Carina. The medium's eyes followed her assistant, but the corner of her mouth twitched up for a fraction of a second. Kat recognized the duper's delight, that spark of joy when a lie goes unnoticed. The difference between her and this medium was that Kat had decades to practice hiding the involuntary spasm.

A woman who looked to be in her forties stood and took the microphone from Layla. "I think that might be my grandfather. His name was Don."

"And what's with the yellow?" Carina asked from the stage.

"It was his favorite color. We used to sing that song, *Tie a Yellow Ribbon*, when we worked in his garden together."

"Okay ... okay ... relax," Carina said to someone only she could see. "He's really persistent. Gah, he's showing me too many things too fast. Calm down, man! He just lit a cigarette. Doesn't he know that can kill him?" The audience erupted into laughter again. "And he just gave me the finger." Laughter again. Kat heard Millie chuckle.

"That is totally something Grampy would do," the woman said.

"He keeps showing me Paris. The Eiffel Tower, the Louvre, and now he's sitting at a café near the Champs-Élysées with a coffee. Are you going to Paris?"

"Oh my god ..." The woman choked. "I've been planning to go to Paris with my husband, but he got sick and we decided not to go."

"Well, Don is saying you should go. Stop dicking around and live your life."

Next to Kat, Farzi gasped. "How can she know such things?" she whispered. "She shouldn't know these things."

Kat looked over at Annalise, whose mouth was opened in an *O*. Millie started tearing up when a man in the audience received a message from his wife, who passed away from lung cancer.

"She wants you to know it's okay that you weren't there when she passed," Carina said, a gentleness in her voice. "She was already gone when you left to pick up your son from the airport. She waited for you to leave so she could too."

The man, seated in the middle of the theater, let out a sob.

"I'm so sorry," he bawled. "I—I—I thought she died alone and that kills me."

"You don't need to hold on to that guilt. You were with her right until her spirit left her body. She's showing me a brown dog? What does that mean to you?"

Kat shook her head. *It means nothing. Even I, who never had a dog, can dig around in my memory for a brown dog.* Kat shook her head again as she recalled the Rottweiler who crawled onto her lap begging for attention as she shared drinks with the Romanian baroness who used children as drug mules. Kat had let the dog into the yard before she slashed the baroness's throat, not wanting to subject the poor animal to anything unsavory.

"We adopted a chocolate lab three months before she was diagnosed," the man said. Kat again rolled her eyes.

"Well, she's telling me you need to put your energy into the dog and not into the other reckless things you are doing to manage your grief. Does that make sense to you?"

"Yes." He nodded. "Thank you."

"There's a boy here," Carina announced. "He's showing me sand and … what?" She looked up to the ceiling and shook her head. "That's not clear. Can you show me something else?"

The entire theater was silent, waiting.

"Oh, okay. I see it now. This is a boy, and he's showing me sand, a paintbrush, and orange paint. The letter *K*. And a soccer ball. Who is this boy connected to?"

Farzi leaned forward in her seat. She rose, placing a hand on Kat's shoulder, as if using it for support.

"That's my son," she said, her voice shaking. "That's my Kalan."

SEVENTEEN

Is she for real?

Kat craned her head back to study Farzi's profile. She watched the emotions playing with the muscles on the woman's face. *That's why she wanted to come.*

"I just need to make sure this spirit is here for you," Carina said. "He's showing me the number fourteen. Does that mean anything to you?"

Farzi nodded, wiping tears from the corners of her eyes. Her hand shook as she took the microphone from the assistant. "He died on the fourteenth of March."

Kat shook her head in disbelief and disgust. People were so gullible. Throwing out a number is random. She had thought Farzi was better than this, but people in pain can't be reasonable.

"He keeps showing me paint. Are you renovating? About to renovate?"

"No," Farzi said, flicking a tear from her cheek.

"Huh, that's weird." Carina scratched her head. "Uh, oh, okay." She was looking at the roof, having another conversation. "All right, I get it! He won't let up on the paint. Why?"

"I guess that's because I'm a painter?" Farzi answered, her voice cracking.

"Not for houses," Carina stated, "but as an artist."

Farzi nodded. "Yes."

"He wants me to ask you why you stopped."

Kat leaned back in her seat, crossing her left leg over her right. She kept her eyes on Carina, looking for more subtle signs that this entire exchange was one hundred percent bull-shit: a change in the rise and fall of her chest, tapping fingers on the lips, a clearing of the throat. These were all natural movements that were easy to miss if you weren't on high alert for deception. During the whole exchange with Farzi, Carina paced back and forth on the stage, stopping and looking directly at Farzi when she had new information to share.

"Did you recently have some grilled apricots?"

"Oh my god," Kat whispered at the same time as Farzi's knees buckled and she collapsed into her seat.

Kat and Annalise looked at each other. Millie crossed herself.

"Yes," Farzi cried. "How do you know that?"

"Your son showed me. You need to do more of that. Not the apricot part, the going-out-with-friends part. That's what will bring change and give you the joy you need."

Holy fuck. This can't be real. Kat swallowed hard.

"Thank you for letting me share this with you today," Carina said, bringing her hands together in front of her chest and bowing slightly. She walked off the stage as a voice announced a twenty-minute intermission.

Kat turned to look at Farzi, but her hands were covering her face. Millie wrapped an arm over Farzi's shaking shoul-ders. Annalise pulled a packet of tissues out of her purse, leaning across Millie to place it on Farzi's leg. Kat wondered if she was supposed to do something as well, offer the woman comfort. But she was paralyzed by her own fear. What if one of her marks made an appearance? What if Carina called out her name?

Kat squeezed her hands into fists. She was being ridiculous. The medium hadn't called out anyone by name. That was part of the illusion and the trickery. People would always pick up what you put down, even if it was as vague as a letter or a number. Kat herself had walked into dangerous situations that could have killed her, but her marks only saw a beguiling and witty redhead or a bubble-assed whore—whoever she chose to be. They were incapable of seeing the cold killer in her. Just like the people in this theater, Farzi included, couldn't see the scam.

EIGHTEEN

"Farzi, I am so sorry for your loss," Annalise said as they stood in a corner of the theater foyer. She put her hand on Farzi's forearm and squeezed.

The audience had filed back to their seats. Kat encouraged them to stay in the lobby, consoling Farzi and skipping the rest of the show, masking her relief as compassion. Carina's voice was muffled through the closed theater doors.

"Thank you." Farzi sniffed. "This isn't exactly the way I imagined I would tell anyone about Kalan. But I feel blessed that he came through Carina."

Millie again put her arm over Farzi's shoulders. "If you don't mind me asking, when did he pass?"

"Thirty-three years ago. He was nine. Shot and killed by the Taliban."

"What? How? Why?" sputtered Annalise.

Farzi swiped at her fresh tears. "The Taliban just do that to keep Afghans in check. They'll sweep through a neighborhood and kill everyone in sight. They drove onto our street in a Jeep with a mounted machine gun and opened fire. My son was outside, playing football—soccer—with his friends. Kalan was one of three to die there. At least now, thanks to Carina, I know he is resting easy in paradise."

"Children have no sin," murmured Millie.

"At least she gave you some peace of mind," Kat said, "even if it isn't real."

"Kat!" Annalise hissed. "Just because you don't believe doesn't mean you have to shit on someone who does."

"It's okay, Annalise," Farzi said. "I wouldn't have believed it either, but her details were unquestionable."

"Really?" Kat wondered aloud. "Psychics are just very intuitive and empathic people. They attract people looking to be validated and heard. Carina threw out some generalities and waited for someone to bite."

"That's how faith works." Millie shot Kat a dirty look.

"Believe whatever you want," Farzi said, taking a step closer to Kat, looking her directly in the eye. "But for a few minutes, Carina made me feel connected to my son. I think about him every day, wondering how his life would be had he not been murdered. He'd be married with children by now. Maybe here in America, or back home in Kabul. Maybe I'd still be married, living out my senior years with a husband I grew to love. I believe our paths are predetermined. I am free to make choices, but it's not going to change the outcome. I was meant to be here, tonight, with all of you."

She turned and nodded at Annalise and Millie. "I'm not sure why yet, but that will become clear. Maybe next week." She turned back to Kat. "Or perhaps when I am standing over your grave."

Slowly, a smile played over Kat's face. "I have no intention of dying soon. I hope you're patient. If Carina brought you comfort, that's what matters."

"Thank you," Farzi murmured. She dropped down into one of the oversized white leather armchairs adjacent to the bar. She looked up to the ceiling, her dark hair spilling over the back of the chair. "I am emotionally exhausted." She closed her eyes and sighed. "But I'm also glad I came. I appreciate you being here with me. All of you."

Annalise leaned against the bar. "Why do people avoid talking about death?" she wondered aloud.

"Because we fear it," Millie answered. "No one wants to consider their death. At church, death comes up only when we talk about living a Christian life of virtue and being welcomed into heaven while avoiding hell. No one ever talks about the nuts and bolts of what happens when you actually die."

"Death is ugly," Kat said. "The last breath is a horrible sound, not the gentle wheeze the movies make us think it is."

"Have you seen a lot of people die?" Annalise asked softly.

"I grew up behind the Iron Curtain," Kat explained, grateful to be able to tell her new friends the truth. "Death was as common as the sunrise."

"That must have been horrible. I can't imagine living like that." Millie shook her head sympathetically.

"It's not so bad when it's the same for everyone," Kat said. "Basic principle of communism. But no one is prepared for death."

"I'd like to finish a lip balm stick just once before I die," Annalise declared. "I always lose them before they're even halfway done."

"We can bury you with one. Then you'll have eternity to finish it," Kat joked.

"Except I want to be cremated. The whole idea of rotting in a coffin grosses me out," Annalise said.

"How much of you would actually disintegrate, though?" Farzi said, coming out of her stupor, glancing at Annalise's breasts. She lifted an eyebrow.

"Touché," Annalise said with a smile. "I'm not even sure cremation is such a good idea. Might be too environmentally destructive."

"They dissolve into a gelatinous goo," Kat said without a

hint of emotion. "Pacemakers and defibrillators are removed. Otherwise, they explode in the chamber."

"All this work, just melting into a sticky mess." Annalise sighed. "What an expensive waste of money."

"Dying is expensive." Millie sighed. "I'm embarrassed to say how much my husband's funeral cost. The casket was as much as a used car. However you look at it, it's throwing good money away."

"My condolences, Millie," Farzi said. "When did your husband pass?"

"A little more than a year ago."

Kat waited for Millie to elaborate, but the woman crossed her arms over her chest and blankly stared out through the lobby windows. She examined the side of Millie's face, looking for the telltale signs of grief. There was no lowering of the corners of the mouth nor drooping eyelids. *Maybe her faith helped her manage her loss. Maybe she had emotionally checked out long before her husband died. She wouldn't be the first woman to be stuck in a loveless marriage.*

"If my ashes are going to spend eternity in a little pewter box," Farzi mused, "at least get it on sale."

"I would like my body to go to science," Kat said. "If I am to disintegrate to dust anyway, I might as well let some medical students learn something before that happens."

"I'll be buried in the cemetery beside my husband," Millie said. "About six months after he died, I went to the funeral home and prepaid for my own plot. I even picked out my casket."

Annalise shook her head. "Oh, Millie, that must have been so hard."

"Actually, it wasn't," she said. "I locked in at those prices. I inflation-proofed my death."

Farzi lifted an eyebrow. "Smart move." She pushed herself out of the armchair. "I'm ready to go. Let's get out of here."

"Farzi, are you okay to drive?" Annalise asked as they walked to the parking lot.

"I can drive you home," Kat offered.

"I'm fine, but thanks for offering. Grief comes and goes. So what shall we do next month?" Farzi asked. "Annalise and Kat, it's your turn to pick."

Annalise looked at Kat, who shrugged.

"I have an idea." Annalise grinned. "Do y'all have hiking boots?"

NINETEEN

"Is this even legal?" Millie, Annalise, Farzi, and Kat stood at what was once probably a clearly marked property line but was now a tangle of twisted wire fencing and overgrown lawn. The air was thick with late-summer heat and buzzing insects. Kat was already sweating in her new hiking pants. She pulled her T-shirt away from her body, allowing some air to flow under the gray cotton.

"I have no idea," Annalise answered. "But clearly, no one comes here. There's no sign of anyone being here recently."

"I can't believe there are other people who do this," Farzi said, wiping sweat from her forehead. "Why would anyone want to go into an abandoned house?"

"I think it's fascinating. How do we get in?" Kat craned her neck, looking for an opening in the fence line.

"We walk until we find a break in the fence links, or we find the front path from the road," Annalise explained. "Half the fun is discovering a way in."

"That is definitely illegal," Millie cautioned. She slid her hands into the pockets of her loose faded khakis. "Are you sure we won't get arrested for trespassing?"

"I don't know, Millie. I've never done this. This is my first time too." Annalise brushed away the gnats flying in front of her face. "I promise, if we get arrested, Matteo will bail us out."

"We won't get arrested," Kat stated. "In order for the police to come, someone has to alert them. The last occupied house we passed is a mile away."

"Maybe I'll stay behind as the lookout," Farzi suggested.

"Bad move." Annalise laughed. "The one who waits alone gets dragged out of the car by her hair and brutally murdered while her friends obliviously carry on."

Alarm crossed Millie's face. "What are you talking about?"

"And then the killer comes into the house to pick them off, one by one," Kat added with a grin. "Until the final girl fights back."

"The final what?" Millie squeaked.

"Have you never watched a horror movie?" Farzi asked.

"No. I can't stomach that kind of violence. I watched one when I was in high school, but I covered my eyes practically the whole time."

"The final girl is the last one standing," Annalise explained. "She's the one who takes on the killer in a bloody fight, with a tool she is suddenly an expert at using. All her rage—for the death of her friends, the chaos in her life, the patriarchy, whatever—is channeled into that final blow. I think I'd make a great final girl."

"Oh, please," Kat scoffed. "Look at you. You're one hundred percent the bad girl."

Annalise put her hands on her denim-clad hips. "Because I have this body?" she said. "I am nowhere near callous enough." She turned to Millie. "The bad girl is the one who sleeps around, who only cares for herself. She is always the first to die, and usually in a horrible way."

"And you … enjoy watching these movies?"

"They're fun," Farzi said. "Even though you know it's not real, it still scares you. I find the violence … I don't know … like a release?"

"Brain stimulation," Kat said. "Fear releases adrenaline at the most horrifying moments. We can watch the darkest parts of humanity from a comfortable couch with a bowl of popcorn in our laps."

"I think you'd be a great final girl," Farzi said to Kat. "A pissed-off, cold-blooded woman who takes out the killer with a baseball bat strapped to the outside of her leg."

Kat's mouth flooded with saliva. Her stomach clenched, and she had to force herself to swallow while fighting the urge to vomit at the same time. Her friend's choice of words had to be mere coincidence.

Annalise laughed, turning to Kat. "Did you bring a bat?"

"If you did, I want it," Farzi declared. "I want to be the F.G.O.C."

"The what?" Millie asked.

"The Final Girl of Color. I'm no trope."

Kat snorted a laugh out her nose. "No, I don't think you are."

"I don't have weapons, but I have these." Annalise unzipped the top of her backpack and handed out face masks, latex gloves, and bright orange safety vests. "We'll need them once we find a way in. Let's go."

Kat stood for a moment longer, examining what she could see of the house between the overgrowth and full trees. She took a quiet but deep breath through her nose. She blinked slowly, then pulled her mouth and eyes into a practiced smile.

Sandwiching herself between Farzi and Millie, Kat followed as Annalise led them along the fence line. Little burrs caught on their pants. A line of sweat was already visible down the back of Annalise's tank top. Millie lifted her hair from her neck and fanned herself. Kat reached down the front of her shirt to wipe away the sweat between her breasts. The only sounds were the occasional fly-by of a bee, the humming of the electrical wires overhead, and their footsteps tamping down the biggest weeds and tallest grasses Kat had ever seen.

The HOA would go crazy if this happened in my neighborhood.

"Annalise, slow down," Kat hissed. "You're going too fast. You might miss a break in the fence."

"Fine." Annalise relented, slowing her pace. "But I don't think I could have missed that." She stopped and pointed. The chain link fence ended at a post, halfway along the side of the house.

"So weird," Farzi said. "Maybe they left before the fence was finished."

"Let's go," Annalise said, pushing her boots through the overgrowth.

"What if we can't get into the house?" Millie asked. "We don't break in, do we?"

Annalise looked back over her shoulder. "There are rules for urban exploring. You only go in if you find an easy entrance. You don't move, break, or steal anything. And you walk slowly and carefully, in case the floors aren't stable."

Kat's pulse quickened. The promise of discovery—not only of what might be inside the house but also the risk of getting caught—was something she deeply missed. She glanced back, seeing the worry etched into Millie's face.

"It's going to be fine, Millie," she said. "We have cell phones if something happens, and I'm fully trained in first aid. I can hear your heart hammering from here."

"Really?"

"No. But I can see your shoulders are raised and your hands have been clenched into fists since we got out of the car."

Millie looked down at her hands and quickly released her squeeze. She forced her shoulders down and took a deep breath.

"I didn't even realize I was doing that."

"It's amazing what body language can reveal."

"Ladies, we have arrived," Annalise called from the front of their line.

Kat moved her eyes up. The two-story house rose like a glass and concrete pillar from the weeds. Annalise marched forward, stomping down the vines and grass, pushing plants out of her way.

When the other three caught up with her, they stood next to each other, forming a wall. This close to the house, Kat could see it wasn't concrete after all. The house had been abandoned for so long, its wood was now bleached gray.

"Let's see if we can find a broken window or a missing door." Annalise turned to her right and they followed her, searching.

"You can't even tell where the backyard ends," Farzi said.

"And is that a shed?" Kat pointed away from the house. They turned to look and could see a gabled orange roof peeking out from behind the leaves of a maple tree. The rest of the building was completely obscured by boxwood and vines.

"How long has this place been empty?" Millie wondered.

"Long enough for nature to reclaim it," Annalise answered.

Farzi turned back toward the house. "Look at the vines creeping across the windows."

A grid of black-framed windows made up the back side of the house to the second floor. The vines climbing the windows to the roof were bursting with pink flowers.

"That's kind of beautiful," Millie whispered. "My house has a wall of windows too."

"It's a common design for Portland," Annalise pointed out. "We have so much greenery to look out onto."

"It's amazing that all these windows are intact," Farzi said. "Even those sliding doors."

"Doors?" Annalise took a few steps back to assess the house.

Kat squinted. "Wow. I can see them now. Wonderful architecture. You can't see them unless you really look."

"I think the windows have that special coating that blocks the view from outside," Farzi said.

"Privacy film," Kat said. "The kind that reflects the sun during the day."

Kat walked up to the sliding doors, pressing her hands on either side of her face. She peered inside, not bothered by the algae and grime coating the glass. She saw a round table and chairs, and beyond that, a kitchen with its cupboards and drawers opened.

Annalise appeared at her side.

"Is it okay to try to open them?" Kat asked.

Annalise nodded. "Any unlocked door is fine."

Kat grasped the metal handle of the sliding door, her glove squishing the moss and algae covering it. She tugged gently, but nothing happened. She leaned her body forward to give her momentum and pushed harder. A creak from the doorframe encouraged her to try again. She pushed once more, and with a hiss and screech, a gap opened.

Annalise also grabbed the handle, pulling as Kat pushed. With a loud shriek, the door began to move, leaving a trail of rust in its track. Once the seal was fully cracked, a plume of dust puffed out, like the house had been holding its breath.

"Well, we won't be needing headlamps," Farzi said as she squeezed in beside Millie.

The house was flooded with natural light from the wall of windows, the floor mottled with shadows of vines and flowers. Annalise stepped in first, followed by Millie and Farzi. When Kat stepped over the threshold, her breath caught.

She had seen many things in her life, but what she saw in front of her was incomprehensible. The opened kitchen cabinets revealed the dishes and glasses still within. A few doors on the lower cabinets were also ajar, and Kat could see pots and pans stacked inside. The kitchen table was grimy with mold, but she could see the shape of the placemats still sitting there. The air smelled musty and full of decay.

"Put your masks on," Annalise instructed them. "We should not be breathing this air unfiltered."

Quietly, they put their masks on and moved deeper into the kitchen.

"Who leaves a house like this?" Kat wondered aloud.

"It's like they fled in the middle of the night," Annalise said.

"Do you think someone has already been here?" Millie asked.

"I don't think so," Annalise said. "Look down." Kat looked down at her feet. Her boots were splattered with dark marks, the blood of her final mark. The others' brand-new boots glowed in contrast to the dust and debris on the kitchen floor.

"There are no other footprints," Annalise said.

Pieces of wallpaper and drywall littered the floor like confetti. Cobwebs draped from the corners and edges of the cabinets and appliances. In a dark corner of the kitchen, Kat spotted an organized pile of twigs, leaves, plastic bags, and fabric.

"That was probably an opossum nest," she said, pointing.

"Why are some of the cupboards open?" Farzi asked.

Annalise walked over to a bank of upper cabinets on either side of the oven, lifting herself onto the tips of her toes to get a better view. "They probably popped open when the house shifted."

"Or when the dampness squeezed them out of shape," Kat added.

They walked carefully across the kitchen, approaching a door sandwiched between a once-white fridge and the oven.

"I'd bet this was the pantry," Kat said. "Look at the mouse

droppings." Without waiting for the others, Kat pulled the door open. The shelves were empty, except for three cans of Spam. *Probably still good.* She laughed to herself.

From the kitchen, they moved into what might have once been a living room or den. A velvet love seat sat facing a grime-covered window that looked out the front of the house. The view was completely obscured by a tangled mess of vines and weeds. A single, tattered curtain hung from a lopsided rod mounted above the window. Kat moved through the living room to the front door. A built-in coat closet sat on the left side of the foyer. Off to her right was another door, fitted with a deadbolt. She turned the bolt and slowly opened the door.

"What the fuck?"

Farzi was beside her, pulling the door wide open. Light filtered in through an algae-covered window, bathing the space in an eerie green glow.

"What'd you find?" Annalise asked.

"*Madar gai,*" Farzi said as she stepped into the garage.

"Motherfucker, indeed," Kat replied without thinking. "Who leaves a Corvette behind?" she added quickly before Farzi could ask how she knew how to swear in Farsi.

"What the hell?" Annalise said from the doorway. She pushed past Kat and Farzi and got closer to the car.

The white car was parked in the middle of the garage, one pop-up headlight raised, as if it were winking. Black mold crept down the walls, but there wasn't a mark on the car. It was covered in a fine layer of dust, and Kat could see the black leather seats through the side window. She walked to the front of the Corvette, where she found a folded-up double stroller.

Something really bad happened here.

"What horrible thing happened to the people who lived here?" Farzi said, as if reading Kat's mind.

"I'm going back into the house." Millie shivered. "This is too weird."

Kat glanced at Millie and saw worry etched on the woman's face. Even in the dim light, she could see Millie's pupils had dilated and she was scratching at the inside of her left elbow. Classic signs of anxiety. Kat couldn't shake the feeling that Millie was feeling something more than creeped out.

"I'll come with you," Kat said.

She followed Millie, leaving Annalise and Farzi in the garage.

"Do you want to go upstairs?" she asked.

Millie stood in the foyer, gazing at the stairs leading to the second floor. "Do you think it's safe? Are the stairs stable?"

Kat looked up at the ceiling. Aside from cobwebs clinging to the popcorn texture, there were no signs of water damage or decay.

"I'll go up first."

Kat climbed the stairs slowly, placing one foot on each step and leaning into it, listening for creaks and testing for stability. Millie followed, placing her own feet in the footprints Kat left on the dust-covered stairs. The staircase curved, ending in an open area with a vaulted ceiling. A crystal chandelier hung from the V, its pieces long ago having lost their sparkle.

To their right, a television was mounted on the wall with built-in bookshelves on either side. Unidentifiable knickknacks sat on the shelves, along with scattered books. Dust blanketed everything.

Millie walked up to the shelves, tilting her head to read the spines. "There are children's books in here."

Kat heard the unmistakable sadness in Millie's voice. Most people would have tried to dig out the reason immediately, but Kat was a professional. She would wait, and Millie would spill her beans when she was ready.

They turned to face the hallway, walking slowly toward the doorways. There were more mouse droppings, and halfway down the hall, the ceiling had collapsed. A pile of yellowed insulation had been shredded and spread, making a nest for a long-gone critter. Millie opened the first door on the right and sucked in her breath.

Kat poked her head past Millie and saw what had once been a playroom. A rocking chair sat near the bay window looking out over the front yard. A toy box rested on its side, trains, dolls, puppets, and building blocks spilling out like the box had puked. Abandoned Lego was half-built on a child-size plastic table with matching chairs. Decaying posters clung to the walls like tree bark.

"Jesus Christ," Kat swore.

"Please don't," Millie whispered.

"Don't what?"

"Use that phrase. It bothers me."

Kat let her eyes drift from the wall to the cross hanging around Millie's neck.

"Can I say holy fuck?"

Millie pressed her lips into a thin smile. "Yes. Sometimes fucks are very much holy."

They left the door to the playroom open, continuing down the hall to the remaining doors. They found a bathroom and three more bedrooms. In the primary bedroom closet, discarded women's clothing was piled on the floor.

"What's that about?" Kat wondered.

"She ran," Millie said, her voice barely above a whisper.

Kat nodded. "That's exactly what it looks like."

Kat watched Millie take in the clothes. She could hear Farzi and Annalise moving around on the main floor, the quiet murmur of their voices.

"Sometimes that's the only way. I hope he never found them. I hope it worked out better for her." Millie pulled off a glove and wiped the sweat from the back of her neck.

When Kat reached out to pull a cobweb from Millie's hair, the woman flinched.

"You have something in your hair," she explained. Millie ran her ungloved hand through her hair, catching the web. Millie furrowed her brow, then walked out of the bedroom. Kat lingered for a moment, knowing better than to push anyone to confess her pain.

TWENTY

Kat and Millie were coming down the stairs as Farzi and Annalise walked into the foyer. The dust and mold had obviously irritated all of them, their eyes red and bloodshot above their masks.

The smell in the house was making Kat feel sick. Most of the walls inside the dining room and the living room were covered with either algae or mold. The dust was thick on every surface, in some cases obscuring shapes and colors.

"I need clean air," she mumbled through her mask. "I've seen enough."

"Me too," Annalise agreed.

Once outside, Kat peeled off her mask and gloves and gulped the fresh air. The headache that had started building when they were in the playroom eased.

"I can't understand how someone just leaves a house like this," she said.

"That's what made me want to try urban exploring." Back at the car, Annalise pulled a plastic bag out of the trunk, holding it open so they could dispose of their gloves and masks. "It's like a hidden art museum. Life, frozen in time, and it's up to us to interpret the story."

"There were dried-up floral centerpieces on the dining room table," Farzi said, pulling off her gloves. "Someone once cared for this house very much. What was upstairs?"

"Bedrooms, bathrooms …" Kat shrugged. "Nothing crazy."

"But the playroom—" Millie shuddered.

"A playroom?"

Kat looked at Farzi and nodded. "In one of the bedrooms. The toys were still in there …"

"It fascinates me how, without human intervention, a place can change from a perfectly normal domestic state to a total wreck." Annalise dropped the garbage bag into the trunk. A small plume of dust puffed out.

Farzi spread her hand over her forehead, massaging her temples. "Back home in Kabul, people fled their homes all the time, but they took what they could carry. The Taliban stole or burned the rest. I think it's sad," she said, lowering her voice to a whisper. "The things in that house must have meant something to those people. To just up and abandon everything like that is not something done by choice, but under duress."

A sob from the front of Annalise's car made them all look up. Millie was standing beside the hood, her back to the house, tears streaking her face.

"Millie, what's going on?" Annalise asked.

Millie shook her head, unable to speak. Farzi glanced at Kat who shrugged her shoulders and raised an eyebrow.

"Millie?" Annalise prodded. "Whatever it is, you'll be okay. You're safe here with us. We're your friends."

"Whatever it is, maybe we can help," Farzi murmured.

Millie pulled up the hem of her T-shirt to wipe her tears, exposing a strip of her fleshy, white belly. Even from where Kat stood, at the back of the car, she could see raised white circles scarring the skin.

Farzi drew in her breath. "Millie, do you want to talk about it?"

Millie shook her head.

"Are you sure?" Annalise asked.

"Leave her be," Kat said. "Sometimes people just get sad." She ducked her head down at the trunk, focusing her attention on carefully tying the handles of the garbage bag. The dust had attached itself to the plastic and crept up the sides. Getting her hands dirty was unavoidable.

Kat looked up just as Farzi stepped away from the car.

"It's okay, Millie. I understand," Farzi said, pulling up her sleeves. The underside of her forearms were peppered with the same circular markings. "I gave myself these cigarette burns. I was trying to manage my grief. But Millie, I saw yours wrap around to your back. Someone else did that to you."

Millie used the back of her hands to wipe the rest of her tears. She turned away from them, silently looking at the abandoned house.

Farzi walked right up to Millie. "Whatever he did, he can't do it anymore," she uttered, her voice just above a whisper.

Millie let out a wail that sounded like it started in her gut. Then she squeezed her eyes closed and screamed, long and loud enough to startle the birds from the trees. Annalise covered her ears. Kat flinched and stepped back. Farzi reached out, palm up, inviting Millie to take her hand when she was ready.

Millie let the scream die and opened her eyes. Farzi nodded, and Millie reached out, clenching the outstretched hand being offered. Farzi squeezed back, acting as an anchor for Millie.

"He beat me," Millie croaked. "For more than thirty years. He said and did horrible things. He broke me. And even though he's dead, he left me with permanent scars inside and out." She took a deep breath. "I thought I would be okay once he died. And I was. I was healing. I was learning how to walk through my own house without having to avoid doing anything that would stir the beast. I could grind coffee without having to wrap the coffee maker in towels and hug it to my chest to stifle the noise. I took showers when I wanted to. I was starting to sleep through the night again without fear of being raped by my own husband."

Millie wiped away fresh tears. "And then I found out that everyone at church knew. Everyone. The women I called friends. The priest I confessed to for sins that I now know weren't really sins at all. They all knew I was being abused, and no one said a word. No one offered me a safe haven. Father David never talked to my husband, ever. His job was to protect and nurture his flock, not avoid making eye contact every time he came to visit me in the hospital. They betrayed me, and I can never forgive them for that."

A bitterness churned inside Kat. After all the horrible things she had witnessed, and all the lives she had snuffed out, wife beaters were one notch above pedophiles on her list of disgusting humans. She didn't even try to calm the rage bubbling up.

Annalise took a few steps toward Millie, then pulled her into a hug. Farzi followed, wrapping her arms around Millie from behind.

"Get in here," Annalise said to Kat.

Kat paused before taking a few tentative steps. Then she stretched her own arms around the three women, closing the circle. Her anger morphed into something far more foreign, yet somehow more comforting: connection. They stood like that for a few moments. Kat pulled away first, then Annalise and Farzi released Millie from their arms.

"We've got your back," Farzi said.

"Always," Annalise confirmed.

Millie's tears started again. Farzi wiped at her own eyes, as did Annalise. Only Kat's eyes remained dry, blazing with fierce protectiveness.

"Anyone who raises a hand to you will have to deal with us," she said, her voice measured and calm. "Now, let's take our dirty, sweaty selves to the bar. We've earned a drink."

TWENTY-ONE

K at sat in the rear seat behind Millie. Why had she said that? Why should she care who hurts a woman she barely knows?

Kat glared into the back of Annalise's head, irritated and getting angrier. How could Annalise be so blind? How could she live across the street from the woman for almost a decade and have no inkling what was going on?

Kat knew the answer. People only see what matters to them. Understanding that was what made her so good at her job.

As they settled into chairs on the patio of the first pub they came across, Kat was still simmering but didn't know what to say. Saying "I'm sorry" didn't feel like the right thing. What was she sorry for? For what Millie endured? For Annalise not noticing her neighbor was being abused? For Farzi only being able to manage her grief by grinding lit cigarettes into her skin?

"People are staring at us," Farzi said, squirming uncomfortably in the cheap white plastic chair.

Kat looked around, meeting the curious gazes of some of the patrons. The corrugated plastic roof covering the patio was so faded, the green was almost transparent. Two fans suspended from the wooden crossbeams spun weakly.

"We don't belong," Kat said. "This is a neighborhood pub, and they know we are not from around here. And you're brown."

"Kat, that's ridiculous—"Annalise started.

"No, it's not," Farzi interrupted. "I can feel the daggers through my back. Good thing I left my hijab at home."

"You wear a hijab?" Millie asked. It was the first time she had spoken since they left the abandoned house.

"Sometimes. Bad hair days. Days when I want to feel the comfort of Islam. I don't wear it in new social situations."

"Why not?" Annalise asked.

"I don't want that to be the first thing people see before they see *me*. No"—she raised her hand to stop Annalise from protesting—"it's the way it is." She craned her neck and turned away. "Anyone see a waiter? I'd really like a drink."

Kat raised her eyebrows. "You must be a loose-practicing Muslim."

"Yes," Farzi agreed, "but don't we all do things we're not supposed to from time to time? Forbidden fruits and all that?"

Kat didn't try to hide her smile. "I love a little risk every now and then."

"That sounds like a challenge," Annalise said. "I'm game."

Millie flagged down the waiter as he walked by. "Do you have lemonade?"

The waiter nodded. "Yes, ma'am."

"I'll have some of that, with ice," Millie said. "And two shots of Crown Royal."

Annalise blinked and shook her head. Kat chuckled quietly. Farzi smiled.

"Do you want the shots on the side?" the waiter asked.

"No," Millie answered. "Mixed in with the lemonade. In a tall glass, please."

"I'll have that too," Kat said.

"Same," Annalise said. "Farzi?"

"Sure. I'll try one."

"Millie!" exclaimed Annalise when the waiter walked away. "Have you been holding out on us? Are you secretly a bartender somewhere?"

The corners of Millie's mouth turned up slightly. "I didn't drink for twenty-seven years. My husband wasn't a big drinker. But he knew if there was less in any of the bottles. The day my daughter moved out, I poured myself a gin and tonic. A small can with a splash. Later that night, when he poured himself a scotch, he noticed the gin bottle had been moved. He cracked one of my ribs for that. That was the last time I touched alcohol. Apart from the sacramental wine, naturally."

"You were punished twice," Kat growled. "By your daughter leaving and by the man who should have helped you through that pain."

"Millie, I wish we had been friends before," Annalise said, pressing a hand to her chest. "Then you would have had a safe place to come to."

Millie's eyes teared up. "That's very kind, Annalise. But I would never have crossed the cul-de-sac."

"Your husband wouldn't have let you," Annalise stated sadly.

"Not only that. Before I knew you, I made some, um, assumptions about the kind of person you were."

Annalise tilted her head. "What kind of assumptions?"

"I, um, I don't really remember specifics," Millie stuttered.

"Yes, you do," Kat said, giving her a hard look.

"It's fine," Annalise reached across the table to pat the top of Millie's hand. "We didn't know each other. Everyone makes assumptions."

Kat frowned. "Don't you want to know?"

"It's fine, really."

"But Millie brought it up. You don't bring something up unless you want to talk about it."

Annalise narrowed her eyes at Kat. "How about we let it go for now and toast our friend for her courage and strength and for allowing us to be the guardians of her hurt?"

Kat ignored Annalise's plea. "If you need to confess and get it off your chest, then go ahead," she said to Millie.

"Let it be," Farzi said as the waiter placed their drinks on the table. "Millie has done enough sharing today."

Kat looked across the table at Millie, whose hands were wrapped around her drink, wiping off the condensation. "Do you not trust us? What have we done to show you anything other than kindness? We are not church ladies, Millie. Whatever you have to say, say it."

"I can take it," Annalise murmured. "Believe me, people have said horrible things behind my back and to my face. Kat's right. Get it off your chest."

"Are you sure?" Millie said. "Annalise, can you promise me you won't get mad?"

"I promise," she said. "I am opening the gates to my vulnerability and inviting you to cross the threshold."

Millie held her glass to her lips and took two gentle sips. "Okay," she started. "Before I got to know you, I thought you were probably a promiscuous woman who lacked any self-control. I made my judgment based solely on your looks. To me, dyed blond hair, big breasts, and clingy clothing were the marks of a whore. When I finally crossed the cul-de-sac, I was so heartbroken over my church friends that I deliberately sought out the biggest sinner I knew. I wanted revenge. I wanted to show those women that I didn't need them and that their lack of support pushed me to the dark side. That's why I knocked on your door."

Annalise turned her face away, squinting into the sunlight. Kat looked over at Farzi, who was suddenly very interested in the scratches and permanent rings on the plastic table. Millie started to cross her arms, then changed her mind, picking up her napkin to wipe away the pool of water under her glass. Annalise turned back to them, dropping her head. Her shoulders were shaking.

"I'm sorry," Millie mewled. "I didn't mean to make you cry."

Annalise looked up, tears in her eyes. "Oh ... my ... god ...," she stuttered. "I'm your whorey revenge friend?" She couldn't hold back another second. A snort blew out her nose. She threw her head back and laughed.

Kat choked on her drink, coughing while the others were laughing. She had thought Annalise was going to storm away in anger, not lose her shit laughing. Retirement had made her sloppy. She used to be able to read body language like a book. She used to be able to catch the twitch of every facial muscle.

"I'm glad you're laughing about this, Annalise," Millie said. "I thought you would have been offended."

"Offended? I am happy to step into the revenge role. Maybe we should all go to church with you and dress as slutty as we can. Ooh, can I go to confession and blow your priest's mind?"

"Annalise!" Millie exclaimed. "We can't do that! I'd never be able to show my face in church again."

"Is that a bad thing?" Kat asked. "It sounds to me like you'd be better off without any of those people."

Millie clinked the ice around in her glass. "It's not so easy to let go of the only life I've ever known."

"I think you did when you crossed that cul-de-sac," Annalise said.

"My father used to say when we take the first step in a new direction, it's because we're ready for change," Farzi added. "You must have been ready, Millie."

Kat sat silently as the waiter placed the appetizers they had ordered on the table. The smell of the hot sauce wafting from the wings made Kat hungry. As they all filled their plates with nutritionally poor but delicious choices, Kat's stomach bubbled. The sensation moved into her chest, and that's when she knew it wasn't hunger. It was happiness. She barely recognized the feeling; it had been so long since she could relax in the presence of others.

But still, there was a familiar humming in Kat's head, like an electrical circuit about to make its connection. She knew this feeling from the moments before the kill, the last seconds of focused calm before the burst of adrenaline. On the wave of a dopamine rush, Kat understood. She was changing. For so much of her life, she had felt pulled tight, like a slingshot ready to fire. She didn't need to launch the rock, she realized. She let herself go slack, relaxing into this new looseness.

"It's nice to have people to do things with," Millie said. "It fills the time."

"And replenishes our lives," said Farzi.

"I don't know about any of you"—Annalise waved a wing at them—"but I find it so damn hard to make friends now. I thought it was because I was so focused on my business, but I think it's just because I'm older and have less patience for–"

"Stupid bullshit," Kat blurted out.

Annalise laughed. "I was going to say drama, but bullshit is accurate too."

"I'm relieved to hear you say that." Millie snapped a carrot in half and dipped it into a plastic pot of ranch dressing. "I thought there was something wrong with me. That I had become a bitter fifty-seven-year-old who was too angry all the time."

"Aww, honey," Farzi said, "that's not you, that's menopause. Have you reached the murderous rage stage yet?"

"The what?" Annalise asked.

Farzi pointed her chin to Kat. "You want to tell them about how anything becomes a viable murder weapon?"

An electrifying jolt snaked up Kat's spine and she smiled wide. "The list is long. A pencil, a loaf of sourdough, even a napkin. You could kill someone with lash extensions, if you wanted to."

Farzi laughed at the look of horror on Annalise's face. "She's not wrong. You'd be surprised by what I think I could do with a paintbrush. Have you not started menopause yet?"

"My periods have been irregular," Annalise answered, "so I guess I'm getting there. I'm a bit scared to ask what else to expect."

"It's different for every woman," Millie said. "I've been postmenopausal for a few years now. I never had that rage, but I tried to pray away the hot flashes and anxiety."

"Maybe if you had some rage, you would have been a widow much sooner," Kat joked. She chomped into a piece of celery, becoming aware that everyone had stopped moving.

"Kat … did you hear yourself?" Farzi was looking at her, worry creasing her brow.

Annalise's mouth hung open, silent for the first time since they'd met. Kat looked across the table at Millie. Her friend's eyes were dry, her hands clenched into fists on the table.

"I—I—it sounded funny in my head. Sometimes I have no filter." She swallowed. The greasy food was boring its way into her bowels.

"We know," Annalise spat.

Millie released her hands, turning to Annalise. "Didn't we just finish saying we have no patience for bullshit? This is what it looks like." She smiled thinly at Kat. "I don't even know how to react to that comment."

Kat shifted in her chair. The plastic offered no ventilation and her rear was sweating. She fought the urge to scowl and walk away. If this were a job, she'd have known what role she should be playing and would have slipped into whatever false persona she created.

"I will not change how I am," she finally said, cracking her knuckles under the table. "But I like doing things with all of you, so I will tell you this—I will say things before I think them through. I won't ask for forgiveness. I will never deliberately hurt you. I know when and how to apologize when I've made a mistake. Millie, I am sorry for being so callous. You can take it or leave it. No bullshit."

"No bullshit," Millie repeated. "I like doing things with you too. You're not off the hook for what you said, though." When Millie reached over to squeeze Kat's shoulder, she didn't flinch. She surprised herself by leaning into it, grasping Millie's hand.

"That *was* a bit too callous," Annalise said.

"But *so* Kat," added Farzi.

Annalise plucked a wing from the serving dish. "I've never wanted to bitch-slap a woman more."

"Where I come from, that is a compliment." Kat smiled as she filled her plate once more. As they ate with gusto, the wall inside Kat crumbled away.

TWENTY-TWO

"That view is spectacular," marveled Millie, looking toward the wall of windows on the far side of Farzi's living room. "I've never seen the Willamette River from this high up."

The women slipped off their shoes in the condo's marble-tiled foyer.

"Please, come in." Farzi smiled, waving them inside.

"Your home is beautiful, Farzi," Annalise said.

"And so welcoming," added Millie. "The colors you've chosen are very warm. This feels like a refuge."

Before coming to Farzi's for lunch, they had spent the morning at Picasso & Percolations, learning step-by-step how to paint a lighthouse. It had been Kat's idea. She had noticed the new business going in down the road from the animal shelter and thought it would be a safe space for Farzi to start painting again.

While sipping herbal tea, they followed the instructor as he showed them each stage of creation. Annalise and Millie were ideal students, following directions as they were given. Farzi didn't even look at the instructor on the elevated platform, painting her own abstract version of the lighthouse. They had laughed themselves to tears when Kat proudly turned her canvas to show them what was apparently a burrito erected upon a deformed turtle.

"Thank you." Farzi opened the fridge, pulling out a platter loaded with charcuterie and a tray full of vegetables. She bent over, reaching into the bar fridge built into the island. "Can I pour anyone a glass of rosé?"

Kat let her eyes roam the kitchen and living room, noticing the high-end black stainless steel appliances, the custom-made furniture, and the million-dollar panoramic view of the riverfront, the city, and Mount Hood.

"You came with money," Kat declared.

Farzi straightened, a bottle in hand, a confused look on her face. "What makes you say that?"

Kat nodded at the wine. "Well, aside from this gorgeous place, you are about to open a $250 bottle of Gérard Bertrand rosé. For lunch. On a Wednesday."

"Is there anything wrong with serving my friends something nice?" The bottle made a soft pop as she uncorked it.

"No. I'm just pointing out you are not a poor refugee fleeing a dangerous country," Kat continued. "You already had money in the bank when you arrived."

Millie stepped up to the island to unwrap the food as Farzi poured wine. "Kat, I don't really think that is any of our business."

"I am pointing out the obvious." Kat shrugged. "Don't tell me either of you didn't assume Farzi was a penniless immigrant."

"I try not to judge others," Millie said.

Annalise snorted. "Please. You totally judged me before you even knew me. It's fine, I'm over it," Annalise said when Millie opened her mouth to protest. "As someone who is constantly assessed based on her looks, it would be hypocritical of me to do that to someone else. Farzi, can we go out onto the balcony?"

"Of course." Farzi nodded. "If you follow it to the right, you'll be able to see downtown."

Annalise collected wine for her and Millie. "Come on, Millie, let's go look."

"We all have our biases," Kat whispered once Annalise and Millie were outside. "I'm sure you were raised with a certain idea about Americans, just as I was."

Farzi clinked her glass with the one she handed Kat. "Infidels everywhere, my father used to say."

Kat chuckled. "When I first came to America, people thought I was a Soviet spy, or that I stood in line for hours for a stale loaf of bread. You and I know better than most what it's like to live in the hyphen. Uzbek-American. Afghan-American."

Which made it really easy for me to do my work. I had no ties to anyone or any country.

"My brother once said something like that," Farzi said. "'Neither here nor there. Not Afghan, not American. You'll always be lost in the middle.'"

The door to the balcony rolled open with a swish. "Farzi, you're kind to open up your home to us," Annalise said, stepping back into the living room. "Does it get hot in here in the summer with all these windows?"

"Not really," Farzi replied. "The windows are responsive. They darken when the sunlight gets too intense."

"See? Money." Kat smirked.

"None of us is hurting. I worked hard for my money, as did you, Kat. There is no shame in that." Farzi handed Kat the vegetable tray. "Let's eat. I'm starving." Picking up the charcuterie board, Farzi led her into the living room. Millie stood at the window, still taking in the view while Annalise examined the books on the built-in shelves in a corner between the kitchen and living room.

"*Flowers in the Attic?*" She pulled the paperback off the shelf, then flipped through the pages. "I read this when I was twelve. I rushed home from school every day for a week to read it. I loved every page. I fell in love with Christopher." Annalise grimaced. "I was mooning over a horny boy who raped his sister."

"I never even saw this book in Afghanistan," Farzi said. "I would have been stoned to death for reading a book like that. The library here had a display for the fortieth anniversary. I was curious why they were making such a big deal about it, so I bought a copy."

"Everyone was reading this in the '80s," Millie said. "I remember when I read the word 'God' in the prologue, I thought it was going to be a pious experience. Boy, did I get that wrong."

"The copy I read as a kid in Uzbekistan was different from the English version," Kat said. "The whole rape scene was removed. I found out when one of my schoolmates smuggled a copy in from Canada." It was one of the better memories Kat had of her childhood. She and three other girls huddled around Sonja, all of them smoking stolen cigarettes, as she read aloud in heavily accented English.

Farzi shook her head. "I cannot understand how a mother turns her back on her children and lets them be locked away in an attic."

"Because she was selfish," Kat said. "She didn't know how to build solid relationships. She was too busy hiding her truths."

"I think she was in pain," Millie speculated, "and hadn't dealt with her grief over losing her husband."

"She was a horrible person and deserved all the bad things that happened to her." Farzi topped up their glasses. "She lied about everything to everyone."

"Not all women are fit to be mothers," Annalise said, her voice wavering. "My mother was exhibit A. She demanded affection and punished me when I refused. She was jealous of me when things went right and gleeful when my life fell apart." Annalise sniffed. "She always had to be the protagonist in my story."

"I know this pain, Annalise," Millie murmured. "I felt it too."

Annalise dabbed her eyes with a napkin. "Did you also have a bad mom?"

"Not like you, no. My mother took religion to the extreme. 'If you're not praying, you're playing' was her favorite saying. When you are seven years old and always moving your lips, kids don't stop to ask what you're doing. They point and whisper and laugh. Instead of hugging me when I was upset, my mother told me to repent. If I was worrying about what the other kids thought, I had obviously stopped praying. I thought I'd be a better mother to my own daughter, but I failed. She left me the second she could get away."

"Kids grow up and move out," Farzi said. "That's parenting, not failure."

Millie shook her head. "She fled. Rachel left the day she turned eighteen. She didn't say goodbye. She never told me she was planning to leave. I haven't laid eyes on my daughter or spoken to her in more than fifteen years. I have no idea where she is or who she became."

"She made a difficult choice," Kat said, surprising herself with how gentle she sounded. "Leaving the way she did was not motivated by fear, but by resolve. She wanted something better for herself, and she learned that from you. She walked away in strength."

Millie turned to look at Kat, who was sitting on one of the oversized armchairs flanking the sofa. "Thank you for saying that, Kat. Why did you never have kids?"

"I knew from a young age I didn't want children."

"Can I ask why?"

"I never felt that maternal pull. I wanted to see the world. From my early twenties, I was focused on my career. Why don't you have kids?" Kat asked Annalise.

"It wasn't in the cards for me." Annalise sighed. "But it's not for lack of trying. I have a rare condition that made my uterus incapable of holding on to an egg. That's why my first marriage ended. My inhospitable womb was a deal-breaker."

"That's awful, Annalise," Millie said.

"I struggled for years with it. But I'm done crying now."

"You've come to accept it," said Kat.

"Not at all. I've got a face full of Botox. Crying makes my face weird." Annalise pointed to her brows, and they hardly budged as she tried to waggle them. She winked instead.

"Okay," Farzi said, pouring more wine into their glasses. "Now I have a whole new set of questions. Aren't you terrified of putting poison into your face?"

"It's not poison, it's a toxin," Annalise answered.

"There's a difference?" Farzi asked.

No, Kat thought. *Both can melt your organs if you know what you're doing.*

"It's a small dose, so it's not harmful," Annalise explained. "But it has a wonderful effect on muscles. Doctors use it for all kinds of treatments. Chronic migraine relief, fixing crossed eyes, overactive bladders ..."

"Really?" Millie said. "I'm probably not far from needing it, then."

"Your face is fine," Farzi said.

"I wasn't talking about my face."

Annalise choked on her wine. Kat smiled. Farzi let out a single laugh.

"Millicent Collins," Annalise exclaimed. "Did you just openly admit to peeing yourself?"

"You must be rubbing off on me. God forgive me."

"You know, our world is full of toxins," Kat said. "A sixteenth-century physician named Paracelsus said that everything is a poison. The right dose differentiates a poison from a remedy.'"

"That's oddly specific knowledge to have," Farzi said. "Are you an expert in poisons?"

Kat turned her head to look out at the Willamette through Farzi's windows. She scratched the back of her neck, as if she could claw away the truth.

"I had an interest at one point in my life," she said. She had wanted to know the best and easiest ways to kill a mark. She researched toxins that could be mistaken for an overdose. Too much acetaminophen could cause fatal liver failure, but it could take two to four days and was not always effective. Benzocaine can choke a body of oxygen, but squeezing and mixing an entire tube of toothache gel into a mark's food was not easy. And then there was the problem of the mouth going numb after five or six bites and the mark not eating the full dose. Methyl salicylate was too smelly to be easily concealed, not to mention the challenge of forcing someone to drink a bottle of mouthwash without complaint. Today's assassins have no appreciation of how easy fentanyl has made their job.

"Let me guess," Annalise said. "When you were in college?"

Kat looked up at the ceiling, like she was struggling to recall. "That sounds about right."

"I was fascinated with serial killers," Annalise joked. "I always walked around campus with my nose in a biography about one killer or another. I met my first husband when I collided with him in front of the student center. He was reading philosophy. I was reading a Charles Manson bio."

"I met my husband at a Bible study group in college," Millie said. "He wasn't even Christian. Just exploring, he told me. Looks like neither of us made good choices back then."

"Nobody in college knew what they were doing." Farzi smirked. "I thought it was a good idea to join the on-campus Marxist youth group. My father advised me not to pick sides. He was right. I was only a year out of university when the

Soviet Union withdrew from Afghanistan and the civil war started. I would have been targeted if I had been a Marxist."

Kat nodded automatically. She remembered that day. On the TV in a hotel room in Qatar, she watched the Russian army tanks roll across the bridge from Afghanistan into Uzbekistan.

Farzi looked at Kat. "How about you? Other than your apparent dalliance with toxins?"

"I allowed myself to be bought. The company I worked for paid for my schooling in exchange for servitude and a guaranteed career. I had to put work first above everything else."

"That sounds lonely," Annalise said quietly.

Kat looked down at her almost empty wine glass. "I never thought about it until later, but it *was* very lonely." Just saying the words released something in her. "I'm trying to fix that now, but maybe it's too late."

Millie stood, grabbing the bottle of wine and pouring a final splash into each of their glasses. "Nonsense. We still have life left to live. I have a lot of years to make up for too. I'd still be a lonely widow if it weren't for you. For all of you."

Kat leaned forward, closing the space between her and these other women who had become an unexpected part of her life. As she raised her glass in a silent toast, her head felt light and bubbly. It wasn't the wine.

For the first time, she belonged.

TWENTY-THREE

As they grazed through the charcuterie, conversation flowed freely. They talked about books Kat had never read, local restaurants she had never visited, and experiences of motherhood she would never have. Annalise looked over at her when Farzi and Millie rambled on about childbirth, opening and closing her fingers and thumbs together like a mouth talking. Kat couldn't suppress her smile.

"Once you have kids, your body is forever changed," Farzi was saying. "Why can't our bodies just stay as they were when we were in our twenties?"

"They can." Annalise winked. She cupped her hands under her breasts. "I bought these as a gift to myself. I was barely a B cup and I wanted to fill out a dress better."

Kat raised her eyebrows. "That's the only reason?"

Annalise smiled. "Not exactly. I was planning ahead to my senior years. I wanted to be like Blanche from *The Golden Girls*."

"Promiscuous and desperate to be loved?" asked Kat.

"No. Confident and sexually satisfied."

"Po-tay-to, po-tah-to." Millie laughed.

"Is it rude to ask how many things you've had done?" Farzi asked.

"I don't mind." Annalise looked up at Farzi's smooth ceiling, moving her lips and counting on her fingers.

"I had a nose job after my second marriage, then an eyelid lift and fillers to get rid of my crow's feet on my fortieth birthday. I started plumping my lips a couple of years ago. I do that and Botox every three months or so."

Kat looked down at her chest. Her breasts had always been average, but the pull of gravity was changing their shape. She sighed.

"Everything okay?" Farzi asked.

Kat nodded. "It feels like I'm kneading bread every time I go to put on my bra. Scooping them in. I can understand why women over fifty start thinking about a breast lift."

"When does it ever end?" Millie moaned. "When do we stop hating how we look and give ourselves permission to age with grace?"

Kat smoothed out the lines on her hands. "This is a very good question."

"I'm. So. Tired." Farzi leaned back into the couch. "I'm angry about the constant vigilance to keep everything stretched, medicated, moisturized, and creamed."

"I lost so much time chasing perfection," Annalise said. "Believe it or not, most days I feel I'm either invisible or a laughingstock."

Kat rose from the couch, then walked toward the large painting mounted over the fireplace. "People will see what they've been taught to see. As a painter, Farzi, you would know that. This painting ... is this one of yours?"

Farzi nodded. "It's one of my favorites. It reminds me of home." The painting was an abstract of undefined shapes in vibrant colors—yellows, greens, and blues separated by fine black lines.

"It looks like a Persian carpet." Annalise came to stand beside Katya, craning her head to examine the painting.

"It makes me think of flowers," Millie said, leaning back on the couch to get a better view.

"See what I mean?" Kat looked over her shoulder. "To me, it looks like chaos and mayhem. What were you imagining when you painted this?"

Farzi uncrossed her legs, then crossed them again. "I was thinking about my family, about the colors of the homes in my neighborhood." She picked at nubs of fabric on her pants that only she could see. "The love that once surrounded me. The flowers my mother-in-law planted. The tallest tree that stood in Kabul for hundreds of years until the Russians cut it down. How my world looked until the Taliban changed it. You're all right about what you see. The black lines were deliberately painted to represent a carpet with all the pieces of my life woven together. All the happiness, the sorrow, the loss."

"Have you ever sold a painting?" Millie asked.

"A few, here and there. Some in Kabul, some in Europe. A handful in America."

"What's the most you've ever sold a painting for?" Kat asked.

Annalise leaned a bit closer to Kat. "None of our business," she muttered out of the side of her mouth.

Kat furrowed her brow. "Why not? If she sells paintings in a show, everyone knows the price."

"It's okay. I don't mind answering. My latest piece sold for two-point-seven."

"*Million?*" Millie gasped.

Farzi shrugged and nodded at the same time. "I sold my first for $100. Years later, an art dealer from Austria saw my work and sold one on my behalf for $375,000. I know I'm lucky to have this success. I also have plenty of unsold paintings stored in the back room of a gallery."

"But you are obviously known in the high-end collector market." Kat peered at the signature on the bottom left hand corner of the canvas. "Would you ever consider selling this one?"

"I'm not sure I'm ready to part with it."

Annalise returned to the couch, still examining the canvas. "You know what would be fun? Slipping a painting into an art show and seeing if we could top the latest sale."

Millie shook her head. "You can't just hang a painting at the art museum and slap a sticker on it."

"No, but we could sneak into a small local art show," Kat said.

Farzi jumped up from her chair and disappeared down the hall. She came back to the living room with an oil painting so large, it obscured her entire body. It was another abstract, but this one was primarily red, with blue and black scraped onto the canvas.

"I did this one on commission last year," she said, "but I made the mistake of letting the buyer into the studio. He wanted to watch me create, he said. What he really wanted to do was slip his hand between my legs from behind. I slapped him with my palette, really leaving him black and blue and red all over."

Millie choked out a laugh, bringing her hand in front of her mouth to stop the wine from bursting out.

"I was not surprised when the painting was done, he tried to pay me less than what was agreed to."

"Why did you keep it and not try to sell it?" Annalise asked.

Farzi leaned the canvas against the fireplace. "He was a big client at the gallery where I usually sell my work. If Koyo, the curator, hung it, the guy would have put her out of business. I thought about throwing it away or painting over it, but I felt that someday it would have a bigger purpose."

"I love this painting, Farzi," Annalise said. "There is so

much movement and texture in the paint. Can I buy it? What was it commissioned for?"

"Two million dollars."

Millie choked again. Kat raised her hand to pat her on the back, pausing before she allowed her hand to rest in between Millie's shoulders.

"That's the one to sell, then," Kat stated.

"Are you *this* Farzi Noor?" Annalise held up her phone. On the screen, Kat saw a collection of paintings.

Farzi's face reddened and she nodded. "Yes."

Kat had pulled out her own phone and did a quick search. She let out a slow whistle. "You not only came here with money, Farzi, you came here with secrets." She glanced up at Farzi, who quickly looked away.

"What are you talking about?" Millie leaned closer to Kat to look at her phone. Kat had the browser opened to a story from *The Kabul Times Daily*.

"*August 12, 2018: The highly regarded Afghan artist, Farzana Noor, disappeared from the art world almost a year ago,*" Millie read out loud, "*amid speculation of inappropriate relations. Once considered Afghanistan's greatest treasure, Noor's reputation suffered greatly among whispers of deviant behavior. Sources say she fled the country in shame and is likely hiding in Europe under a different name.*"

"Ooo, you're naughty," Annalise mewled.

"What's the story, Farzi?" Kat asked.

"I'll need more wine for this." Farzi walked to the fridge and pulled out another bottle. The others watched silently as she uncorked a different rosé and filled her glass. She drank deeply, topped up her glass again, and took another deep drink.

"I fled Afghanistan because I had an affair," Farzi announced. "With an older woman." She averted her eyes, looking at the floor.

"You're a lesbian?" Millie gasped.

130   DANA GOLDSTEIN

Farzi shook her head. "No, I don't think so. Bisexual, maybe? Curious? I don't know. I had to leave. My family found out and my uncle wanted me stoned to death."

Annalise gasped. "They really still do that over there?"

"Sadly, yes. That article tells you all you need to know about what the Muslim community thinks of a bisexual woman."

"And a famous artist has nowhere to hide," Kat said.

"How did you end up in Portland?" Millie asked.

Farzi sat on the couch and grinned. "That was thanks to an immigration officer in San Francisco. When he asked me what my final destination was, I answered honestly and said I didn't really know yet. I told him I wanted to go somewhere colorful and unusual, where people chased their art dreams, unbound by the conventions of what is usually considered normal. Without hesitation, he said, 'You want weird? Go to Portland.'"

"Do we live up to the hype?" Annalise asked, trying to waggle her eyebrows.

"You are your own category, Annalise," Kat said, "one that defies explanation." She brought her hand to her mouth, shocked by the words flying out of her mouth. "I didn't mean … I don't know why—"

Annalise winked. "I take that as a compliment. Are you happy you came here, Farzi?"

Farzi paused reflectively. "I was surprised by a few things, actually. So many unhoused people. So much racism. Not always overtly, but microaggressions that fall easily from people's lips. I thought Portland was more progressive and liberal. But"—she shrugged—"I love the art scene, the summers, the festivals, and there is so much moss. Afghanistan is so brown, and Oregon is so green. I tolerate the rainy, damp winters because I know the gray will yield to colors in spring."

"Spoken like a true artist," Millie said. "I'm sorry you have to endure racism."

Farzi waved her off. "It's part of being brown. But everything is tolerable, now that I've met all of you. Now, tell me about this art show idea."

TWENTY-FOUR

From the moment she entered the vestibule of Arts Commons, Kat knew Annalise had made the right choice for where to sell the painting. The sandstone building, located in the heart of a residential neighborhood, had been completely reimagined into a creative hub and artist coworking space.

Between the main doors and the doors to the first floor sat a wildly decorated piano. Every inch, except the keys, had been painted, appliquéd, or decorated with plastic jewels. On top of the key lid sat a happy, hand-lettered sign: PLEASE PLAY. Kat swiped her fingers over the keys, playing a short glissando and was pleasantly surprised to hear it in tune.

She passed through the doors to the main hallway, examining the artwork hung at equal intervals. Above her, glass panels hung from the high ceiling, diffusing light and letting it spill onto the paintings and drawings on the walls.

"It's beautiful, isn't it?"

Kat startled, not having heard Annalise approach. She was irritated at herself for having been caught off guard, but also relieved that she was learning to be in a space without scanning for a threat or target.

"I feel like I've walked into a surreal landscape," Kat said. "Everywhere I look, it's something different to capture my attention."

Annalise nodded. "This place is an arts utopia. It used to be a school, then the city bought it with some private investors and they converted it into a coworking space. There are affordable studios and salons on all four floors for creatives to share. Wait until you see the third floor."

At the end of the hall, a coffee shop was tucked into a corner. Kat heard the hiss of the espresso machine's steam wand, instantly making her crave a flat white. She had knocked back more than a few while tracking a mark in Brisbane.

"Should we get coffee?" she asked. Annalise nodded and Kat placed an order for all of them. While they watched the barista steam milk, Annalise's phone buzzed inside her handbag. She reached in, fishing around.

"Millie is lost." She laughed. "She's here, but she came in the doors on the other side of the building and is now on the second floor. I'll go get her. You'll wait here for Farzi?"

Kat didn't have the chance to answer. Annalise walked off, turning into a doorway Kat assumed led to stairs.

Kat took the tray of coffees from the barista. Six months ago, these women weren't even on her radar. Now she knew how each preferred their coffee. The void that had plagued her since she retired was no longer gaping. The days when she did not receive a text from one of these women were long. She found herself smiling more and scowling less.

"Got her!" Annalise sang out.

"This place is like a maze," Millie said. "I don't understand how I got to the second floor. There are only eight steps at the entrance on the other side."

"Well, you're here now." Kat handed her a decaf latte. "Anyone hear from Farzi?" Kat asked.

Both Millie and Annalise shook their heads.

"I hope she didn't change her mind," Annalise said, looking toward the main entrance.

"She'll be here," Kat said with confidence. "She was ready to get rid of that painting."

"I don't know how she could keep it, given its history," Millie said, pulling her cardigan around her. "I got rid of everything within a couple of months of my husband's passing."

"But you stayed in the house," Kat pointed out, "and I'm sure his ghost is in every corner."

Millie shrugged. "Some days, yes. It gets easier every year to ignore the bad things that happened in each room. I love my house, and I love the neighborhood. There are some good people there." She smiled shyly at Annalise.

"*Salaam alaikum!*" Farzi waved at them from down the hall. "Can you guys help me? I got the painting into the car, but I can't seem to get it out."

"Where's the Honda?" Kat asked as they followed Farzi to the parking lot. Farzi was standing beside a bright red MINI Cooper.

"It was making a loud clunking sound. I took it to the shop and this was the only car they had as a loaner. Is that coffee for me?" She took the cup Kat offered.

Annalise peered into the back window. "How did you get this in here?"

"Could you even see out the rearview mirror?" Millie laughed.

"Not at all. Thank Allah I wasn't pulled over."

Farzi set her coffee cup on the pavement, then opened the hatch, holding it so it couldn't fully open. She reached underneath to press carefully on the canvas. "The door will pull it up if I don't push the painting out of the way," she explained.

Once the hatch was safely opened, the four women stood at the back of the car, sipping their coffees, assessing the dilemma. The canvas was wedged horizontally in the narrow space, tilted so that half of it was resting on top of the front passenger seat.

Millie took a corner of the canvas and tried to pull. "This will require some careful calculations," she said. "Good thing I was almost an engineer."

"This is more of a physics problem," Kat said, crouching to examine the painting from underneath.

"I ask again—Farzi, how did you get this in here without ruining it?" Annalise asked.

Farzi took their empty cups to the trash, then pulled her hair back, tying it off in a loose ponytail. "It went in pretty easily, but now it won't come out. I guess when I was driving, it settled and got stuck."

"Okay, Kat, you grab that part." Millie pointed to the rear corner on the passenger side of the car. "I'll take this one. Annalise, you crawl into the front passenger seat and maneuver from there. Farzi, you'll be the navigator from the driver's seat, watching for any potential damage we can't see."

"I like this version of you, Millie," Annalise said as she opened the passenger-side door. "So bossy and determined. I didn't even know you had it in you."

Farzi kneeled in the driver's seat. "I want to know why you were *almost* an engineer."

"It's what I took in college. The plan was for me to get my certification as a chemical engineer after my husband finished law school and passed the bar exam, but …" Millie shrugged, her face drooping for a moment. "I never had the chance. Water under the bridge, now. Let's get this thing out of here. Kat, you lift from your corner and I'll push down from mine."

They pushed and pulled, wriggled and wobbled, careful not to rip the canvas or break the frame. Bit by bit, the canvas loosened. Annalise leaned over the passenger seat, her arms awkwardly wrapped around the back, a hand on each side of the painting.

"We need to get this more on its side. Push deeper, but not harder!" ordered Farzi.

Kat looked at Annalise and the two started cackling.

"Harder is sometimes better, no?" Kat smirked.

Annalise was laughing so hard, she lost her grip and fell forward. Her face smacked the headrest with a worrisome thud and her cheek was smushed against the leather.

"I think one more push-pull-twist combo, and this thing will come out," Millie said.

Farzi reached between the seats and lifted the canvas from the edge. "I can see a tiny bit of space near the roof on your corner, Kat. I'll lift, then you lift a bit, and it should come out."

As Farzi and Kat raised the painting, Annalise pushed and Millie pulled. The canvas brushed softly against the roof of the car, and then it was free from the MINI.

"Maybe this is a bad idea," Farzi said, examining the painting that was now leaning against the closed hatch.

"Are you kidding?" exclaimed Annalise. "After all that effort? No way. We are doing this, Farzi."

"I feel really weird about sneaking this in. What if we get caught?"

Millie's face brightened and she raised her eyebrows. "Annalise, do you have those safety vests we wore at that abandoned house? No one questions a safety vest."

"We don't need them. No one will question us, anyway," Kat said as Annalise shook her head. "People are either too afraid of confrontation or too absorbed in their own problems and don't want more. We could lift a painting from the wall and walk out and no one would say a word."

"How can you be so sure?" Farzi asked.

"You know, I think she's right," Annalise said. There was a gleam in her eye as she bounced on her toes again. "Let's go."

Annalise took the back end of the painting while Farzi held the front. Millie led the way, holding open the front door so they could sidestep into the building. Kat followed them, head up and fully confident they could pull this off. They rode the elevator to the third floor, emerging into the middle of the hallway. From end to end, art hung on the walls.

There were only two other people on the floor, a young couple who Kat guessed were in their late twenties, walking slowly and talking quietly as they looked at the artwork. A door was propped open at the far end, a sign to the left of the entrance reading TOSSERS & POTTERS. From where she stood, Kat saw a few people, heads down, hands covered in clay, hunched over potter's wheels. They would not be a problem.

Millie was looking back and forth down the hall. "Does anyone see any open spaces?"

"Maybe down there?" Annalise pointed to the opposite end of the hall, where the wall was made entirely of glass.

"Hmm, west facing," Farzi mused. "Not exactly a good choice for hanging art. Too much sun."

Kat strode away down the hall, turning her head left and right, scanning for a spot.

"What about here?" Millie's voice came from behind.

Kat turned to see Millie standing at the wall, holding up two pieces of wire hanging from the ceiling. Two hooks were attached to the end of each piece, one bigger than the other to accommodate different sizes of art.

"There's not enough space," Kat stated, frustrated. "Farzi's painting is too large."

"The wires are on a track."

Kat followed Millie's pointed finger to the ceiling where all the wires were attached to a track built into the concrete above them.

Farzi and Annalise leaned the painting against the wall. Farzi stood back, examining the paintings and photographs hanging on both sides of the small spot.

"If we move all the artwork on either side," she said, "there should be enough space."

Annalise and Farzi started sliding the hung art to the left of the space, while Kat and Millie worked from the opposite end. Half a dozen people passed them, none of whom uttered a word.

"I can't believe we're getting away with this," whispered Farzi when they met at the enlarged empty space. "You were right, Kat."

Under Millie's instruction, Annalise and Farzi lifted the painting while Millie and Kat got the hooks under the wire running across the back of the framed canvas. Once the painting was hung, Farzi stuck an object label to the left with blue putty.

Annalise leaned forward to read the card.

"Title: *Hands Off Me* / Artist: Farzana Noor / Price: $750."

"You put your real name on it." Millie smiled approvingly. "I thought you might have tried to hide that. And $750? That's a steal. Now I *really* want to buy it."

"I thought about putting a fake name on it, but then I thought how nice it would be if someone bought the painting because they liked it and had no idea who I was," she said. "Wouldn't it be a great reward for someone ordinary to take this home and one day discover it's actually worth three thousand times what they paid?"

Kat walked up to the hanging canvas. "I think that's a fine way for this painting to live its life. You can move on now, yes?" She turned to look at Farzi, who had tears in her eyes.

"I wish winning my family back was this easy," she said, pulling a tissue from her purse. "I can't just rid myself of who I am, though. I embarrassed them and they shunned me. I send money home every month, but my mother still hangs up on me when I call. I never get an answer to my emails or to the letters I send. Maybe when I find a new husband, they'll finally welcome me back."

"Is that why you went to speed dating?" Annalise asked.

"Yes." Farzi sniffed. "I thought speed dating would expedite finding a man. Any man would do. He doesn't even have to be Afghan. I haven't seen or spoken to my family in three years, and if I can go visit with a husband, they might forgive me for chasing a woman."

Millie placed her hand on Farzi's shoulder. "Is that what you really want?"

"Yes and no. I want my family back, but I want to live my life on my terms."

"Even if you do marry a man, will your family ever accept you, Farzi?" Kat caught Annalise shaking her head. "Isn't the shame going to follow them around forever?"

"Kat," Annalise hissed, "can't you show some compassion for a change?"

"I'm just trying to point out that we are worthy of being loved for who we are. Marrying a man won't change what people believe. Farzi, if marrying a man will truly make you happy, then I support you. I'm your friend no matter who you have sex with."

Farzi wiped the last of her tears away. "I don't know what I want. And you're not wrong, Kat. The shame *will* follow me and my family. If I even so much as go out for lunch with a female friend back home, the gossip will start all over again." She sighed heavily, as if letting go of her pain.

"Well, you're here in America with three women who adore you," Annalise said.

"Who will keep you safe," Millie added.

"Who will kill anyone who tries to hurt you," said Kat.

The others laughed, but Kat meant every word.

TWENTY-FIVE

K at hadn't fully realized how much Annalise, Farzi, and Millie had impacted her life until she visited the Saturday Market in Portland's Old Town. She had been fidgety that day, but no one was free to accompany her. She walked the stalls alone, asking the artisans questions about their work. She tried on earrings and hats and bought bamboo underwear. She took the time to smell handmade soaps, tasted her first bubble tea, and got a henna tattoo. She did it all in the daylight, without having to hide in the shadows. And she was yearning to tell her friends about all of it.

She texted them photos of her discoveries. As she walked through the market, she sent pictures, asking for opinions on blouses she considered buying. She bought a cactus in a planter stamped with the words *Don't be a prick* because it made her laugh, and she felt it was time to try taking care of another living thing. She asked a vendor to take a photo of her sampling his chocolate-covered caramels with a look of ecstasy on her face and smiled with satisfaction when Annalise texted back, *I'll take a hundred of those.* She bought eight bags, two for each of them. When she left the market, she didn't feel so alone after all.

It felt like a lifetime ago that Kat had walked into Fireside Restaurant in search of a hookup. She had been completely caught off guard by these women, and she still could not understand why they welcomed her into the fold. Over the last six months, they'd wormed their way into her life. She looked forward to seeing them, smiling to herself when a new text arrived and struggling with restlessness when they didn't have plans.

She was relaxing in the tub with a calming lavender bath bomb she bought at the market when her phone buzzed on the bathroom floor.

ANNALISE

If you have plans next Saturday, cancel them

Kat wiped her hands on the bath mat before picking up her phone.

Why?

ANNALISE

We're crashing a gala.

FARZI

Oooh, fun.

MILLIE

We can't do that. Can we?

FARZI

How do we get into a gala without a ticket?

Kat knew the deception and evasion required to sneak into a private event. Alone, it was easy. With three other women accompanying her, not a chance. Still, a ripple of excitement shook her at the thought of trying.

ANNALISE

I have a ticket. I'm going to sneak YOU in.

FARZI

Are we going to run through the kitchen on the way in or the way out? I'm in either way.

ANNALISE

Someone very clever told me people are too busy in their own lives to notice anyone else. Kat smiled at Annalise repeating her own words back at her.

MILLIE

I have nothing to wear :(

Kat started typing, then deleted, then tapped again, then deleted again.

I have a closet full of dresses you are welcome to come try.

She leaned her head back against the steamy tiles and closed her eyes. Different dress sizes wouldn't be hard to explain.

ANNALISE

You're crushing my dream of a shopping montage.

FARZI

LOL, take me along and I guarantee a Pretty Woman experience, but with a POC instead of a prostitute.

Kat watched the text dots appear and disappear. A few more seconds and the silence would become awkward.

I bet that happens even when you go to buy milk.

FARZI

It's worse when I wear my hijab.

ANNALISE

We've never seen you wear it.

FARZI

I wore it every day of my life until speed dating. I took it off that night to try something new. Take my life in a new direction. It worked.

A memory flashed through Kat's mind. She had passed Farzi sitting in her car in the parking lot and had noticed her taking off the hijab.

MILLIE

We'd be friends even if you wore it. Some things are destined to be.

She shook her head, but a smile tugged at her lips.

Let me guess, Millie. God's work?

MILLIE

Naturally. He brought me to a woman who might have a beautiful dress I can borrow.

KAT

If you find a dress in my closet, you can keep it.

ANNALISE

Really crushing my dream of a massive makeover over here.

FARZI

I'll let you take me gown shopping, Annalise.

ANNALISE

You need a dress?

FARZI

No. But think of all the tongues we can get wagging. Your big boobs and my brown skin. We can hold hands and pretend to be a couple.

ANNALISE

They've seen it all in Mario's. Trust me.

In all the years Kat had lived in Portland, she hadn't ever been to the high-end department store.

KAT

Now I want to go. Trying on couture dresses could be fun.

Kat stared at her phone, waiting for a response, but there weren't any active dots. She reread what she sent, trying to decipher if she said something wrong. Did she invite herself to something Annalise and Farzi were going to do together?

The blank space glared back at her, the blinking cursor taunting. Biding time had never been hard for her. Patience was a requirement for an assassin. But waiting for her friends to respond was torture. Her mind spun with worry and paranoia. Were the three of them having a conversation without her? Were they throwing her out of the group? Maybe they didn't like her at all. Maybe they felt sorry for her.

She was deciding how to keep the conversation going when the dots appeared. She waited, but the dots disappeared again.

KAT

Where did everyone go?

ANNALISE

Just ran to the bathroom.

MILLIE

I thought my phone stopped working.

FARZI

Oh my Allah, I thought I offended you with the big boobs comment.

ANNALISE

LOL, I'd be offended if you didn't mention them.

KAT

I hate texting

Broken, illogical conversations. When are we going shopping?

They picked a date and made a plan. They would go to Mario's first, then for fondue lunch at the Melting Pot.

Kat put her phone down and drained the tub. Wearing only a towel, she went into the kitchen to brew herself a celebratory espresso. The range of emotions from a five-minute text conversation exhausted but also exhilarated her. She had friends. And they were going to spend a morning shopping, just like in a movie montage.

As she brought the steaming demitasse to her lips, one more thought flitted through her mind.

Don't fuck this up.

TWENTY-SIX

"What the hell?" Annalise pulled on the doors at Mario's, but they were locked.

"It's after ten," Kat said. "Why aren't they open?"

"Do you need to book an appointment?" Farzi asked.

"No." Annalise shook her head. "I shopped here for years and never had to do that."

"Maybe we should ring that bell." Millie pointed to a small button built into the doorframe.

Annalise frowned, then pushed the button. Not hearing the chime of a bell, she leaned her ear against the door and pushed again.

"I didn't hear anything. Do you think it's broken?"

Kat shrugged, as did Millie. They stood on SW Broadway, under the canopy of oranges, reds, and yellows from the trees.

"Oh, someone's coming," Annalise said as she stepped back from the doors.

A security guard flipped the lock, then pushed the door open. "Good morning, ladies." He smiled.

"Is the store not open?" Annalise asked.

"It's open," he answered, "but we keep the doors locked at all times. That's just how it is now downtown."

The store was an open plan, enabling Kat to see every corner of the menswear department filling the floor from front to back. In the center, a wide set of quartz stairs split the space.

"Women's is upstairs," Annalise said.

They followed Annalise up, emerging into the wide open space that mirrored the main floor. Two associates, a man and a woman, stood chatting behind a bleached hardwood cash desk with a white quartz counter to match the floors. Neither salesperson looked up.

"This is different," Annalise whispered. "It's so … sparse."

Kay looked at the racks hung with minimal clothing. Perfectly folded shirts and jeans were displayed on tables. Jewelry was locked in clear cases on pedestals. A small selection of shoes and boots were spread out on a shelving unit that reminded Kat of a lazy Susan. Handbags and accessories were scattered among the clothing, as if they were a last-minute thought.

"Where are the dresses?" Millie asked quietly.

"I don't know," Annalise said, shaking her head. "I haven't been here for years. It's not the same. The whole front half used to be couture gowns. Everything here is so—"

"Young," Kat finished.

"I was going to say modern, but yeah, young works too."

"Who on earth is this small?" Farzi held up a black leather miniskirt. "I mean, this waist is the same size as an opened book. Will this even cover anyone's rear?"

"I have dish towels bigger than that." Millie chuckled.

Kat glanced over at Annalise. Her friend was moving from rack to table, confusion and disappointment written all over her face.

"Excuse me?" Kat said to the associates who had still not acknowledged them. "Where can we find ball gowns?"

The young man turned his head unnaturally slowly, letting his eyes travel over Katya from feet to head. "We don't carry gowns here."

"Since when?" Annalise asked. "I used to get my gowns here all the time."

"Well, not since I've been here," he sneered. "And I've been working here for more than two years."

The young lady looked up from her phone. "Maybe you can get gift cards for your granddaughters and they can come shop on their own. That's what most of the old people do."

Millie's face reddened. Annalise opened her mouth, but no words came out. Farzi raised a single eyebrow.

Kat strode to the counter, placing her hands flat on the cool stone to calm the rage building inside her. "I've been called worse by better. I can only imagine how spectacular you'd both be with personality." She tilted her head, pressing her lips into a tight smile. "Have a super day!" Kat turned to her friends. "Let's go someplace more welcoming?"

Annalise's frown disappeared and her face lit up. "Let's go to the Portland Food Hall. It's a five-minute walk. They have mini doughnuts."

They walked past the steel and stone office towers, the boarded-up shops and restaurants. There were few pedestrians, but both sides of the street were filled with parked cars. When they got to the food hall, the brick and concrete space was already bustling. Most of the tables were taken by entrepreneurs tapping on their laptops, moms bouncing babies on their laps, people in yoga pants, ripped jeans, and crop tops. The din of voices made it impossible to pick up any one conversation.

"Young crowd," Millie noted. "Don't people work anymore?"

"Lots of people work remotely," Annalise said. "It's also that magical time between the start of the workday and lunch. Coffee time. Is that the line for the doughnuts?"

Kat craned her neck, following the line of people snaking toward a sign reading THOSE LITTLE DONUTS. "Not a highly creative name, is it?"

"At least there's no confusion about what they sell," Farzi said.

"I'll queue up," Kat volunteered. "Why don't you guys go find a table?"

Kat wandered to the end of the line, watching the activity around her. The food hall was about the size of a large house, if all the walls had been removed, but it had the energy of a carnival. Flashing lights from signs, people laughing, espresso machines hissing, a bell being rung every time a plate was ready at the Mexican takeout counter.

As the doughnut line shuffled forward, Kat relaxed into the chaos, listening to the women in front of her share parenting tips. She examined the exposed brick walls, seeing the patched mortar and wondering what stories they held.

"What are you hiding underneath these clothes?"

Kat startled at the gruff voice at her ear.

"No, don't turn around," he said as she tried to look at the source. "It's better if you don't see what's coming."

Kat's heart raced and she struggled to fill her lungs with air. *This is it, then. They've finally sent someone. I'm going to die standing in line for mini doughnuts.*

He put his hands on her hips, then moved them down to her rear. He handled her roughly, just as she would if she was searching someone for a weapon. He was silent, breathing into her hair. He moved his hands around her back, tracing the sides of her jacket, skimming the sides of her breasts.

"You're very handsome," a familiar voice said, "but way too hands-on for my liking. Please step away from my friend."

Kat managed a glance over her shoulder and saw Annalise standing behind the man, a purple jeweled can of pepper spray at the ready.

The man turned away from Kat and laughed. "Please, little girl, take your tiny spray bottle somewhere else."

Annalise walked in front of him, put her pepper spray into the front pocket of her jeans, and kicked the man in the balls. He went down to his knees with a loud moan.

"I should spit a thousand curses on your head." Farzi appeared, standing next to Annalise. She leaned over, pulling off her ballet flat. Raising her arm, she brought the flat down onto the man's head. "You ... stupid ... *khar*." Each word was punctuated with a slap of her shoe.

The hand not protecting his privates went up to his head, trying to stop the assault. People broke out of the mini doughnut line, holding up their phones, recording. Kat turned her back on the crowd, keeping her head down, watching Farzi unleash her rage.

With a roar, the man rose, pushing Farzi into the spectators. He slapped Annalise across the face. She staggered backward, falling on her ass. Millie was there in an instant, charging at the man, her fists raised. Kat saw him reach into his inner jacket pocket and she made her move. She stepped in front of the man, and using the flesh between her thumb and forefinger, Kat punched him in the middle of the throat. She heard the familiar snap of cartilage fracturing in the trachea. His hand came out of his jacket. He dropped like a rag doll, a bottle labeled ketamine—an anesthetic popular among rapists—rolling out of his open palm. He hadn't come to kill her at all.

"We need to go," Kat said. She locked eyes with one of the moms who'd stood in front of her in line. "You should call 911."

Without another word, they marched out of the building, the sun on SW 2nd Avenue momentarily blinding them.

"Fucking men," Annalise hissed. "What the hell did you do to him, and can you teach us how to do that?"

"Did you kill him?" Millie whispered.

A wry smile pulled up the corners of Kat's mouth. "No. He's not dead, just incapacitated for a few moments." *About twenty seconds. Enough time to run.* "I learned that move in a self-defense class." *KGB training that taught us how to crack a windpipe so air leaks into the neck and chest and your mark passes out.*

"I hate that anyone thinks they can touch us however they wish," Farzi said.

"You'd think at our age, we'd be immune to this," Millie said.

"You'd think at our age, my friends wouldn't be so damn fearless." Kat laughed. "Thank you. That was something else. Remind me to never piss any of you off."

Annalise laughed. "I don't know about you, but I am *starving*. I could murder some fondue right now."

TWENTY-SEVEN

"Well, that sucks," Annalise said, standing in front of the ornately carved portico of the Melting Pot. "Can this day get any worse?"

"They don't open until 3:00 p.m.," Kat said, reading the sign on the other side of the columned entrance.

"I never thought to check." Annalise pulled on the door, like the sign was a mistake and the restaurant was actually open. "I'm really sorry."

"Don't be silly, Annalise," Farzi said. "All of us were capable of checking their hours online."

Millie looked left and right down the busy street. "So, what now?"

"Fogo is a block north of here." Annalise pointed with her chin. "And Bangkok Palace is about three blocks east."

"What kind of food do they have?" Millie asked.

"Fogo de Chão is Brazilian churrasco. Bangkok Palace is Thai."

"Brazilian what?" Millie asked.

"They come around to your table with various cuts of barbecued meat. It's all-you-can-eat," Annalise explained. "Steak, pork, chicken …"

"That sounds like a lot." Millie brought her hand to her throat. "I'm not sure I can eat that much heavy food."

"They have a gorgeous appetizer bar with charcuteries, soups. You don't have to have the churrasco," Annalise told her.

"Are they open?" Kat asked.

"I've been to both for lunch, but I'll check." Annalise reached into her bag.

"Already on it." Farzi was scrolling her phone. "I vote Brazilian," she said. "They have a seafood tower I am drooling over."

A light drizzle had just started when they reached the restaurant. They were the only customers.

"Is it always this quiet at lunch?" Millie asked their waiter.

"We only opened ten minutes ago. Soon, the office people come. After noon."

"It's kind of funny that none of us ordered the all-you-can-eat." Farzi laughed after the waiter left.

"I used to be able to eat what I want, when I want." Annalise sighed. "But lately … not so much."

"Wait until you pass fifty," Millie said. "It gets worse."

"I *am* past fifty. I'm fifty-two, actually."

"Your Botox works, then," said Kat. "You look at least a decade younger."

Annalise beamed. "Glad to know my money isn't wasted."

"I'd like to get through a day without excessive gas," Millie said. "Everything I eat, it doesn't matter what or how much …"

"You fart all the time," Kat finished.

"My grandmother was always gassy," Farzi added. "It was a symphony from both ends."

"And if it's not gas, it's indigestion. Heartburn like crazy." Kat brought a fist to her chest, rubbing like the reflux had already started. "There's no Botox for that."

"You guys make aging sound horrible," Annalise whined.

"Surely there's a supplement you can take that helps digestive issues."

Farzi and Kat looked at each other, then burst out laughing.

"There is no end of vitamins and supplements," Kat said when she caught her breath. "Pills you've never heard of."

"Names you can't pronounce," added Farzi. "Plants you never knew existed."

"Lies all over the internet," Kat continued. "Oils … oh my god, don't get me started on the oils."

"Ugh, so many lies there," Farzi said. "How can an essential oil you rub on your elbow make bowel movements easier?"

"They don't really claim that." Millie looked from Farzi to Kat. "Do they?"

Kat nodded. "The really unconscionable ones will promise a cure for infertility."

"That's horrible," Annalise said.

"What's horrible is that every time we go out to eat, we talk about bodily functions." Farzi shook her head. "It's like you wake up one morning and everyone under thirty looks like a teenager and you and your friends commiserate about various ailments. I miss youth."

"Youth is stupid." Kat waved her hand, dismissing the idea.

"You're right. I have a different awareness of life now that I'm sixty." Farzi nodded.

"Youth is not having to make a single tough decision," Annalise said.

"But it's also not knowing who you are and bending to the will of others." Millie smiled ruefully.

The waiter appeared with glasses of water and a round of caipirinhas. Each glass was stuffed with limes. The sugarcane spirit gave the drink a light golden color.

"What's the dumbest thing you did as a kid?" Annalise asked.

"When I was six," Millie said, "I wrote my name in wet concrete, but I had just learned my address so I added that too. The city knocked on our door and my dad had to pay a fine."

"I stole a piece of sheer pira from a shop—it's like a mix of fudge and nougat—and shoved it into the pocket of my shorts. Then went to play with my friends. In the Afghan summer heat." The corners of Farzi's eyes crinkled. "I got in trouble twice. For the theft when my mother found out and for the mess in my shorts."

Kat took a sip of her drink. "I wanted to be more like the boys I played with in my neighborhood, so I cut off all my hair. Then I took my father's razor and shaved my head to get rid of all the choppy bits. My mother cried for three days."

"Once on a road trip to Mexico," Annalise started, "I got pissed at my dad for not buying me a soda, so when the car was stopped, I jumped out of the car and ran away."

"What's so stupid about that?" Millie asked.

Annalise picked up her drink and wiped the condensation from the glass. She smiled. "We were at the border and I was making a run for it, *into* Mexico. The border guards were much faster than I was. I think I made it four steps before someone grabbed me. We spent the next ten hours in Customs and Immigration. My dad was fuming. But the best part?" She grinned. "While my parents were being interrogated, the immigration guards brought me a Coke."

"You're lucky it didn't go badly," Kat said, shaking her head. "Mexican authorities are not known for their fair treatment."

"I was six. Not exactly a national threat."

"Everything is so much bigger when you're a kid," Millie said. "Emotions, desires, dreams …" She sighed. "I wish I could be that innocent and free again." She pushed her chair back and stood. "No sense pining for the past. I'm starving. Let's eat." She led the way to the appetizer bar where they filled their plates with things they couldn't pronounce and dishes they couldn't identify.

"This is such an adventure," Farzi gushed once they were seated again. "I have no idea what I'm eating." She tasted some soup, licking the dark liquid off her lips.

Annalise was trying to pierce an elusive chickpea with her fork. "I was such an idiot in my twenties. I married the wrong man. Then I did it again. I thought the third time would be the charm, but I woke up one morning in my mid-thirties and had nothing to show for it." She gave up on the legume and speared a piece of smoked salmon. "No children, no purpose, and absolutely zero love."

"Is that when you started getting plastic surgery?" Millie asked gently.

"You know, I never thought about it, but yeah. I believed changing how I looked on the outside would improve how I felt on the inside. You're right, Kat." She smiled at her across the table. "Youth *is* stupid. I bet you had it all figured out before you were thirty."

Kat lowered her eyes to her kale and beet salad, pretending not to have heard. How could she tell her friends that by the time she was twenty-five, she'd already lost track of how many assassinations she had carried out? She speared a beet and looked up. Annalise, Farzi, and Millie were looking at her expectantly.

She raised a shoulder in a shrug. "I only could do what Mother Russia allowed me to do—build my career in service of the politburo. There was no room for fantasies or big dreams."

Millie placed a hand on her chest. "That's so sad. It must have been horrible."

"It wasn't." Kat shook her head. "It was the only life I knew. The only regret I have is I was so focused on building my career that I never made the time for life. For living."

"Surely you've had relationships?" Farzi asked.

"Not really, no." Kat paused, deciding which way to move the conversation. Something told her if she wanted to keep these women as friends she would have to give them something more than a vague response.

"I had … lovers. Men who only want a night or two of sex are easy to find."

"Amen to that." Annalise nodded in agreement. "I want to hear your slutty stories, Kat. Spill."

Kat scraped her mind for a rendezvous she felt okay sharing, one that wouldn't invite a lot of questions.

"I had an affair with a classmate in university," she started. "It was short-lived, a little more than two months. He was the man who taught me how to figure out what I liked." Kat put her knife and fork down. "How much do you want to know?"

"All of it." Annalise smirked.

Both Millie and Farzi were watching, waiting for her to continue. "The day after we had sex for the first time, I put on my favorite body-hugging spandex dress. When I passed by him in a lecture, I whispered, 'I'm not wearing any underwear today.' I could feel his eyes burning into the back of my dress, examining my rear for the telltale signs. All day, we passed by each other in the halls, and I could see the hunger in his eyes. At the end of the day, we went out for drinks with some other schoolmates. We were sitting in a booth, and he sat next to me. Under the table, I took his hand and forced it between my legs, guiding his finger inside me."

"Oh. My. God." Annalise panted. "That is the hottest thing I've ever heard."

"I would never have the courage to do that." Millie blushed.

"I wasn't that kind of person either, Millie. Sexually, I was active, but I never had the confidence to do anything like that. He allowed me to taste how it feels when you have all the power in a sexual relationship. When the term was over, we ended things, but he mailed me letters for a few months after school finished. Dirty letters."

Annalise used her napkin to fan her face. "So spicy!"

"I thought those kinds of things only happened in the movies," Farzi said. "You've given me hope, Kat."

"What's the craziest place you ever had sex?" Annalise took her first bite of the seared tofu dish she ordered.

"Oh, that's easy," Kat said. "On a trampoline at the Moscow Circus."

Farzi sputtered on an oyster she'd just poured down her throat. "How does that even work?"

"Like regular sex, but with more bounce." Kat smiled. Sergey, an acrobat, was so ridiculously flexible. And so was she, at the time.

"I never made love anywhere remotely interesting," admitted Millie, "but Aaron Mark did kiss me in front of the rhinoceros exhibit at the zoo."

"And what happened to the man with two first names?" Annalise asked.

"Not a man, but a boy in my sixth grade class. We were on a field trip. I didn't even know he liked me. His family moved away the next week, and I was grateful I didn't have to tell him I didn't like him that way."

"That's the worst, when someone wants more from you than you can give," Kat said.

Farzi cracked a crab claw. "That was me, the first time I fell for a woman. I didn't know I was attracted to women at the time. All I knew was I wanted to spend more time with this woman. She let me kiss her because she was curious, but made it clear she was not interested."

"Ouch." Annalise grimaced.

"No big deal. It turns out she was spying for the French and she was executed by the Taliban. Guess I dodged a bullet. Literally."

Kat whipped her head up, watching Farzi tear the crab's

shell apart. She realized she really knew very little about this woman from Afghanistan and wondered what other surprises she held locked up.

"You never answered the question, Farzi," Annalise pointed out. "Craziest place …"

Farzi peeled the shell from a shrimp and held the tail as she dipped it in seafood sauce. She paused to think, gazing off at nothing while the sauce dripped onto her plate.

"You know, I can't think of anything. For me, kissing a woman was crazy enough. What's your story, Annalise?"

"Maybe not the craziest place, but certainly the most interesting. Deep inside a cave in an inactive volcano in Hawaii. I've never shared that with anyone."

"Were you deeply moved?" Kat quipped.

"Was it mind-blowingly explosive?" Farzi added.

"Were you worried about premature eruption?" Millie said.

"Millie!" Annalise exclaimed. "Two drinks and your dirty mind is set free?"

Millie grinned with the side of her mouth. "What can I say? You ladies bring out the wickedness in me. God forgive me."

"I don't understand how you still have faith." Kat locked eyes with Millie. "You served your god and in return, he let people hurt you. Yet you still believe and forgive. You've earned your place in heaven, as far as I am concerned." Kat looked away, hoping no one had noticed her eyes started to glisten.

Millie gently placed her fork on her plate and rose from her chair. She walked to the other side of the table, leaned over Kat, then wrapped her arms around her from behind. Kat tensed, then reached up to pat Millie's forearm.

"I know we'll see each other in heaven." Millie sighed. She went back to her seat, a satisfied smile painted on her face.

"Doubtful," Kat said under her breath.

"Millie, can I ask you a question?" Farzi's voice faltered. "About your husband?"

"Yes, of course."

"How did he die?"

Millie put her glass down on the table and looked off into the heart of the restaurant. She watched a waiter slice steak onto a patron's plate before she spoke again. "He had a heart attack. Sudden cardiac arrest caused by an unidentified condition. A bunch of words I can't pronounce."

Kat glanced up from her couscous salad, looking for the lie written on Millie's face. Her friend was not a stupid woman. She had gone to university to study chemical engineering. She would know big words.

"Was it cardiomyopathy? An arrhythmia? Ventricular fibrillation?" Kat fired the terms at her. "Do you remember what the doctor told you?"

"Kat," Annalise said, lowering her voice just above a whisper, "why does it matter if Millie remembers the words? Sometimes shock can make us forget things or tune them out completely."

"That happened to me when I first saw Kalan's body. I cradled him, and the noise around me vanished. I'm sorry for your loss." Farzi sighed. "Even with what he did to you, that must have been hard."

"I'm still mostly angry." Millie scowled. "I'm mad at my church and the women I thought were my friends. But I'm also so very, very mad at myself for not having the courage to leave."

"My mother had a saying," Kat said. "Be more sponge and less rock. A sponge can grow and change. A rock is stuck as it is. It was one of her best lessons." Kat felt the sting of a thousand knives. She'd waited too long to listen to her mother. "Sometimes, the only way to survive is to be the rock."

"Well, this rock still needs a dress," Millie said.

"I'm sure we can find something," Annalise said. "We can walk off our lunch and roam the stores down here."

"My offer to browse my closet still stands, Millie. If you find a gown in my closet, you can keep it. I never wear them and it would make me happy to see you happy."

"Kat …" Annalise breathed. "I knew you had a gooey core."

Kat put a beet in her mouth but had a hard time swallowing past the lump lodged in her throat. "Yeah, I'll disintegrate to dust, unlike your plastic ass."

"Not true," Annalise said, pushing her hair behind her shoulders. "I've not done anything with my ass. Yet."

Millie raised her nearly empty glass. "Amen to that!"

Farzi lifted her own glass in a toast and smiled widely. "I can't remember the last time I felt so … happy. I wish everyone in the world could feel as fulfilled as I do now."

As Millie and Annalise murmured their agreement, Kat paused with a forkful of salad and beets hovering over the tablecloth, letting red juice drip down to stain the linen. She wanted to say something, but she lacked the vocabulary to express how she was feeling without inviting more questions. She was less agitated and spring-loaded these days. More curious and sure of herself.

"Hey," Farzi exclaimed suddenly. "Have any of you ever done a random act of kindness?"

"I've done plenty," Millie continued. "It's practically a church requirement."

"I'd love to do something more than pay for a car or two behind me in a drive-thru," Annalise said.

Kat rested her cutlery on her plate. This conversation was becoming far more intriguing than her somewhat disappointing salad. *Should have had the meat,* she thought. "Let's do one right now. Together."

"Oh, I *love* that idea," Millie gushed. "The power of many. What should we do?"

The ideas flew across the table.

"Buy doughnuts and cookies and take them to a police or fire station."

"We could leave a bowl of quarters at a laundromat."

"Pay everyone we see a compliment."

"Buy bouquets of flowers and leave them at random front doors."

"Or get grocery gift cards and hand them out."

"I feel like we should do something bigger," Annalise said. "Something that can make a huge difference in someone's life."

"Hold on." Kat squinted. "How much do you want to spend?"

"I don't know ... $300?" Annalise said.

"Is that really life-changing?" Farzi wondered.

"I meant $300 each," Annalise clarified, "unless that's too much? Just throwing out a number."

"We clearly all have the means," Kat pointed out. "So what should we do?"

The table fell silent as the waiter cleared their plates, smiling politely when they declined dessert.

"How about him?" Farzi pointed her chin to the retreating waiter.

Annalise's eyes brightened. "Oh! That's perfect. A $1,200 tip is a great idea."

"If we time it right, we can be long gone before he realizes it," Kat said. "I don't want any gushing and sob stories."

"Of course not, Kat," Millie joked. "I think you'd contribute more money just to avoid anyone getting their feelings all over you."

"Ha ha, very funny. Go ahead and make fun of the woman who spent most of her adult life without being good at making friends." She glanced sideways at Millie. "Maybe solo life is better."

Millie grimaced. "I didn't mean to offend you."

"Relax, my friend. I am just teasing back. I need to work on that too, I guess."

Annalise asked the waiter for separate checks, and they each diligently added $300 to the tip line on their credit card slips. Kat was giddy with the thrill, and judging by the looks on her friends' faces, they were too. They watched their waiter emerge from the kitchen, arms loaded with plates for another table.

"Time to go," Kat announced, her chair scraping the floor as she pushed back.

They ran out of the restaurant, down the block, and around the corner. They stopped, all except Kat out of breath and wheezing.

"I think I pulled a muscle," Farzi said, rubbing the front of her thigh.

"I know I've triggered my sciatica." Millie rubbed the left side of her rump.

Annalise was bent over, trying to catch her breath. "Oh my god!" she exclaimed. "What if he thought we were running away and skipping out on the bill?"

They looked at one another for a moment, holding the gaze, before the laughter dam burst.

TWENTY-EIGHT

Kat paced back and forth in front of the bow window in her living room. Every time she heard a car on her quiet residential street, she looked up, like an expectant teenager on a first date. It was a fruitless exercise, she realized, since she didn't even know what kind of car Millie drove.

Kat had cleaned her house from front to back last night. It hadn't taken her long—the bungalow was compact and not filled with the kinds of knickknacks others were fond of. Her furnishings were sparse since she'd never bothered to get more furniture than what was actually needed.

Her nerves were jangled, and she wasn't able to calm them. The last time she'd felt so unhinged, she was on a plane to Berlin, about to fulfill her first solo job. Before she became an independent contractor, she had been trained by the best in the business—in her opinion, anyway. Vasily's kill count and stoic demeanor were legendary among assassins. He taught her to focus on the task, to envision only success.

Missing is not an option, he said, his voice flat and distant. *Play it out in your mind. Plan every move to perfection.*

Doing so, she discovered, evaporated her anxiety and ensured the job went well.

But with Millie coming over, there were too many variables. First of all, Kat had *never* had anyone in her house. She knew the basics of etiquette—offer a drink, have something to eat, be a gracious host—but she had never put any of that into practice in her own home. Secondly, even though she'd known Millie for almost a year, they'd never spent one-on-one time together. Kat wasn't sure she would like Millie outside the safety net of the others.

When she'd first met Millie, she saw only insipid meekness that seemed pathetic. She wanted to grab the woman by the shoulders and shake the shit out of her. She wanted to yell, *Use your outdoor voice, woman!* Instead, Kat retreated into her own silence, doing what she did best: observing and learning. She decided Millie was careful with her words, and not because she didn't know how to engage in conversation, but because she was fearful of speaking up. By the time they left Lulu Bar that first night, Kat figured Millie had grown up in a home, or had married into one, where her voice was continually silenced. She took no pride in being right about that.

Kat turned a wing chair toward the front window, dropping into it to wait. She closed her eyes and took a few deep breaths. Her upper body was relaxed, but her legs were restless. She crossed one over the other but could not stop her top leg from swinging. She stood, watching the road again, making eye contact with the driver of a passing car.

Kat went into the kitchen, pulling the olive and pickle tray she bought out of the fridge. She plated crackers, fanning them into a spiral. She cubed cheese and placed the little flags the cheese shop gave her, marking the white cheddar, the balsamic BellaVitano, and the Muenster. She double-checked to confirm a bottle of white wine and cans of diet soda were chilling. She was wiping the spots off her salad plates when the doorbell rang.

"This is a great neighborhood." Millie stood on the front stoop, hugging a bottle of wine.

"Did you have to come far?" Kat glanced over Millie's shoulder, seeing the curved rear of a silver car in her driveway.

Millie stepped inside the foyer. "I'm just on the other side of the 205. It took me a little more than twenty minutes. I brought some wine."

Kat examined the label. "Oh my—Millie … how—where —" she sputtered.

Millie shrugged. Her face reddened. "It wasn't easy, but I made some calls and found a tiny little liquor store in East Portland that imports Slavic wines."

Kat brought a hand to her heart. "I haven't seen an Uzbek wine in decades. Come, let's drink!" She glanced at Millie. "You *will* have a glass, yes?"

Millie nodded, following Kat into the kitchen. "A small sip would be great."

As she uncorked the pinot noir and decanted it, Kat watched Millie in her peripheral vision. The woman was trying to look around the kitchen without appearing nosy, twirling a loose thread at the bottom of her sweater around her index finger.

"Do you want to eat something?" Kat pointed to the assortment of food on her kitchen table. "Or do you want to look at the dresses now?"

"I could eat," Millie said, gesturing with the half-full glass of wine Kat handed her. "Thank you for doing this."

"I have too many dresses. One or two won't be missed."

The floors creaked as they went to sit at the table. Millie looked down at the oak as she pulled out a chair.

"Are these original floors?"

"They are forty-six years old." Kat nodded. "They were black with dirt when I bought the house. The nice thing about hardwood is it cleans up easily. Sanded and restained and they look like new again."

"They do look great." Millie took the salad plate Kat offered her and chose a few olives.

"Eat, Millie. You're in your fifties. And your husband is not here anymore."

Millie held Kat's gaze for a moment, then nodded. "I love these little flags," she said, slicing off a chunk of the BellaVitano. She took a bite, closing her eyes. A smile slowly spread across her face and she nodded to herself.

Kat hadn't yet had a sip of wine, but her chest warmed. She had chosen the cheese carefully, curating a mix of hard and soft cheeses that she'd learned were appealing to any palate.

Millie sliced off another piece. "I love this nutty flavor. But it's also sweet and tangy." She peered at the flag sticking up from the wedge. "I've never heard of BellaVitano. It sounds so deliciously Italian."

"It comes from Wisconsin, actually."

"You're making that up."

"It's true. It was created by a master cheesemaker in Plymouth."

"Come on. How do you know these kinds of details?"

"I like to know things. I want to make informed decisions."

"The devil is in the details," Millie murmured.

"I never understood that phrase. English is so strange sometimes."

"I always thought it was the opposite of 'ignorance is bliss.' Sometimes knowing more about something ruins it for you."

Kat picked up her glass of wine, swirling the bloodred liquid. She popped a gherkin in her mouth, watching the wine's legs slither down the sides of the glass. Millie picked a good one.

"Is that what happened with your church friends?"

Millie was cutting into the Muenster and Kat noticed the slight pause before Millie continued to cut, adding some cheddar, a few crackers, and three pimento-stuffed olives to her salad plate.

"You don't mince words, do you?"

Kat shrugged but remained silent.

"I never thought about it, but you're right," Millie continued, filling the silence. "Once I found out they all knew about what I had suffered, the curtain was pulled back and I didn't like what I saw. I tried to ignore it. Tried to return to the community. But I could never trust any of them ever again. Do you know how that feels?" Millie took a healthy sip of her wine, and Kat watched her swallow.

"Try the BellaVitano again," Kat instructed, ignoring the question, "and see how it tastes now that you've had some wine."

Millie squinted and tilted her head. "Ooohkay," she drawled, then popped a piece in her mouth. Her eyebrows went up. "It tastes fruity now! How—why?"

"Now take another sip of the wine. And let it rest on your tongue for a moment."

Millie finished chewing, then brought the glass to her lips. She sipped slower this time and paused with a mouthful. Her eyes widened. After she swallowed, she blew out a short breath.

"It tastes so much sweeter now. If only Jesus had cheese when he turned water into wine." She grinned, then took another deep drink. Kat saluted her with her own glass.

"Come," Kat said, after draining her wine. "Let's go look at dresses."

Millie took another sip, then Kat led her into the primary suite and slid open the glossy white door in front of her walk-in closet.

"All the dresses are there." She waved to the left side.

Millie walked in ahead of Kat. "It's so cozy in here," she said. "I love these built-ins."

Millie turned around, examining the shelves, drawers, and hanging bars. "You organize your clothes by color?"

"Of course. And also by season. Too much time is wasted in an unorganized closet." She stood with her hands on her hips, following Millie's eyes with her own.

"That's, um, efficient?"

Kat rested her hand on the first gown to the left. "I sorted the gowns from smallest to largest," she said.

"Well, I'll start at the end, then." Millie reached out to touch the largest-size dress, a peach gown with long sleeves made of gauzy, metallic fabric.

"You're so lean, I can never imagine you having to wear anything this large," Millie said, pulling the next dress out of the line. It was a dark navy velvet gown with an empire waist. "When were you ever this size?"

"It was a long time ago." Kat caressed the skirt, the memory of the pressure from the weight suit she wore underneath the dress still vivid.

"There have to be thirty gowns here. I'm amazed you kept them all."

"I had planned to sell them but never got around to it. I have some great memories attached to these dresses." *Like the cream spaghetti strap I wore in Monte Carlo.* She felt a flush of heat between her legs at the memory of Jules sliding off the straps and pushing the bodice down so he could take her breast in his mouth.

"I don't even know what would fit me."

Kat looked Millie up and down, then pulled out a black, off-the-shoulder gown. "Try this one."

"I don't think that will fit. That bodice looks really tight."

"It'll fit. It matches your shape perfectly. Smaller chest, narrow waist, big hips."

Millie's shoulders rounded as she dropped her arms to her sides. She was looking at the dress, avoiding Kat's gaze.

"This is just the way my body is," Millie whispered. "You don't have to be so callous."

Kat sighed. "How long have we known each other? More than six months, right?"

Millie nodded.

"Have I ever not spoken my mind? Have I ever been dishonest?"

Millie shook her head.

"This is how I speak. How I will always speak. I worked around the world for more than forty years. I'm not skilled in friendship like you and Annalise and probably even Farzi. If I am hurting you, it's not on purpose. I hope you'd tell me when I'm being an asshole."

"You're not an asshole." Millie sighed, looking at the dress draped over her arm. "I'm overly sensitive, I guess. I've been trying to lose weight my whole life. Even at my thinnest, my husband convinced me I was a fat cow."

Kat huffed and yanked the dress from Millie. "Enough! He's gone! Why are you letting that demon run your life even now? All the things he called you, all the times he beat you, that was him feeling scared and needing to control someone. Abusers always try to beat their own inadequacies into their partners."

Millie used her thumb to wipe the tears from her eyes. "I'm just going to go. I'll find a dress somewhere. I'm sorry to be such a nuisance."

"You are not leaving," Kat barked. "I don't stick with people I don't like, and I would never invite them into my home. Millie, you are a lovely lady who is broken. We are all a little broken. You can dust the pieces under the carpet or try to glue yourself back together. Do you know what *kintsugi* is?"

"No," Millie squeaked.

"It's a Japanese philosophy about broken things. They

repair broken pottery with gold or silver epoxy. It changes the object into something different. The Japanese believe that when something is damaged, it still has history, and it becomes even more beautiful. You are stronger now than you have ever been, Millie. That's what I think."

"I don't feel that way," Millie said. "I've got decades of hateful words to unwind from my head. It's just as hard as shedding the actual weight."

Kat rehung the black gown and placed her hands on either side of Millie's face. She tilted her friend's head back, forcing her to look at her. "I have been so many sizes. I know what it's like to feel uncomfortable in your own skin." *Fake skin, but still, I felt the weight and judgment.* "It's just packaging, Millie. You are more than that."

"I wish I had known you before I got married. I think you would have stopped me from making that colossal mistake."

Kat let go of Millie's cheeks. "No, I don't know that I would." The truth was she didn't know what kind of person she would have been if she had never become an assassin. She always had had a vein of violence pumping through her. Even as a child, she had no fear, smacking a boy two years older for lifting girls' skirts on the playground. "I would not have sat by silently like your church people did. Of that I am certain."

"You're a wonderful friend, Katya Noskov." Millie smiled shyly. "I hope we're friends until the day we die."

Kat turned away to hide the blush in her face. "I have the *perfect* gown for you," she exclaimed, changing the subject. She shuffled through a few dresses, stopping at a scarlet gown with an organza skirt. "If this doesn't fit you and make you look like a goddess, I'll buy you whatever gown you want."

Millie brought her fingers to her lips, then reached out to touch the gold brocade on the silk bodice. The front of the dress was a crossover, cinching at the waist.

"I've never seen anything more beautiful. It must have cost a fortune."

"It did. Now get in there"—Kat pointed to the ensuite bathroom—"and put it on. I'll wait out here." Kat settled into a wingback chair in the far corner of her bedroom.

Kat smiled with satisfaction when Millie emerged. The crossover fit Millie's chest perfectly, settling into a sexy, but not too revealing V just above her breasts. The cowl of the off-the-shoulder collar accentuated the feminine curve of her neck. The organza skirt skimmed her hips, flaring out gently into a perfect A-line. The red fabric warmed her pale skin and gave her a glow.

Kat leaned back in the chair, assessing the woman from head to toe. "Millie, you are stunning."

"Really?" Millie drew her hands over her torso, looking down. "It feels a bit tight on top."

Kat shook her head. "It's supposed to fit close, to highlight your shape. You are very curvy."

"Oh. Is that good?"

"Yes, Millie. This is good. You will take this dress and wear it to the gala. I think many men, and probably some women, will fall all over you."

Millie brought her hand to her mouth and giggled. "I've never worn or owned anything like this. Thank you, Kat, for being so generous and kind."

Kat swallowed, then cleared her throat. "Get changed and let's get shit-faced."

TWENTY-NINE

K at's phone buzzed on her nightstand, waking her from a deep sleep. She didn't even have to open her eyes to know she was still a little drunk from last night. When she proposed getting shit-faced, she hadn't planned on doing it alone. Millie had one more glass of wine, and she was certainly tipsy, but not the silly, over-the-top drunk Kat was aiming for. She should have known her Bible-toting friend could not go from teetotaler to lush in one night. Kat had finished off the Uzbek pinot noir mostly on her own and then moved onto cognac.

Millie's glass and a half loosened her tongue. She talked about the church ladies, gossiping like a high-brow character in a Jane Austen novel. It was a kind of retaliatory gossip, Millie lashing out and revealing their secrets in response to their betrayal. Kat nodded and laughed eagerly, listening to the indiscretions of people she would never meet, keeping Millie talking long enough to make it safe for her to drive home. She wondered if Millie woke up this morning with the realization of what she'd said and regret for having said it.

Kat's phone buzzed again. She reached for it, opening one eye to peer at the screen. It took a moment for her vision to focus, and she had to fight to keep her eye open. Why was Farzi calling her so early? She dropped her phone next to her on the bed, rolling onto her side, pulling her comforter over her head. She needed more time to sleep off the wine.

She tossed and turned for the next hour, finally giving up when her thick tongue and her thirst became too distracting. She wobbled into the bathroom, placing her face sideways under the tap to catch water in her mouth. The cold dribbled across her cheek, waking her up even more. When she was done, she stood at the foot of her bed, debating whether to try going back to sleep.

You can nap later, she told herself. *An unexpected gift of retirement.*

From the window above the kitchen sink, Kat stared out into her backyard. The maple and oak trees that took up most of the far end of the yard blazed with fall colors of red and yellow. This was the perfect time in Portland, in Kat's view, that space between summer and fall, when the rich hues of the leaves made you forget about the rains of winter just around the corner. She had missed so much of this change in seasons, having never spent more than a stretch of a few weeks in her house.

With no plan for the day, Kat took a luxuriously long shower, steaming away the rest of her hangover. When she walked into her closet, wrapped in a short towel, she realized she hadn't even chosen her own gown for the gala. One by one, she slid the dresses apart, considering and remembering. Her fingers brushed the lavender taffeta of her favorite, and she took in a sharp breath when she pulled it off the bar. The side of the dress was splattered and stained with very, very old blood.

That could have been very, very bad. Good thing Millie is not a size 8.

The day the dress was ruined, she decided she couldn't burn it like she had so many others. She thought she would try to clean it, scrub out the blood, and make it look like new. It had never happened. She hadn't a clue how to treat taffeta, and the cartels of the mid-'90s kept her too busy to try. She had carefully folded the gown in her carry-on, then hung it back in her closet when she got home.

Kat pulled the gown off the Barneys hanger, rolled it up, and shoved it into the kitchen garbage. She stared at the sheen of the fabric sitting among the deli paper and plastic wrap. She squinted, angry with herself for attaching any kind of sentimental value to a dress. That had been an easy job in the early days of her freelance career. She had made the rookie mistake of buying a gown she fell in love with instead of one that could be considered disposable, but sometimes a woman just wants to feel beautiful for her special day. Kat dropped the lid of the trash can, the gown now removed from her history.

As she was getting dressed, Farzi called again.

"Good morning!" Farzi sang. "I hope I didn't wake you."

"You did."

"Oh, uh, I'm sorry about that. Do you want me to call you later?"

"Why?"

"So you can go back to sleep?"

"No. I am awake now. What's up?"

"We've made a plan for today. Since Millie has a gown, we're going to skip shopping and just go for lunch."

Something squeezed in Kat's gut. *They made plans without me?*

"Yes, Millie has a gown," she said, considering her words carefully. "She told you?"

"Annalise told me." Kat felt another squeeze. "She's very upset that we aren't going shopping together," Farzi continued. "I think that woman loves spending money."

Why didn't you ask her when you had a private conversation with her? she wanted to say. Kat held her tongue, letting Farzi fill the silence.

"What does the gown you gave Millie look like?"

Ah, okay, so no details were shared.

"It's a scarlet crossover with an organza skirt. It brightened her whole face."

"I can't wait to see it. Did you get my text?"

"No." Kat pulled her phone away from her ear, only now noticing fourteen missed texts. They had tried to include her in the decision, but she had been deep in wine-soaked sleep.

"I can pick you up," Farzi offered.

"I'll drive us," Kat said. "It doesn't make sense for you to come to the other side of the river only to go back downtown."

Farzi laughed. "That's fine. As long as you let me pay for parking."

"Deal!" She clicked off the phone, relieved the sting of rejection was misplaced.

After getting dressed, Kat shuffled into the kitchen to make a pot of coffee. The lid of the trash can hadn't fully closed and lavender taffeta spilled out. She opened the bin to push down the fabric and saw a tiny cheese flag waving next to the bloodied bodice. She reached in, turning it to read the label. BellaVitano. Kat couldn't stop the smile from spreading across her face.

She hadn't messed up. Millie had hugged her on the way out the door, thanking her for a wonderful evening and the gown. Kat was being genuine when she told Millie she was glad she had come over. She had really listened to her, asking questions and offering advice. She wanted Millie to leave feeling assured and happy.

For the first time in her life, Kat wasn't isolated, she was invested.

THIRTY

K at had been ready for forty-five minutes and spent all that time alternating between pacing in front of the living room window and sitting on the edge of the couch trying not to crease her black Valentino. Her freshly dyed hair was swept back into curls in a half updo the stylist talked her into. And she had been right. Kat's dark brown hair looked fuller and feminine. She stood tall, her two-inch heels an extension of her body. The slit up to her thigh allowed for a glimpse of her lean, muscled leg. She ran her hands over the bodice, down to her slight hips, reveling in her womanhood.

She threw back a few shots of vodka to calm her nerves. Without a script to follow or a mark to watch, her heart pounded in her chest. Kat kept returning to the bathroom to blot the beads of sweat from her forehead and the nape of her neck.

She was relieved when a sleek, black limousine pulled up to her house. *Of course Annalise would hire a limo.* She paused at the full-length mirror beside the front door, nodding her approval. Kat pulled a pashmina over her shoulders and stepped out into the fresh October air.

Kat settled into the soft leather seat, her back to the driver, and graciously accepted the glass of champagne Annalise handed her. Millie sat beside Annalise, looking so stunning it took Kat a moment to process. Millie's mousy hair had been colored gray-blond and it shone with silver strands, all of it pulled into a chignon pinned with black pearls. She was wrapped in a cashmere duster. Annalise wore a fur shawl, the sheer tulle of her gown flaring out around her.

"Millicent, why have you been hiding this stunner from us?" Kat said.

"I know, right?" Annalise said. "I can't tell you how many times I had to tell her she wasn't a harlot."

Millie's face reddened. "I've never, not once in my life, worn this much makeup. I feel like I'm on display. Even my cleavage is sparkling."

Kat couldn't help but shift her eyes to Millie's chest. "I presume that is your doing." She tilted her chin toward Annalise, who nodded and shrugged in response. "Pardon me if this is abrupt, Millie, but you look very fuckable."

"Well, that's a first." Millie beamed. "Thank you, Kat. For everything. I needed this boost."

When they stopped to pick up Farzi, the woman walked out of her condo lobby in a black duster, its golden lining matching her gown. Her hair, pulled to the side, swept her shoulder in waves.

"That color!" Annalise clapped her hands. "It really brings out the golden flecks in your eyes. Just gorgeous."

"Are you flirting with me?"

"One hundred percent, yes." She handed Farzi a filled flute, raising her own glass. "We all still got it, ladies."

"Millie, if you ever decide to come to the other side …" Farzi's eyes glistened.

"Told you," Kat mouthed to Millie.

"Where are we going?" Farzi asked as the limo pulled away from her building.

"The Benson," Annalise answered.

Kat bit down on her tongue and forced her hands to lay flat on her lap. She hadn't thought to ask where the gala was being held, letting herself be swept up in the excitement of a night out with her friends. More than three years had passed since she'd last been to the hotel, trailing what turned out to be her final mark into the lobby bar.

Kat spent the six-minute drive mentally chastising herself for walking into a situation blindly. She pasted a smile on her face, watching the others in animated chit-chat. They were oblivious to her silence, having become accustomed to Kat's conservative conversational skills.

When they pulled up to the front of the hotel, Kat was calmer, her self-directed anger simmering down. The valet opened the door, helping Annalise and Millie out. Farzi followed, and the three of them stood under the porte cochère waiting for Kat. Inside the limo, Kat started to move forward. Without warning, like someone or something was there, she was pushed back into the seat.

You're getting old, she thought dismissively, *and it's harder to get moving.*

Reaching out to grab hold of the handle above the door, Kat slid across the seat and pulled herself forward. She lost her momentum again and fell back into the seat.

"Are you okay?" Millie poked her head into the limo.

"I can't seem to find my footing," Kat said.

"Madam?" the valet asked, holding his gloved hand out to help. Kat took it, and the valet reached for her other hand. With his assistance, Kat unfolded herself from the back of the car.

"That was weird," she said, smoothing down the front of her gown.

"Getting up is getting tricky, isn't it?" Farzi mused. "Aging is terrible."

"No more old lady talk," Annalise ordered, shrugging off

her shawl and handing it to the coat check attendant. Kat let her eyes travel over Annalise from head to toe. Her hair spilled over her shoulders in soft waves; her gauzy, cream-colored gown was embroidered with delicate silk flowers on the bodice and through the skirt. "We are here to dazzle, to dance, and to donate."

"And you will, in that Dior." Kat smiled.

"You know your couture," Annalise said. Kat heard approval in her voice.

"I've shopped for one or two in my life." *And that gown cost more than a compact car.* "You look gorgeous, Annalise."

"She's gorgeous in a paper sack." Farzi laughed.

"Thank you, my beautiful friends." Annalise beamed.

Annalise walked up to the registration desk, distracting the volunteers. She flapped a hand behind her, waving Kat, Farzi, and Millie into the ballroom. Kat's heart thumped harder for a few beats as they snuck past the gatekeeping greeters at the door.

The Ross Weaver Cancer Center Gala was held in the hotel's famed Mayfair Ballroom. Kat had never been beyond the main bar and lobby of The Benson, and she couldn't help but gawk. She had read online about the hundred and fifty crystal chandeliers lighting the room, but the photographs did not prepare her for the splendor. The lights shimmered, splashing prisms of color across the linen-covered tables and the cream wallpaper. It was elegant and sophisticated, the perfect place for two hundred guests to dress in their best and give their money away.

Once Annalise joined them, they walked through the atrium, examining the various items, experiences, and services available for silent auction. Annalise bid on a flight simulation for Matteo and a curated wine-of-the-month package for herself. Farzi placed a generous bid on tickets to every special exhibit at the art museum for the next two years. Millie put her money down on a long-weekend vacation package, and

Kat bid on a gaming pack with video and board games that, should she win it, she planned to donate to the children's ward of the cancer center.

Millie and Farzi wandered away, while Annalise moved through the ballroom with purpose, shaking hands and air-kissing cheeks. Kat watched with envy. Her friend was clearly in her element, a social butterfly flitting from person to person, floating around the room capturing everyone's attention. Kat looked for Farzi and Millie, spotting them standing near the photo booth at the back of the ballroom, watching people pose with props. Millie tugged at the crossover bodice, ensuring she wasn't showing too much cleavage. Farzi pressed herself up against the wall, her eyes nervously scanning. Unlike those two, Kat felt at ease sneaking around the ballroom as an uninvited guest.

When the cocktail hour was over, everyone made their way to their assigned tables in the ballroom. Annalise beckoned Farzi and Millie to the table where she sat with six other people. Kat slinked over, claiming a chair. Annalise introduced the people in the other chairs: Blink's top-performing managers and their partners.

Kat narrowed her eyes. "Annalise, you bought this table, didn't you?"

Annalise shrugged a shoulder. "Busted."

"And now this is going to be so much less fun." Kat faked a pout. "I was looking forward to a night of deception and subterfuge."

"Well, I, for one, am relieved." Millie's face relaxed and she smiled. "I was so nervous about being thrown out."

"I'm with Kat," Farzi added. "I was secretly hoping to be challenged. I had imagined us running out the door to escape capture."

Kat raised her eyebrows, then looked down at Farzi's feet. "I would love to see you run in those heels."

"Likewise." Farzi laughed.

After the opening speeches, dinner was served, an uninspired choice of steak, chicken, salmon, or vegan entrées. The drinks came fast and freely, and by the time dessert—a tiny orange chocolate soufflé—was served, Kat was still sober but very happy. She laughed when Annalise pulled them all onto the dance floor, mimicking the moves of the much younger guests.

"The last gala I went to," she shouted at her dance partners, "the dancing was all waltzes and foxtrots."

"When was that?" Millie asked. "1895?"

Kat threw her head back and laughed. "It was in Vienna, so you're not far off."

Annalise sidled over, bumping her hips on Kat's. "Fundraising ... galas ... are ... different." She punctuated each word and thump in time to the music. "They want people to have fun. It encourages the flow of money. Speaking of which, I'm going to check on my auctions."

As the song ended and blended into the next, they refreshed their drinks, then made their way back into the atrium, increasing their bids.

"Millie, do you know that's a Valentine's weekend you're bidding on?" Farzi said, reading the information off the bid sheet.

Millie nodded. "I know. I thought a little romance with my besties would be nice." She wrapped her mouth over the straw of her piña colada and cast her eyes down into the drink, her cheeks flushed.

Kat sipped her chocolate martini. "Who says we can't turn a romantic getaway into a girls' weekend?" She then looked away, blinking, unsure why and when she decided she wanted to be part of this plan.

"I've never been on a girls' trip," Farzi said.

"Does heading to the Christian Jamboree count?"

"NO!" Annalise shouted. "Any mention of Jesus automatically nulls and voids the girls' weekend covenant."

Kat raised her eyebrows. "The covenant?"

"Yes." Annalise nodded, frowning and turning serious. "There are rules that must be followed. You must bring more alcohol than is safe to consume. You must commit to lounging in yoga pants during the day and dressing in revealing clothing when we go out in the evening. Underwear and bras are optional, as are dietary restrictions."

"You are making this up." Kat waved her hand dismissively. "I've traveled the world and never heard of such things."

"That's because the most important rule of girls' weekend is that you never talk about what happened on girls' weekend to or around anyone else. The secrets die with you."

Millie bent over the bid sheet, writing down a number that far exceeded the package's estimated value. "Think anyone is fool enough to outbid me?"

Farzi whistled when she looked at Millie's bid. "You know, we could probably pay for three girls' trips out of pocket for that amount."

"I know. But this is for a good cause. And I'll get a tax receipt, right?"

"Cheers to benevolent acts with a tax break!" Farzi raised her glass, then pouted. "My glass is empty. Round of strawberry shortcake shots?"

The drinks flowed freely for the rest of the night. They danced with men whose names they forgot as soon as they heard them. They watched the entertainment—a famous ventriloquist only Kat had never heard of—and laughed themselves to tears.

When the DJ started playing music, Annalise grabbed Millie's arm. "I *love* this song," she yelled, pulling Millie onto the dance floor. Millie's drink sloshed over the sides of the glass as she handed it off to Kat.

Kat looked around the room, trying to see all the people without analyzing them, but the ability to read people was deeply ingrained. At the table next to theirs, a wife appeared to be smiling, but her eyes cold with rage as she watched her husband ogle every woman. A man standing at the bar was having a conversation with another gentleman, but the way he exaggerated his nods and laughter told Kat he was speaking with his boss. Kat knew from the way a young lady plucked empty glasses from her table and placed them on a passing tray that she had worked as a waitress herself.

When the emcee announced the silent auction would be closing in ten minutes, they all revisited their bid sheets. Millie was still on top; Kat had been outbid, so she topped up again; Farzi did the same. Annalise tottered at the bid sheet for the wine, pen in hand. Kat watched her squint at the paper, obviously unable to focus.

Kat stepped up beside Annalise. "Can I help you with that?"

"I can write a number." Annalise waved her off. She put the pen to the paper, but the tip was retracted. She tried clicking the top, staring at it contemptuously, as if the nib was being purposefully belligerent in its refusal to come out.

Kat took the pen from Annalise, twisted the barrel, and handed it back without uttering a word.

Annalise narrowed her eyes at Kat and stuck out her tongue. "Why are they ushing trick penss?" She turned her back to Kat to bend over the sheet and add her new bid.

"What about the flight simulations?" Farzi reminded her. "Do you want to go back to that?"

"Nope-uh," Annalise said, popping out the *p*. "Matteo can fly a real plane. I think. He did the stimulation before."

"You mean *simulation*," Millie corrected.

"Feh, it's the same thing to men." Annalise craned her neck, looking toward the bar. "Let's have another drink!" She swayed, unsure which way to go.

"Why don't you go back to our table and I'll get the drinks," Kat said.

"I've got you," Farzi said, guiding Annalise by the elbow into the ballroom.

Millie trailed behind, but stopped to turn to Kat. "Please get her some water. I think she's had enough."

"She's an adult, Millie. She can decide for herself."

"I don't want her to puke all over the limo," Millie said.

"I'll get her a virgin gin and tonic," Kat said. "In her state, she won't be able to tell the difference." Millie nodded once, then caught up with the others.

When Kat returned to her friends, virgin cocktail and a glass of water in hand, petit fours were being served. Tiered plates had been placed in the center of each table with an assortment of small chocolates and truffles.

"This is the cutest!" squealed Annalise, pointing to a dark chocolate with a tiny candy octopus floating on top. Plucking it off the plate, Annalise popped it past her lips, her eyes widening immediately.

"It jus' explooded in my mouth!" She held her hand in front of her full mouth.

"What's inside?" Farzi asked, choosing a similar chocolate with a lighthouse painted on top.

"Salted caramel, the bess."

Farzi took a bite of hers. Her hand flew up to catch the chocolate ganache dribbling onto her chin. She closed her eyes and moaned.

Millie sat back in her chair, eyeing the desserts, her clasped hands resting on her lap.

"You should try these, Millie," said Farzi.

Millie shook her head. "I'm afraid if I start, I won't be able to stop."

"Caloriesss don't count at a fundraising gala." Annalise waved her hand in front of her, hitting the dessert display.

Kat's reflexes kicked in and she was out of her seat in an instant, catching the tiered plates before the chocolates flew off. She overcorrected, and a single chocolate launched itself off the top tier, landing in Millie's lap.

"Now you *have* to eat that one." Annalise snorted.

Millie picked up the chocolate, examining the blue and gold swirl on top. She shrugged before putting the whole thing into her mouth. She chewed, then swallowed, then grimaced.

"Not good?" Kat asked. "What was in it?"

"Lavender cream," Millie answered. "There was a sweet burst and then I tasted the lavender. Too much flower."

Kat selected a fiery red octagon. As soon as her front teeth carved into the chocolate, she could smell and taste the smoky heat of chipotle.

"Mmm," she moaned, tilting her head back to swallow. "Mexican chocolate. Velvet and fire at the same time. *Es la fuego muy bien.* Heat is good."

Farzi, Millie, and Annalise were staring at her.

"How many languages *do* you speak, Kat?" Farzi asked. "And why do you know so many?"

"It was my job." She shrugged. "It was easier to communicate and negotiate in a client's mother tongue. If you want a number, I speak twelve languages, including three dialects."

"That's amazing!" Millie exclaimed. "How do you keep them all straight in your head?"

"Practice. But now that I am retired and no longer use them, I can feel the words fading from my mind." Kat laughed. "I can't imagine I'll have much need for Papiamento anymore. Unless I go back to Curaçao, Aruba, or Bonaire." *Which I won't. Small islands with long memories. They still mourn that gangster singer who sold children.*

"Pa-pi-ah-men-too …" Annalise worked the word around her tongue. "I like that. Just saying that sounds like I'm speaking another language. Am I speaking another language?"

Kat laughed. "Kind of. Papiamento is a mix of Portuguese and Spanish."

"Say something fun. Can you swear in Papi … papima … mom?" Annalise was bouncing on the edge of her chair.

"Kat's not going to teach you how to swear at a gala for kids' cancer," Millie pointed out.

Annalise pouted. "Just one word? Pleeeasse?"

Kat pursed her lips. "Okay. One word. Are you ready?"

Annalise nodded enthusiastically, shaking some of her hair out of its chignon.

"Okay." Kat glanced from side to side. She leaned forward, getting close to Annalise's face and whispered, "*Kaka*."

"Kaka?" Annalise screeched. "Kaka? Like … poo?"

"Exactly," Kat said.

"What kind of swear word is poo?" Annalise sat back in her chair and crossed her arms in front of her chest. "I feel cheated. What kind of shit is this?"

"Exactly," Kat repeated.

Millie was already shaking with laughter. They watched their drunk friend struggle to work it out. Annalise scratched the back of her head. Farzi tilted hers to the side. Kat waited.

Watching drunk Annalise put the pieces together was like waiting for the lamp in a lighthouse to make a full circle.

"Oh. OH. OH. I get it! Shit," she blurted out. "Shit. *Kaka*." Annalise threw her head back and laughed so hard, she gasped for breath.

"You're a fun drunk," Kat said, "but a slow one."

The emcee was back, announcing the end of the silent auction. The gala volunteers would be delivering vouchers to the winners.

"Please make sure to complete your payment before you leave," the emcee explained. "You can collect your items tonight or make arrangements for delivery if needed. The Ross Weaver Cancer Center thanks you for your continued support. We hope you enjoyed your evening and look forward to seeing you at next year's gala."

The music fired up, and Annalise's managers and their partners headed out to the dance floor. A volunteer appeared at the table.

"I have winning bids for Annalise Onofrio and Millicent—"

"That's us," Annalise screamed. "WOOHOO!" She threw her arms up over her head. "Pass them over." She was opening and closing her hands, gesturing at the smiling volunteer.

"You can pay for and pick up your items in the room next to the coat check. Congratulations." The volunteer gave them each a slip of paper.

"Someone must have outbid me at the last minute." Farzi pouted. "I knew I should have checked again."

"Same," Kat agreed.

Millie looked down at her slip. Her shoulders rounded and she bit her bottom lip. "When Darren was alive, I would never have spent this amount of money at once. It feels … uncomfortable."

Kat leaned over to look at Millie's slip. "I can cover it if you need me to."

"I have the money," said Millie, "thank the Lord. Thank my husband, actually. I cowered when I had to ask him for money to buy clothes. He gave me a tight grocery budget and forced a lemon into my mouth if I went over. And now, here I am, with more money than I know what to do with. He was a complete piece of shit, but he was a smart investor. The son of a bitch never dreamed he would die so young, and he never bothered with a will. Every penny went to me. But I still feel sick spending anything."

Kat watched Millie's face. There was an involuntary twitch near the corner of her right eye. *Could be pain. Could be she's hiding something.* Kat pushed her suspicion aside. Millie was her friend. A woman who had endured horrible things, who knew the heartache of having her trust violated and her foundations rocked. *Of course she's twitchy.*

Kat took Millie's hand, squeezing it and bringing it to her chest. "We will help you. We will go on this trip you won together. You'll be okay, Millie. I'll—we'll—make sure of that. Now, let's go collect your goods and call it a night. This old lady needs some sleep."

THIRTY-ONE

"This can't be right." Annalise held a large rectangular basket in front of her, squinting through the cellophane. "I thought I won the wine thing."

The volunteer looked as confused as Annalise. "Um, let me double-check." She leafed through all the papers, pulling out the sheet marked WINE-OF-THE-MONTH. "Oh, I see you did have a few bids, but then other people outbid you."

"No, no, no. Check again. I upped my bid at the last minute. There is no way this many people came after me."

The woman shook her head, her messy bun bouncing. "You were the last bidder on this one." She held out the paper, marked Merry Jane Society at the top. "These two items were right next to each other. Maybe you got confused?"

Annalise took the paper and squinted. Kat pointed out the drunken scrawl spread over two lines halfway down the page. There was no mistake. Annalise was the final bidder on whatever this was.

"Never drink and bid, I guess," Kat said.

Annalise brought her face closer to the basket. "Is it food?" She used the flat of her hand to push her hair off her cheeks and spit away the strands stuck to her lips. "Looks nice. I hope it's not crap."

"It happens all the time at these events," the woman soothed. "The last guy who paid bought a full image makeover, including a makeup session." She leaned forward. "Not sure how he's gonna explain that to his wife," she whispered conspiratorially. "If it's for her, well …"

Annalise widened her eyes. "What kind of asshole buys a makeover for someone else?"

"Maybe it's for him," Kat chimed in from behind. "He wouldn't be the first married man with a secret."

Annalise's face paled, and she ran her hand over the bodice of her gown.

"Are you going to be sick?" Kat asked, looking around for the nearest bathroom.

"No, I'm fine." Annalise shook her head. "Just tired, dehydrated, and drunk." She tapped her credit card over the terminal the volunteer held out, then tucked the basket under one arm.

Millie and Farzi waited for them in the vestibule between the hotel lobby and the portico.

"I am so excited," Millie gushed. "I have never won anything in my life. And I get to spend three nights in a luxurious cabin with my best friends. You're all coming, right? I mean, I don't mean to be pushy, but that's why I bid big. I *really* want to go with all of you. You'll come, right? Annalise, you can bring the wine you won."

"Umm, except, I didn't win the wine."

"What?" exclaimed Farzi. "You were super aggressive with your bidding. You were stalking the table like a lioness hunting an antelope."

"But this lioness was a little tipsy and was sniffing around the hyenas." Kat laughed.

"I *thought* I was bidding on the wine, and I was. But I guess

I got a little drunker than I planned and I bid on the wrong item at the last minute."

"So, what's in the basket?" Millie asked.

"I'm not sure." Annalise scratched her head. "Whatever it is, we'll have fun with it."

Once they were in the back of the limo, Annalise tore open the cellophane. She pulled out the items one by one, not caring about the crinkled paper shreds falling all around them.

"Oh, Merry Jane … I get it." Annalise chuckled. "Mary-jane … clever. It's a basket full of cannabis edibles."

"It's all marijuana?" Millie whispered. "Oh my …"

"Look at this." Annalise held out a powder-filled jar. "It's an instant latte. Vanilla chai."

"Why is there a hole in the bottom of this cup?" Kat asked, pulling out a tall red mug with a cave-like opening at the bottom.

Farzi dug around in the basket on Annalise's lap. "That hole is for a tea candle." She held out a small bag with two tea lights inside. "It's a fondue mug. There are probably a couple of forks in here …" She continued digging around, pulling out a pair of mini two-prong forks. "See?"

"I found the chocolate," Annalise said, holding up two small rectangles, one white, one milk.

"I didn't even know they could make so many things with marijuana," Millie said, holding up two bottles, one labeled Sauced and the other Spiced. "This is wing sauce. And this is jam. 'Red Pepper Pot Jelly,' to be exact."

"Oh, this is clever," Kat said, examining a round metal tin. "Wake and Bake Instant Coffee."

"We should bring all of this for our girls' weekend." Annalise winked.

"I like that idea," Millie agreed. "I haven't gotten high since that one time in high school. I *think* I had fun."

"I'm glad it's all edibles," Annalise said, stuffing the items back into the basket. "I hate the smell of weed. I smoked some in high school, but now, the smell turns my stomach. I get why they call it skunk weed."

"I've never smoked it or tried an edible," Farzi confessed. "I've never done drugs of any kind."

"Not even once?" Kat questioned, passing the coffee tin back to Annalise.

Farzi shook her head. "Opium was the big deal when I was a kid, but as a way to make money. Why would you smoke your profits?"

"Well, that, and you could go to prison for using," Kat said.

"Farzi, it's okay if you don't want to do this," said Millie. "Come for the weekend, anyway. It won't be complete without you."

The limo stopped, and Kat looked out the window. They were on a cul-de-sac, the road and houses barely visible in the dim streetlamps.

"Where are we?" she asked.

"This is our street," Annalise answered. "Millie and I live closest to the hotel, so it made sense for the driver to drop us first. This has been so much fun! Thanks for being the best dates. Good night." Annalise put her hand on the door, but the driver opened it first. She climbed out, the crinkle of the cellophane drowning out the chirp of fall crickets. Millie followed behind, turning back to blow kisses to Kat and Farzi.

"Please wait until they are both in their homes," Kat instructed the driver. Annalise and Millie hugged in front of the limousine's headlights, then turned and walked to their houses.

She watched Annalise for a moment before turning to watch Millie walk toward her house. The motion-detection lights went on when she stepped onto the driveway, illuminating Millie and the borrowed gown like a flame.

I am absolutely going to let her keep that, she thought.

Kat turned her head to check on Annalise. When she

opened the front door and turned back to wave, Kat raised her own hand in response, forgetting for a moment the limo's windows were tinted.

She leaned back, her head thumping against the headrest. Farzi reached across the seat, taking Kat's hand and squeezing it.

"That was a truly spectacular night." Farzi sighed. "I'm so glad I met you all."

Still looking out the window, Kat squeezed back. "So am I, Farzi. So. Am. I."

THIRTY-TWO

There was the slightest hint of daybreak when Kat woke up the next morning. Still under the covers, she turned toward the bedroom window, letting the glow of last night warm her.

She kept her eyes closed, replaying the highlights. The exhilaration of bypassing the registration desk and gliding into the ballroom like they belonged. Millie's panicked face when an usher asked for their table number. Farzi realizing the woman with the silver locs twisted down her back was actually flirting with her and not merely being friendly. Kat throwing her shoes off to dance and not caring about the sticky floor. Annalise trying to convince the gala's organizers to set up another table so she could run a poker game.

Kat burrowed herself further into the covers, holding on to the warmth of feelings that were new to her. When Farzi squeezed her hand in the limo last night, something simultaneously opened and slid closed inside Kat. She asked the driver to take her home before Farzi, not wanting to ride solo at the end of their evening. She had spent enough of her life alone. She was done with that now.

Her phone buzzed on the kitchen island, pulling her out

of bed. When she saw a text from Millie glowing on her home screen, her brain flooded with dopamine.

MILLIE

> Taking your gown to the dry cleaners today. Any special instructions they need?

KAT

> No. And correction—it's your gown now. Please keep it. I have more than I will ever wear again.

MILLIE

> Are you serious?

KAT

> Very. It fit you perfectly. Wear that to speed dating next time and you'll have a dozen proposals.

MILLIE

> I don't think I want to get married again.

KAT

> I didn't say marriage proposals.

MILLIE

> Good Christian women don't do those kinds of things.

KAT

> You need to stop being good.

MILLIE

> LOL. Thank you, K. For the gown and for being a wonderful friend. TTYL.

Kat read and reread the text. Despite the last seven months, she still felt like she was on the periphery, watching Annalise, Farzi, and Millie bond while she observed, contributing little. A fish out of water. A wolf in sheep's clothing. A woman who could meticulously plan a clean kill but couldn't figure out how to fully open herself up to her friends.

After filling her espresso maker with water and ground coffee, Kat realized she didn't want to be sitting alone at home. She got dressed to make the fifteen-minute walk to her favorite local coffee shop. The crisp air confirmed the arrival of fall, her favorite season. She grabbed a sweater from the coat rack by the door. It was old and worn, a piece of the past when she needed to be invisible, to be overlooked like a grandma. She tossed the sweater over the back of the couch, no longer content to be that kind of person.

She went into her closet, pulling out a dark gray full-zip velour hoodie. She brought it into the sunlight, examining it for any stains. The last and only time she wore this hoodie was when she was tracking a mark in Venice Beach. Death by steroid overdose, that one. It was a warm and lush hoodie with thumbholes in the cuff, so different from the old sweater where she could stuff tissues up the sleeve.

Just as she sat down with a flat white at the café, her phone buzzed again. Millie had sent a new text, this time with the group.

MILLIE

I got the email from the resort. Has anyone been to Sweetgrass by the Sea?

KAT

Never

She let her coffee sit, allowing the milk froth to thicken. The first sip of a settled flat white, she learned in Italy, was worth the wait.

FARZI

I just Googled it. It looks amazing. Those ocean views! Have you been?

Kat brought the small mug to her lips and sipped. The espresso was cut perfectly with the creamy steamed milk. She opened a browser and looked up the resort. Set on the Oregon Coast, every cabin had a spectacular view of the Pacific Ocean.

MILLIE

Never even heard of it. I'm glad I didn't bid on some crappy place in the middle of nowhere.

KAT

Which cabin do we have?

MILLIE

I don't know. I'm going to call later this morning and find out.

FARZI

I guess Annalise is still asleep.

KAT

Of course she is, it's Sunday morning. And she was very drunk.

MILLIE

I think we were all a bit above our normal limit. Might go to confession this afternoon.

Kat raised an eyebrow.

Drinking is not a sin, Millie.

FARZI

I thought you were done with church.

MILLIE

I know. But I miss the ritual.

ANNALISE

Good morning and fuck that. Those assholes stabbed you in the back. Come on over and you can confess to me over Bloody Marys.

FARZI

Good morning! Hungover?

ANNALISE

Mild headache. Are we planning our girls' weekend?

MILLIE

I've never had a Bloody Mary. I don't like tomato juice.

KAT

Me neither, Millie.

ANNALISE

So when are we going away?

FARZI

Back home, my babu made fresh tomato juice with salt and lime.

MILLIE

I'm getting confused with this mixed-up convo. Why don't you all come over for brunch today? 11?

Millie's suggestion of brunch made Kat's stomach rumble.

KAT

I will make obi non and suzma, a tradition at Uzbek breakfast.

ANNALISE

Sounds fancy.

KAT

Bread and seasoned yogurt. Not fancy. Only delicious.

Farzi offered to bring smoked salmon, cream cheese, and capers. Annalise would supply crackers and cheeses, plus some

Bloody Mary mix. Millie was in charge of non-Bloody Mary beverages and vegetables.

Farzi texted Kat in a new message.

FARZI
Want to carpool? I'll pick you up at 10:30.

KAT
Yes. Thank you. See you later.

Kat finished her coffee, then walked another two blocks to the grocery store. She wouldn't have time to make homemade suzma, a process that required fifteen hours to drain the yogurt, but she could use a thick *labneh*. She would add her own crushed garlic and fresh, fragrant dill.

When she got home, Kat set her oven to proof the obi non. She turned her kitchen drawers inside out, searching for both the large and small *chekich*, the stamps her mother long ago used to decorate the bread. She found them in the back of a junk drawer.

Kat didn't need a recipe. The process was imprinted into her like the flower stamps she'd pressed into the bread with her mother every Sunday. This was the only lasting memory she had of her mother who had died of cancer the year before Kat finished boarding school. Her father kept the truth from her, and the school did the same. When Kat returned home for the weekend before her graduation ceremony, both her parents were gone, another family lived in her house, and her aunt had moved to Europe. Penniless and angry, Kat moved out of the school dorms and into the arms of the KGB.

Shaking away the painful memories, Kat found peace in the repetitive kneading of the dough and rolling out bagel-sized disks. She took her time stamping flowers into the middle of each flattened piece, humming an old Uzbek folk song as she pressed the larger stamp into the dough, forming swirls around the central flowers. She glanced at the microwave clock, thankful for the modern appliances that reduced a six-hour process to an hour and a half. She had plenty of time to make twelve salad plate-sized loaves.

Once the breads were in the oven, Kat brewed herself a sweet tea, then sat at her kitchen table, assessing the mess on the island. It took only a few minutes for the smell of the baking bread to reach her.

A warmth spread through her chest. She had forgotten how good it felt to bake for others, to know that she could provide nourishment through her own hands.

Without warning, a wave of sadness washed over her and her eyes burned with tears. She had wasted her life, telling herself she was performing a noble job, ridding the world of very terrible people. But at what cost? She was almost halfway through her sixties and had passed through life never knowing how valuable a friend—friends—could be. Dropping her face into her hands, Kat let the tears flow, unsure if she was grieving or relieved.

When the oven timer beeped, Kat straightened up, wiping her tears away before checking the bread. The obi non were perfect, their sunken middles soft, the bottoms crispy and the tops golden. She inhaled the sweet scent of the fresh-baked bread. It was nothing but milled wheat a couple of hours ago, but now it was a work of art.

THIRTY-THREE

"Allah, that smells *SO GOOD*," Farzi exclaimed as Kat climbed into the front seat of the Honda and placed the obi non and suzma on her lap. "Is there anything better than homemade bread?"

"I don't think so." Kat smiled. That was exactly the response she'd been hoping for.

"How mad would you be if I reached into that"—Farzi pointed to the cloth sack holding the loaves—"and ripped off a chunk?"

"Let me make it easy." Kat loosened the drawstring and pulled out the top loaf. "It's still warm, which makes it even better."

Kat offered the bread to Farzi, who threw the car into park and used both hands to rip off a chunk.

"Do you want some suzma dip to go with it?" Kat asked.

Farzi held the bread under her nose. "I'm a bit of a purist when it comes to bread. First bite should be clean. What's in the dip?"

"I made it with store-bought labneh, but normally, it's Greek yogurt drained through a sieve so it thickens like cheese.

I didn't have time to make it from scratch, but I added dill, garlic, and parsley."

"That sounds like the *sabse borani* dip we make in Afghanistan. Also drained yogurt, but we add caramelized onions and garlic or spinach." Farzi bit into the bread and closed her eyes, moaning. "This obi … what do you call it?"

"Obi non."

"It's amazing. Soft and chewy in the middle and crispy on the outside. I wasn't expecting that. One day, I will make you my grandmother's flatbread."

Still chewing, Farzi pulled away from Kat's house.

"That's *noni Afghani*, right?"

Farzi nodded. "Exactly. Just how much time have you spent in Afghanistan? You seem to know a lot about it."

Kat tore off another chunk of obi non. She ripped it in two, handing half to Farzi. Kat held the bread in her mouth for a moment, letting it melt there.

"I was a foodie in my late twenties and early thirties. Before there was a term for it. My work took me all over the world. I rarely had time to be a tourist, but I always made time for at least one good meal. I ate from so many street carts and in hundreds of back alley, hole-in-the-wall food stalls, it's a miracle I never once got food poisoning. But you know what the biggest thing I learned was?"

"What?"

"That we are not so culturally different when it comes to food. Did you know that nearly every culture has a version of dumplings? Afghanistan has *mantu*—Uzbeks call them *manti*. There's gyoza, kreplach, samosas, ravioli. The list is long."

"You're making me hungrier than I already am."

Farzi pulled onto the highway. Kat realized she didn't even know where they were going. Correction: She knew where they were going, she just didn't know how to get there.

"I always suspected food united us as much as art or

music," said Farzi. "Have you ever broken bread with people you didn't really know and then, by the end of the meal, you've found a new best friend?"

"Not until recently, no." Kat picked at the drawstring on the bread bag. She took a deep breath. "I spent most of my life on the move, working. I bought my house when I was thirty-three and never stayed in it for more than three weeks in a row. Always on the move."

"It's not any better for an artist," Farzi said. "I work in isolation all the time. But I know myself well enough to recognize when I need to be with people. I'm not an extrovert, but breaking bread with people fills my cup."

"I'm happy to break bread with you anytime, Farzi."

Farzi took her right hand off the steering wheel to wiggle her fingers. "Can you tear another hunk off for me?"

Kat tore the last piece of the loaf in half again, handing the larger piece to Farzi.

"I don't know how you are still single," Farzi mumbled around the bread in her mouth, "being able to bake like this."

Kat turned away, looking out the window, to hide her sadness.

"I want to tell you something, but I'm worried it might make you feel differently about being my friend."

Farzi took her eyes off the road to glance at Kat. "Whatever it is, I'm sure our friendship can handle it."

"I went to speed dating night because when I retired, I realized I was completely alone. I didn't have a single friend. I'd never married. I thought maybe I would meet some men, go out on some dates, and maybe settle down. At age sixty-three." Kat rolled her eyes. "Like a horny and desperate teenager."

A smile spread slowly over Farzi's face. "Can I tell *you* something? I'm only three years younger than you and I was also fishing. And a closeted bisexual who was looking for a husband so her family would love her again."

"Was? Have you stopped looking?"

Farzi nodded. "I have something better now." She reached over to pat Kat's thigh. "I have some very close friends who, I think, accept me for who I am. I have never laughed as hard as I laugh with you guys. We do crazy things, and I've never lived my life that way. I did what I was supposed to, playing by the rules of my faith, my culture, and my family. I lost my son, and I wasn't allowed to grieve the way I wanted to. For decades, I felt like a twisted piece of rope pulled tight. I always expected the rope to snap and for me to have a nervous break-down. But meeting you ladies … my rope unwound slowly. One little bit unraveled at a time. I don't feel so clenched anymore. You know what I mean?"

Kat looked down at the cloth bag resting on her lap. She had been wrapping and unwrapping the drawstring around her index finger.

"I do," she said, dropping the string. "I went from real-izing I wouldn't have anyone to invite to my wedding to having the best bridal party a woman could ask for."

"Aren't we a pathetic pair? Wait, are you getting married? You met someone? How did we not know this?"

Kat threw her head back and laughed. "God, no. I was just trying to say I'm happy to have you all in my life too."

After they had passed through an industrial zone, Farzi pulled off the highway. They were now moving toward the residential area. The houses started small—wartime bunga-lows, mostly—peppered with newer and larger infill homes. The landscape changed, and they slowed to gawk at some of the much larger homes built much farther apart from one another.

"Until I came to America, I never knew a house could be so big. In Kabul, if you were well-off, you had a two-story house built behind a wall. If you were really wealthy, you had barbed wire on top of that wall."

"Is that how you grew up?"

"I grew up in an apartment in the city. We didn't have much, but most of the time we had enough. There was never extra money for luxuries. How about you?"

"Communism." Kat shrugged. "Everyone was poor, but we didn't know it. By the time Uzbekistan declared independence in 1991, I had been gone for more than a decade."

Farzi was alternating watching the road and the navigation. "Can you imagine living on the same cul-de-sac for so many years and never talking to each other?"

"Millie probably didn't have a choice. Abusive relationships are like that," Kat said.

"And she thought Annalise was a godless harlot, so there's that."

"I'm sure it's how she justified never making contact. It's easier to not invest yourself in someone when you make them a villain."

"I guess so." Farzi shrugged. She turned right, then right again. "We're here."

Kat looked out the front windshield. They were pulling into Millie's driveway, and what she saw caused the obi non to claw its way up her throat. In the driveway sat a custom pearl-painted BMW X3, similar to the one she had seen almost four years ago, this one silver instead of white.

It can't be the same one, she told herself. *There are other BMWs exactly like that.*

Kat's hands were shaking as she reached to unbuckle her seat belt. Her insides vibrated and she silently admonished herself. She shook off the sick feeling in her gut. She would have recognized the house when they dropped Millie off after the gala.

But you weren't paying attention.

It had been dark outside and she was swooning from the alcohol, the laughter, and the friendship. It was like being in love for the first time. It had to be coincidence that Millie had the same car as Kat's last mark.

There's no way I missed that. Yes, I'm retired, but surely my instincts are still intact.

"Are you coming?" Farzi was already out of the car, leaning back in through the driver-side door.

"Um, er, yes." Kat cleared her throat, trying to hide the sandpaper she heard in her own voice.

"Are you okay?" Farzi asked, obviously hearing it too.

Kat nodded once. As Farzi walked to the house, Kat opened the car door, using the frame as support, because her legs were rubber. She felt a separation between mind and body, like she was present, but her body was drifting. Her thoughts flew all over the place, searching for words, trying to convince herself that this was *not* the same house, and wishing for a stroke.

This can't be happening.

But as soon as Millie opened the front door, Kat's worst fears were confirmed. As she walked toward the stoop, Kat was able to see inside the house. Behind Millie, whose excitement at their arrival was written on every delicate line of her face, Kat saw the familiar wall of windows at the back.

Beyond the windows was the ravine where she remained hidden, watching her mark and his wife move throughout the house. She carried her sack of obi non to the kitchen island where the wife fell when her husband backhanded her. In the bright sunshine, Kat could see the pool, covered for the winter. She knew that off to the right was the pool house where the mark's brains had been splattered over everything.

There was a buzzing in her ears as she followed Farzi and Millie into the kitchen. Annalise was already there, stirring a pitcher of Bloody Marys.

As Kat stared at the swirling alcohol, visions of the last time she was here flashed before her. The spray of blood on the kayaks. The bits of flesh on the window looking out to the pool. The puddle forming under the body. She heard snippets: "Glad you're here," "Want a tour?" "Coffee or Bloody

Mary?" In a haze, she walked to the kitchen island, putting down the bread and dip, but holding on to the granite like it could anchor her.

"Millie," she heard herself say, "was this your marriage home? The one you moved into after ... I'm sorry, I forgot your husband's name."

"Darren."

Kat swallowed, forcing her voice to remain steady. "After you and Darren married?"

Kat didn't hear the answer. She nodded, but her mind was racing. This had to be a coincidence. Millie's last name was different from the mark's.

Annalise asked the question for her. "You went back to your maiden name, didn't you? I noticed the name on the mailbox changed."

Millie nodded. "I made that decision a little more than a year ago. My therapist said it was a healthy sign that I was ready to move on. I discarded Zucca and went back to Collins."

The air around Kat went still. She was sucked into a vacuum, voices muffled, but the roar of her blood pumping was deafening. She felt as if she had leaned back too far in a chair and was starting to fall backward. She grabbed onto the edge of the island to steady herself. This could not be happening.

Kat swept her eyes around the kitchen, searching for something to ground her. It took a few seconds for her to refocus her mind. The question ticking in her brain came forward.

Why did Millie lie about how Darren died?

She snorted quietly when her eyes landed on the cross mounted on the wall above the kitchen window. *Of course.* Millie wouldn't be the first Christian to hide a suicide. For a moment, Kat felt pride for having done the job right, and then immediately felt nauseated with shame. She swallowed back the ball lodged in her throat, closed her eyes, and massaged her temples.

"Are you okay?" Annalise asked this time.

Kat only nodded, unable to speak. She forced out a smile, praying it didn't look like a grimace. "A delayed hangover, I think."

Annalise scanned Kat's face for a moment before turning toward the windows.

"You know, Millie, I wish we had bought a house on this side, then we'd have a huge-ass lawn too."

"But there is so much lawn to mow," Farzi pointed out.

"You don't think I actually do it myself, do you?" Millie laughed. "Darren did it, but only because he was one of those guys who was particular about his lawn."

"Do you use the pool much?" asked Farzi.

All words entered Kat's ears like they were passing through cotton balls.

"Not really," she heard Millie say. "Truthfully, I barely used it when Darren was alive. He did laps occasionally. Maybe I'll start doing that this summer."

"I'll come over every day and swim with you," said Annalise.

"Me too, if the invitation is open," added Farzi.

"How about you, Kat? Are you in for a summer swim camp?"

Kat looked over at her friends standing around the kitchen, unsure which one asked the question.

"I can't swim," she blurted.

"We'll hire a hot instructor to teach you," mused Annalise. "Private lessons."

The conversation moved forward with Kat not saying a word. Food was spread out on the island. Drinks were poured. Millie led them through the house, giving them a tour. Kat followed, completely mute. In the walk-out basement, Kat gasped involuntarily. She knew that tree line.

"I know." Millie sighed. "The backyard goes on forever. Wait until summer when the maples and silver birch are in full bloom. You could hide among the trees and no one would know you were there."

Please stop talking. Please. No more.

Kat stood behind her friends, wondering if she should retreat and leave.

Go to ground, Vasily told her. *If anything ever goes wrong, burn down your house. Set fire to anything that can connect you to the world. Then lie low until the heat dies down.*

"It looks like a fairy-tale forest," Farzi said. "Let's go look." Farzi grabbed Kat's hand and pulled her out to the patio.

"Careful! There might be a wicked witch hiding in those trees," Annalise joked.

"Probably a wolf or two," Kat heard herself say.

"No wolves," Millie assured her, "but I've seen a few coyotes cut across my lawn. One even dragged a very large and very dead rabbit into the ravine."

"Is that what that stain is?" Annalise stood next to Millie, pointing to a dark smear to their right.

Kat followed Annalise's finger. The smudge was right beside where the pool house used to be. Her mind raced, trying to determine if the stain mimicked the shape and size of a body. Her muscles coiled tightly, preparing to flee.

"Ew, no," Millie winced. "That's black mildew. Someone is coming in the spring to kill and clean it."

Kat watched Millie's face, but nothing changed. There was no tick, no blinking, no flush in the cheeks. There was not a hint that Millie was lying.

"I hope they get it all," Kat said. "That stuff is sneaky and stubborn."

The words were coming out of her mouth without any emotion, but in her head, she was fighting the swirl of panic and agitation. Her friends were oblivious to her tension and her silence, moaning over the freshness of her obi non and the savory flavor of her suzma.

As she chewed on a carrot, a headache was building. She was trying to figure out how she would tell Millie, a woman she had grown to love and admire, that she was the one who killed her husband.

THIRTY-FOUR

What should have been a lovely brunch with her friends turned into the worst kind of torture for Kat. She barely ate, her stomach aching with hunger and fear. She fought the urge to drown herself in Annalise's Bloody Marys. She melted into the shadows in the brightness of the quartz and stainless steel kitchen.

She was stuck with no way out. She vacillated between being angry for allowing herself to be ambushed—her own doing!—and feeling hurt that her friends didn't even notice she had withdrawn. They carried on conversations, accepting her shrugged shoulders and short responses. When they laughed, she pressed her lips into a tight smile. Her annoyance built, smoldering like a spurned lover.

Kat mentally flipped through her repertoire of characters, searching for one who could help her manage this situation. Maybe Alina, the woman with a limp caused by a childhood illness. Alina was great at being helpless and getting close to a mark who loved to be the savior. Maybe Eloise, the master at diverting attention. She was klutzy and empty-headed, perfect for a job that called for distraction. As fast as the ideas flooded her mind, Kat dismissed them. It was too late to pretend to be someone else.

"Kat? Hello?" Annalise's voice cut into her thoughts. "Are you going to weigh in on this?"

"Sorry, what?"

"We're trying to pick a weekend for our girls' trip," Millie explained.

They were all watching her, phones in hand, expectant looks on their faces. A plate of macarons and tiny chocolate tarts had somehow found their way onto the coffee table.

"Okay. Let me get my phone." Kat went to the foyer, where she had dropped her purse on a bench. She looked at the front door, considering if she should just open it and walk away.

"How about sometime in the new year?" Millie asked her when she came back to them sitting in the living room. "Maybe late January or February? After the Christmas season and before spring break."

"I don't know," said Annalise. "Winter on the Oregon Coast can be awful. Cold and rainy for sure. It might be depressing."

"Or it might be nice and cozy to bundle up with blankets," said Farzi. "Imagine it … the fireplace burning, the wine flowing, hiking in the rain. What do you think, Kat?"

Get out now. Abort.

"I don't really care when we go."

Millie winced. "Ouch. Do you not want to go at all?"

Kat very much wanted to go, but she couldn't look Millie in the eye without feeling overwhelming guilt. If she told the truth, she risked losing the only friends she'd ever had. If she kept to the lie, she would never be able to fully let go and be herself around these women. Either way posed a potentially shitty outcome.

"No. Why would I want to sleep in a strange bed and sit around while it pours?"

"I think Farzi makes it sound nice," said Millie.

Kat swirled the tomato pulp at the bottom of her glass. "You all go ahead without me. I'll ruin the mood. I am miserable when it's dark and cloudy."

"Kat, you have to come," Farzi pleaded. "Millie bid on a weekend for four, not three. It won't be right if you don't come."

"Truth," agreed Annalise. "Besides, I've seen you drink vodka and you are the only one who can keep up with me." She tipped her glass to Millie and Farzi. "Not like these lightweights."

"I will pass on this one, but thank you." Kat pinched the bridge of her nose. "I think I'm just going to go home. I'm not feeling very well. My sinuses feel like they are inflamed." She sniffed, forcing a rough gargle from her throat.

Annalise narrowed her eyes. "I call bullshit. You were fine a minute ago."

Kat opened her mouth to protest, but Annalise held up her hand. "Don't say anything. I know you're new at this whole friendship thing. You can't run away from intimacy anymore, Kat."

"I'm not running—"

"Yes, you are," Farzi interrupted her. "I don't know why. If you want to be the one to drive, fine. If you want to stay inside the whole time, that's okay. I *like* your company, Kat. Please, come."

"Three is a terrible number," Millie added. "What if we want to rent tandem bikes? Who should be the one left to pedal alone? That's as sad as not having a friend to target on bumper cars. You are an important part of this group, Kat. I trust you with my life."

Those words started a new battle inside her, between dread and delight. She held Millie's pleading gaze for a moment, then made her decision. Millie's secret was hers too. Kat would do whatever she could to protect them both.

With a new mission—and an unwitting ally—in mind, a warmth spread through Kat's chest, radiating through her arms and down her legs. If she were a different person, she might have run over to hug Millie.

"Well, I don't want Annalise getting drunk or high alone," she said, relenting. "I will come."

"I don't want to wait months to go, though," said Farzi. "What if something happens between now and then? Do we really have the luxury of waiting? What if one of us gets sick? What if I slip and fall and break my hip? No"—she shook her head—"I want to go sooner rather than later."

Annalise burst out laughing. "Morbid much? We're not ancient. I don't know about any of you, but I didn't get out of bed this morning thinking I'd be going casket shopping later today. I have zero plans of dying anytime soon. The edibles will expire long before any of us do."

"Good to know you have your priorities," Kat said, smiling thinly.

"But you know," said Millie, "Farzi's not wrong. We don't have to wait. It's not like any of us have very busy schedules. I think it would be great to go next month. I've always wanted to watch a storm roll in off the Pacific." Millie looked down at her phone. "Uh-oh."

"What? They are booked?" asked Kat.

"No, they're wide open, but the voucher I won only covers a small cabin. Two bedrooms and a pull-out couch in the living room. A king-size bed in one bedroom and the other has a bunk bed."

"Oh, hell no. I cannot do a bunk bed," Annalise protested. "That is a recipe for disaster."

"I'll sleep on top. I don't mind," said Farzi. "It'll be like a true sleepover."

"Have you ever slept in a bunk bed?" Millie asked. Farzi shook her head. "Well, do you think you could navigate *this* for the middle-of-the-night pee?"

Millie held up her phone, open to photos of the cabin's second bedroom. The wood-framed bunk held two double mattresses. Steps were bolted to the wall, but they were narrow, with no handrails.

"That's a hip replacement waiting to happen," Kat cautioned. "It would be safer on the sofa bed."

"No need. There is a three-bedroom cottage where the third bedroom has two queen beds."

Annalise took Millie's phone to look at the pictures. "*Cottage* is not the right word. This looks like a seaside villa. Oh my god!" Annalise swiped through the photos. "There's a hot tub and a sauna. And a wraparound deck overlooking the ocean! With a fire pit. Okay, we're staying in this one."

"It's going to cost extra," Millie told them, "and I'm okay to cover that."

"That's silly," Farzi said. "We can all pitch in. Can we see the pictures?"

Annalise handed the phone back to Millie.

"Sending you the link."

Kat watched her friends scrolling through the images, their faces glowing with blue light, listening to their exclamations.

"This is a chef's dream kitchen!"

"I love the Scandinavian look!"

"The view from the living room is making me cry. That entire wall of windows is amazing."

"And it faces west, so the sunsets will be fantastic."

Millie looked up, plucking a pistachio macaron from the plate, her eyes bright. "Kat, how come you're not looking at the photos?"

"I don't need to see everything," Kat said, surprising herself. "I trust that you have chosen a good place. It will be nice to walk in without knowing what to expect. It's my experience that expectations usually do not match reality."

"That happened to me with speed dating." Farzi sighed. "My expectations were very much misaligned with reality."

"Mine too," Millie said, laughing, "but I still want to do another one in the new year. I won't need you to be my wing woman, Annalise. I think I can navigate those waters on my own now."

Annalise brought her hand to her heart. "Look at my babies! All grown up and going out into the world without me." She reached over to the plate, picking up a chocolate-filled tart topped with what looked like salted caramel.

"May the rest of our lives continue to be sweet and salty, the best of both worlds." She raised the tart in a toast before popping it into her mouth. Her eyes went wide.

"These are incredible, Millie. I have to know where you got them."

Millie's cheeks reddened. "I, uh, made them."

"Excuse me?" Annalise exclaimed. "This is one hell of a secret talent. All of you, with your painting and baking skills. Makes me wonder what other secrets you all are holding back."

Kat kept her eyes locked on the tray of treats, trying to look like she was assessing the macarons. She plucked a bright yellow one from the plate. The lemon curd was exquisitely tart, with a perfect hint of sweetness.

"Did you make these too?" she asked, hoping to divert the conversation.

Millie chose a dark green macaron. "I wish," she said, taking a small bite. "These are beyond my skill level."

"We should take a baking class together!" Farzi said, helping herself to one of the tarts. "I'm sure we can find one that will teach us to make macarons."

"I'm more interested in the eating than the baking," said Annalise.

The conversation turned to wine tasting, cooking classes,

spa weekends, and trail rides. Kat put the rest of the macaron in her mouth and swallowed, hoping the sweetness would settle the acid bubbling in her stomach. It wouldn't take much effort to figure out what secrets her friends were hiding. But it was getting harder to let go of the fact that she was harboring the biggest secret of all.

THIRTY-FIVE

Kat stayed quiet for most of the two-hour drive from Portland to Manzanita. She sat in the back of Annalise's SUV, watching the scenery go by as she tried to calm her racing mind. How could she tell Millie the truth about what she had done? Could her friend forgive her for pulling the trigger?

The pressure built up so quickly, Kat found herself contemplating jumping out of the moving vehicle. Killing without conscience had been easy because she loathed her marks. They were extremely shitty people, the worst of the human race. The man who beat her friend was no exception.

"I think this road ends at the beach house," Annalise said, turning off the GPS navigation. Within seconds, she slammed on the brakes. Kat's hands flew up, her palms on the back of Annalise's seat.

"Oopsies." Annalise chuckled.

Kat tilted her head to look between the seats. They were at the edge of a cliff, the ocean straight ahead. Millie, in the front passenger seat, was crossing herself and mouthing prayers.

"Oopsies?" Kat snapped. "You almost drive us over a cliff and all you can say is *oopsies*?"

"We're not dead." Farzi patted Kat's thigh. "Have you never made a wrong turn? Just back up and turn around, Annalise."

Silently, Annalise began maneuvering a three-point turn. It rapidly became an eighteen-point turn as she tried to avoid hitting the trees that lined the road.

"Just trust the backup camera," Farzi said from the back seat. "The lines tell you where to go so you don't hit anything."

"I know, but when the lines curve, it messes me up!" Annalise said, frustration clear in her voice. "It's like I have a mental block for this."

"I'll get out of the car and guide you," offered Millie.

"It's fine. I've been driving for thirty-eight years, since way before cameras were a thing. I'll trust my mirrors, thank you very much."

On the first pass, Annalise nearly hit a tree. When she pulled forward, she veered too hard to the left and *did* hit a tree. Gently, but still. Millie, Farzi, and Kat sat silently while Annalise backed up and drove forward, cursing and not making any progress.

"Can I just do it?" Kat said, exasperated by Annalise's lack of skill. She turned her head to look out the rear window, biting her bottom lip as Annalise edged the car closer to the trees.

"I think I got it now ... hang on."

Annalise kept backing up, this time nudging a pine that rained cones and needles onto the car.

"Should never have turned off the GPS," muttered Millie.

When Annalise finally maneuvered the SUV out of the tight spot, she drove for less than a hundred yards, then slammed on the brakes. Everyone in the car lurched forward, their seat belts cutting into them.

"It's right here," Annalise said, pointing out the wind-shield. "I must have missed the driveway."

Kat craned her neck to look out the front windshield. "How did you miss the paved driveway? And the big sign?" A large metal sign stamped WINDWARD COTTAGE was staked into the lawn.

"Oh my fucking god." Annalise shook her head. "I really *am* blond sometimes."

"I think I should drive us home," Millie said. "I don't want to end up in Seattle."

"Or worse. Mexico," joked Farzi. "With Annalise making another run at the border."

"Screw you all," Annalise grumbled. She gunned the car up the steep driveway so fast, she had to brake hard to avoid hitting the cottage.

Millie was the one who started laughing first, her shoulders shaking. When Kat looked at Farzi, they both burst out laughing. Annalise glared at them through the rearview mirror, trying to hold a scowl. Her lips were pressed tightly together, but her face betrayed her as she tried not to laugh. Little snorts came out of her in short staccato bursts, until the dam broke, and she joined them.

Still giggling, they climbed out to unload. Kat shook her head at the volume of groceries piled in the back of the car.

"You know we are only here for three nights, yes? Why so much food?"

"I like to be prepared," Annalise answered. "I wanted to make sure I covered all the bases for snacks. The last time I smoked pot, I ate an entire bag of corn chips, a family-size chocolate bar, and then inhaled a burger that had been sitting on a cold grill for like four hours."

"Well, that's disgusting," said Millie.

"Exactly. I'd rather eat things that don't come with the risk of salmonella or E. coli."

"Can we do this in one trip?" Farzi asked.

Annalise reached in to collect her wheeled suitcase. "We can try."

"There is no way." Kat shook her head.

"Load me up," Millie said, standing with her arms outstretched, her oversized weekender bag hanging off her shoulder. Annalise started slipping bags onto Millie's forearms.

Still shaking her head, Kat threw her own bag over her shoulder and took a grocery bag in each hand. She made her way up the stairs, flexing her arms to work the muscles. Behind her, she heard the chaos of the three women trying to maneuver everything out and up the stairs at once.

"Oh, oh—help!" she heard Millie cry.

Kat dropped her bags and turned. Annalise was bracing a loaded-down Millie, who was inches away from toppling ass over tea kettle down the stairs.

Farzi grabbed Millie's shirt from the front, letting go of her own rolling suitcase, on top of which she had piled two bags of groceries. The bags fell, sending the contents tumbling out and down the stairs. As Farzi pulled, a loose can of hard cider rolled away, bouncing and rolling down the concrete steps. They all froze, watching the can slowly roll its way to Millie. It veered off to Millie's left, landing on the weedy hillside right next to the steps. They let out a collective breath.

Millie slipped from Farzi's grasp, tumbled backward, bringing the entire weight of her body, the food, and her overnight bag crashing down. Annalise fell onto her bottom and then her back. Millie toppled on top of her, the weight of the grocery bags forcing her into the least graceful pirouette Kat had ever seen. She face-planted right into Annalise's chest.

Farzi started laughing, but then lost her footing as she stepped down to pull Millie out of Annalise's breasts. Kat scurried down, reaching to stop her. Her hands landed firmly on Farzi's shoulders and she guided her off the steps. Farzi's foot nudged the can of cider, causing it to spin twice, then tap gently against the side of the concrete steps.

They heard a hiss coming from the can. Annalise lifted her head to look at the can, Millie extricated hers and turned, Farzi glanced down, and Kat closed her eyes, sensing what was coming next.

A gush of cider arced into the air, dousing the side of Kat's face, her ear, and her head. She stood there, eyes still closed, and waited. It took just a moment for the flow to die down to a trickle, but it was enough to leave Kat soaked, cider dripping off her chin.

Kat wiped her face with the hem of her shirt. "It's been a long time since I've been sprayed in the face. Is it bad that I'm a little aroused right now?"

"Is it bad that *I'm* also a little aroused right now?" Millie repeated, waggling her eyebrows as she rolled off Annalise.

Farzi threw her head back. "Oh, Allah!" she exclaimed, hands raised to the sky. She started laughing and when she brought her head forward, she snorted.

Annalise dropped her head back to the ground and covered her face with her hands. Her whole body was shaking, and she was gasping through her giggles. "I … can't … can't … get … up."

Millie slid her arms out from the handles of the grocery bags and pushed herself off the ground. She reached down, grabbing both of Annalise's hands to pull her up.

"Huh." She smirked. "Given the buoyancy up top, I thought you'd be lighter."

They were still laughing like drunkards as they hauled their weekend bags and groceries up the stairs to the cottage's front door. This time, they made sure the load was reasonable, taking three trips to get everything inside.

After the food was piled on the kitchen island, Kat pulled a fresh shirt out of her bag and found the bathroom. She smiled as she washed the cider from her face and chest, the wisps of hysterical laughter still lingering.

Maybe I don't have to say anything at all. It can all be like this.

Standing in her bra, Kat examined her reflection in the mirror above the sink. Her chest bore the marks of a life not many people would ever experience. She had a peppering of darkened spots where shattered glass had cut her up. Kat touched a fingertip to the raised keloid scar from the one time she was stabbed. This tangible part of her history was easy to hide. Keeping secrets from these women—*her friends*—was a more difficult pain to manage.

With a sigh, Kat pulled the clean shirt over her head. She walked back into the main living area where Annalise, Millie, and Farzi stood at a wall of windows, the Pacific Ocean wide open in front of them.

She joined them, looking past the six bright yellow Adirondack chairs sitting on the uncovered deck. She stood quietly, watching the long beach grass dance in the breeze. Beyond that, the waves gently rolled over each other.

"It's better than I imagined," Millie said, popping open a bottle of Prosecco.

"I don't want to move," Kat whispered. "It feels like I've come home."

"The ocean does that to me too," Annalise said.

Farzi opened the windows on both sides of the living room and the soft roar of the ocean drifted in.

"How do we get out there?" Millie turned, looking for a door.

"Out the door we came in," Farzi said. "The deck wraps around. Come."

Because the deck had no railing, the view to the ocean was unobstructed. Kat sank into one of the Adirondacks, listening to the rush of the water, the squawk of seagulls, and the rustling of the grass on the low dunes.

"There is nothing to hear and so much to listen to." Farzi sighed.

"That's beautiful. Is that a proverb from Afghanistan?" asked Annalise.

Farzi laughed. "No. That's just me."

"An artist and a poet. I can see you painting this one day," said Millie.

They sat in silence, watching the waves lap at the sand. Kat breathed deeply, filling her nostrils with the smell of pine and pungent brine. Fresh new life and death, all in one breath. She was about to share her bad poetry when Annalise interrupted.

"Who's hungry?" Annalise asked. "Nachos for dinner? I'll go fry the beef and get everything ready." She drained her wine and headed back to the door.

"Do you need help?" Millie shouted after her, but Annalise was already in the kitchen, unpacking groceries and opening cupboards.

"Should we go help her? I should go help her."

"Relax, Millie," Kat said. "She runs a multi-million-dollar company, she can handle this. Sit back and drink more."

"I don't feel right sitting out here while Annalise does all the work." Farzi turned to look back into the house. "Let's go help."

Once they were all in the kitchen, Annalise began delegating. "Okay, Farzi, can you chop the tomatoes? Millie, please sauté the beef. Kat, would you like to cut up onions or jalapeños?"

"I'll do both. I can handle the sting," she bragged.

Annalise took on the job of making guacamole, shredding cheese, and spreading the chips on a baking sheet. Kat focused her attention on the chopping as the others chatted about their favorite songs, the best holidays they ever took, and their first loves. Kat had little to contribute but was grateful that no one seemed to mind.

Once the nachos were in the oven on the cookie sheet Annalise brought, they went back out onto the deck, watching the sun drop over the ocean. Ten minutes later, Farzi and Annalise went inside and came out with a fresh bottle of wine and a steaming tray of fully loaded nachos. Kat followed Annalise back in to help bring out the plates, salsa, guacamole, and sour cream.

"These look great," Millie said. "You know, if you help with the prep, the calories don't count."

Those were the last words spoken as the sun made its descent. The crunch of chips and cheese was muffled by the ocean's roar. Gradually, the waves grew smaller and the clouds broke away from the horizon, allowing the sun to paint the sky in brilliant shades of red, orange, and purple. The clouds still hovering in the sky were dark blue. The air chilled, and their breaths puffed out of their mouths.

Kat let her eyes follow the curve of the shore, watching as the water darkened. In the distance, a mountain jutted into the ocean. A few birds flew over the ocean, disappearing as they landed in the dunes. It was the most peaceful Kat had felt in a long time.

She glanced over at Annalise and Farzi. Both of them had their eyes locked on the colors in the clouds. When she looked at Millie, Kat felt a pressure in her chest. Her friend's face was glowing in the sunset. *She looks like she's found the rapture*, Kat thought. Her stomach clenched and a sour taste filled her mouth. *How can I ever tell her what I've done?*

Sitting on the deck with the only friends she'd ever had, Kat's thoughts ran wild. These women had accepted her into the fold, putting up with her curt responses and lack of communication skills. They didn't pry into the dark corners of her life that she deliberately kept hidden. Every time they were together, she laughed more than she ever had. Just being with them allowed her to learn what happiness meant.

Kat hadn't known how much her loneliness stung until she

met these women. Her days at home alone now seemed endless. If she ever confessed to being the one who took Darren's life, she would lose everything. But if she said nothing, wouldn't the truth taint everything to come?

In the silence, there had been comfort, but now Kat felt something else. A frisson of fear. A sense of doom that this new way of living was going to come to a crashing end. As if to punctuate her thought, thunder rumbled in the south. They were in near darkness, lit from behind by the lights in the house.

"That was really something," Farzi said, keeping her voice low. "I wish I had paint and a canvas right now."

Millie stretched her legs in front of her. "What is it about a sunset that makes us want to watch?"

"It's a reminder of how small we are in this world. That nature and the course of life is bigger than we are," said Annalise.

"It's not just the sunset we enjoy," said Kat. "It's the luxury of time to enjoy the sunset. It takes nothing more than to look outside, no matter where in the world you are, to see it. We all get to see it, every single day."

All three of them looked at her. "What?" she asked.

"That was almost poetic, Kat," said Millie.

"See? We all have a little bit of art inside," said Farzi.

"I'm freezing," said Annalise, crossing her arms over her chest. "Who's ready for some edibles?"

THIRTY-SIX

"I'm in," Farzi said without hesitation.

"I thought that was for tomorrow night," said Kat.

"Trust me." Annalise smirked. "There's enough in that basket for a week. And probably a few more days after that. What's stopping us from eating them now? Do we have big plans for tomorrow?"

Millie shook her head. "I thought a walk from one end of the beach to the other would be lovely. It's seven miles from end to end."

"How long would that take?" asked Farzi.

"At a slow pace, maybe a couple of hours," answered Kat. "Even if we sleep late, we can still walk."

Millie turned to Annalise. "Do you know what the right dosage is? Do we just eat one? Do we need to take it with water?"

"Isn't that info on the label?" Farzi asked. "Does it go by body weight?"

Annalise threw her hands up in the air. "Are we really talking about this like we're trying to figure out how much fiber we need?"

"Do we even know where this cannabis came from?" Millie's fingers twitched. "Are we sure it's safe?"

"It's fine, Millie. I won it at a charity auction. I didn't sneak into some back alley and buy it from a drug dealer."

"What if we take too much?" Farzi asked, a hint of panic in her voice.

"For fuck's sake," Kat groaned. "Annalise, where are the edibles?"

"Next to the coffee maker." She pointed without looking up.

As they came into the cottage, her friends were still arguing over dosage and side effects. Kat ripped open a pouch labeled Campfire S'mores, 10 mg THC. She put her nose to the open package and sniffed, surprised by the strong smell of chocolate, marshmallows, and graham crackers. She tapped one out into her hand, took a knife from the kitchen block, then cut the caramel-colored candy in half. Without hesitation, she popped the gummy into her mouth.

Kat raised her eyebrows. "These really taste like s'mores."

In the living room, her friends fell silent.

"You took one already?" Annalise asked, turning to look at Kat over the back of the couch.

Kat nodded. "While you senior citizens were stalling, I took matters into my own hands." She cut a second gummy into two. "Is anyone going to join me?"

Annalise leapt off the couch. "Me! Why did you cut them in half?"

"My instinct is telling me to go gently. Maybe not take the whole thing the first time."

Farzi had followed Annalise and was now examining the edible. "What will this do?"

Kat looked at the package. "Get us high. Isn't that the goal?"

Farzi chewed the gummy slowly and Kat smiled at the

surprise on her face. "I had the same reaction. I don't know how they get it to taste like that."

"It's delicious! I could eat them all in one sitting." Annalise plucked another pouch from the bag. "Look at all these flavors." She started reading the labels aloud. "Pineapple mango. Milk chocolate. Sour grape. Ooooh … salted caramel. That one's next for me."

"Millie, do you want to try?" Kat asked gently. "I understand if you've changed your mind."

Millie furrowed her brow as she looked out the now-dark window. Her face relaxed as she watched Annalise and Farzi, who were still pulling packets out of the bag, calling out the flavors. Kat kept her own face neutral, not wanting to influence her friend one way or another.

"You know what?" Millie said, striding into the kitchen. "I've had enough of not doing things." She picked up the gummy. "As long as you all promise not to let me walk out into the middle of the ocean …" She smiled, then took the edible. "Are you sure there's pot in here? I can't taste anything. What happens now? Am I supposed to feel something?"

"It takes time. If nothing happens in an hour, we'll eat the other half."

"So, what should we do? Can we still drink?" Annalise was looking at Kat, waiting for her answer.

"I don't know. Why are you asking me all the questions?"

"You seem to know what you're doing," answered Farzi.

"I have no idea what I'm doing." Kat snorted. "I've never done edibles before."

"Drinking may enhance the effects," Annalise announced, holding up her phone. "It says so right here on the internet."

"Let's build a fire in the pit outside," Millie suggested. "I want to sit out there, listen to the ocean, and talk with my friends."

"No more wine, I think," said Kat. "Do we have stuff for real s'mores?"

Farzi grabbed Millie's hand. "Let's go get some logs from the front."

While Farzi and Millie collected wood, Kat joined Annalise in opening every cupboard in the kitchen. The kitchen was fully stocked with everything they would need for cooking. There was a cabinet filled with spices, and another one with oils and vinegars.

"Oh, look at this!" Annalise stood beside the fridge. "It's a hidden door." She demonstrated by closing the door and gently pushing. When closed, it looked like a wall panel. "I only found it because I leaned against it and heard something click."

Kat pushed and the door popped ajar. Taped on the inside was a sign: "Take some, leave some. Enjoy." She scanned the shelves, which were well stocked with baking supplies.

"We could bake cookies when we get the munchies," said Annalise. "Oooh, popcorn!" Kat stood beside Annalise, who pulled out a box of microwave popcorn. There were unopened boxes of pasta, snack-size cookie packets, as well as instant coffee, boxes of tea, and a canister of sugar.

Annalise was moving things around when she squealed. "You won't believe this! Look!" She took a step back and raised a boxed s'mores kit over her head. "This one comes with caramel sauce to drizzle."

"That was unexpected," Kat said. "Are there roasting sticks in there?"

Annalise looked around, then shook her head. They'd rummaged through every cupboard and hadn't seen anything they could use to roast marshmallows. Kat started pressing on the parts of the kitchen that looked like panels, searching for another hidden door. When she pressed on the wood next to the oven, the panel popped.

"Well, look what we have here!" Reaching inside, she pulled out a narrow rolling drawer, sectioned to house baking sheets. From a hook inside the cabinet hung a set of four roasting sticks.

"Fantastic! They really did think of everything," said Annalise.

When they went out onto the back deck, Millie and Farzi were crouched on the sand in front of the firepit, trying to light a heap of logs with a match.

Kat and Annalise carried Adirondacks from the deck and placed them around the concrete block circle. Kat sat down, watching the other two fail spectacularly at fire-building.

"Does anyone feel anything yet?" Annalise asked.

Millie and Farzi shook their heads.

"I'm not sure." Kat scratched her chin. "But I'm watching the two of you and I don't feel the need to push in and take over. Maybe the edibles make me less of a control freak."

"Control freak?" Millie turned away from the pit to look at Kat. "Please. It's like pulling teeth to get you to come out with us."

"You're not exactly forthcoming," agreed Annalise. "I sometimes wonder if you even like us."

"She just has one of those faces," said Farzi. "You know, looks angry all the time. Or bored. Maybe judgy? I'm not sure which. It's so hard to tell."

"Is it 'Pick on Kat' night?" Kat tried to sneer, but her lips formed a smile and she giggled.

"Oooh, there it is," exclaimed Annalise. "I think it's starting to work!"

"I'm not high," she protested, narrowing her eyes. She knew there was something she wanted to say to them, but the thought left her head. "At least I know how to build a fire. It's obvious neither of you have done this."

"Do you want to do it?"

Kat pushed out of the chair, peering into the firepit. "Not a control freak," she said. "I'm so thirsty. Does anybody want something to drink?"

"No alcohol," Annalise reminded her. "I didn't know what everyone likes for soda, so I brought one of those mixed cases. I'll take a ginger ale, please."

"Is there Diet Coke?" Millie asked, abandoning the firepit and taking a seat.

"Yup. Also, cream soda, Coke Zero, and Sprite," answered Annalise. "Maybe Sprite Zero and something else."

"Sprite for me," said Farzi, still crouched at the firepit, pulling out all the logs.

Kat went back inside. She stood in the kitchen, looking around, completely confused about why she was there. She saw the cut edibles and picked them up, wrapping them in a paper towel.

"Are we ready for the second half?" she asked when she was back outside.

"Isn't it too soon?" Farzi was now placing the logs back into the firepit, building a teepee.

"I have no idea," she answered. "But we didn't take a full dose. We should be okay." Kat walked the circle, holding out the paper towel.

"I won't die, will I?" Millie asked, looking up at Kat for reassurance.

"I won't let you die," cried Annalise. "We've only been friends for two years, Mil. I'm too young to start going to my friends' funerals."

"I'll toast to that," Kat said, raising her edible.

Annalise took her portion and tapped it to Kat's. "Mmm, toast," she moaned. "Toast with peanut butter is the best."

"Crunchy peanut butter!" cried Millie.

"I'm thirsty. Does anybody want something to drink?" Kat heard her own voice like it was coming from outside her head.

"Why won't this fire work?" Farzi whined. "Kat, where's the fire starter?"

"Shit. I forgot." Kat marched back into the house, repeating *fire starter, fire starter* over and over in her head. She stopped at the fridge, pulled out a Coke Zero, and popped the tab. She gulped until her thirst was quenched.

"You need to relax," Annalise was telling Millie when Kat returned outside.

"Relax? You haven't said anything to make me annoyed."

Kat handed the fire starter to Farzi. "What did I miss?"

"I have no idea." Farzi took the fire starter and stared at it.

"You need to put that in the middle of the teepee," Kat advised. "That is the only way."

Farzi nodded, lighting the wood wick of the waxy puck before placing it under the teepee. Her hand knocked a leaning piece of wood and the whole thing collapsed. "*Bilach!*" she snapped.

"I don't need to speak Farsi to know what that might mean." Annalise laughed.

"I can't take it," Kat said, reaching into the pit. "Let me fix this." She righted the logs, then relit the smothered fire starter.

They were all quiet, watching the small flame lick at the logs, teasing the wood. They cheered loudly when the first log caught and the flame flared.

"Kat, where did you put our sodas?" Millie asked.

"Shit," Kat huffed. She marched back into the cabin, locking her eyes onto the fridge so she wouldn't get distracted. Picking up the case of soda, Kat tucked the open end up under her arm.

Back outside, Kat sat and leaned back in an Adirondack chair. The fire warmed her legs pleasantly. She closed her eyes, paying close attention to what she was feeling in every part of her body. The muscles in her face relaxed. She sank farther into the chair, aware she could no longer feel any discomfort from her bones poking into the hard plastic. Her skin wrapped her in a pillowy pelt, and she felt safer and more comfortable than she had in years.

"Kat, are you asleep?"

She rolled her head lazily from side to side. "*Nyet*. I am pillow, squish like marshmallow."

"Why are you talking like that?"

Kat opened one eye, peering in the direction of the voice.

"Is how I speak, Annalise."

"No it's not." Millie frowned. "Is it?"

Kat swiveled her head to look at Millie. The woman was smiling, leaning forward, holding her hands over the fire.

"Everything looks brighter," said Millie.

Farzi nodded. "I know what you mean. I can feel the yellow."

"Why am I wearing a headband?" Annalise's hands were on either side of her head, her fingers lost in her hair.

"I can't see it," said Farzi, "but can you guys help me? I'm falling."

In what felt like slow motion, Kat turned to look at Farzi. "You're not even out of your chair."

"I've got you!" Millie screamed, pushing out of her seat. She leapt over the firepit and wrapped her arms tightly around Farzi.

Kat turned her gaze to Annalise, who looked as shocked as Kat felt. "I didn't know she could move like that," Kat whispered. "Did you?"

Annalise burst into laughter. Kat felt the giddiness bubble up from her chest and she let loose. Millie caught the laughter bug and when she snorted, Farzi lost control, her whole body shaking with howls.

"Ladies, I would say we are most definitely high," said Annalise. She stood up and turned back toward the house. "I'll be right back." She returned with the leftover nachos.

"Who wants to eat?" she asked.

"Hey, weren't we going to make s'mores?" Millie stood behind Farzi's chair, holding on to the back.

Kat blinked, trying to figure out when Millie had moved to

that side of the fire. "Yes, s'mores ..." She looked around her and under her own seat, but she couldn't find the kit.

Annalise, holding the cookie sheet like a serving tray, walked over to Millie and Farzi. "Can I interest you in some nachos?"

"Are they still hot?" Farzi asked.

Annalise shook her head.

Kat got out of her chair, her sudden hunger compelling her. She looked at the nachos, not in the least bothered by the hardened and congealed cheese. The white fat solids on the ground beef didn't deter her either. Using both hands, she ripped off a large chunk of stuck-together nachos.

Millie grimaced. "You're not really going to eat that, are you?"

"Why not? I'm hungry and these are already cooked."

"But they're cold. Nachos shouldn't be eaten cold."

Kat carefully assessed the glob, deciding which side to bite from. Farzi was suddenly beside her, her hand resting on top of Kat's, pushing Kat's hand away from her mouth.

"You deserve better," Farzi whispered.

Annalise placed the tray on Farzi's now-empty chair and backed away from the nachos. "Farzi's right. You never have to settle for cold nachos."

"Fuck it. I'm eating them."

"I'll pray for you," cried Millie. "I love you, Kat. Please don't die."

Before anyone could stop her, Kat shoved the whole mess into her mouth. Little bits of corn chips and ground beef cascaded down the front of her shirt. When she was done chewing, she smiled, satisfied with both her defiance and the food. "That was delicious," she confirmed. "You should eat some."

Annalise backed away from them, shaking her head. "No. No. No. This is all wrong."

Farzi pushed the sleeves of her hoodie up to her elbows. "I

must be strong," she said. She strode to the tray, tore off some nachos, and defiantly took a bite. "Oh," she moaned, "these are the best nachos I have ever had."

Millie hovered over the tray, reaching for nachos and then pulling her hand back. "I want a small taste, but I can't find just one. Ugh, screw it." Using both hands, Millie pulled off a cold slab, smiling after the first bite.

Annalise shook her head, still backing away, still muttering. When her legs hit her chair, she lost her balance and fell with an audible thud.

"Annalise, why did it sound like rice cereal crackling when you sat?" Millie asked.

Annalise shrugged. "Don't know. Can you bring over the nachos? I just got my period and I'm craving something salty."

Kat grabbed more nachos as Millie passed by. "I'm glad to be done with that whole part of womanhood. Menopause was no picnic, but at least I'll never have another period."

"Oh, me too," agreed Annalise.

Farzi gave her head a shake. "If you're menopausal, how are you bleeding?"

Annalise spread her legs and looked down. She lifted her hips from the chair, then put her hand on the seat beneath her bottom.

"What the …" She pulled her hand out and held it up, showing her palm to the others.

Farzi was squinting. "What the heck is that?"

"Is that caramel sauce?" Kat exclaimed. "Annalise, did you sit on the s'mores kit?"

Annalise nodded once, slowly, and then let out a long and loud groan. "I squished the whole box," she whined. "I wrecked it. I'm sticky *and* now I can't have any s'mores."

Farzi barked out a laugh. Millie hooted. They looked at each other and started laughing like hyenas. Annalise, still gazing at her hand, brought it close to her face. When she stuck out her tongue and licked the caramel running down the inside of her wrist, Kat lost control. Her laughter bubbled up and out, her whole body shaking.

"I ... I ... can't ... believe ... you ..." she sputtered, "you ... licked ... your ... hand ..."

"I've licked worse." Annalise laughed. "And never quite so sweet." She stuck a finger in her mouth, slowly sucking the sauce off.

A fresh round of laughter erupted. None of them was capable of speaking coherently. Kat's whole body was relaxed and energized at the same time. It was a euphoria close to how she felt after a successful job.

Annalise was still licking caramel off her hand when Millie stopped laughing and her face got serious.

"Millie, are you okay?" Kat asked.

"I peed my pants," she blurted out. She looked down at her crotch. Kat tried to force herself not to look, but she had to. Millie was wearing a tunic that came down to her mid-thighs, hiding any wetness in her leggings.

"Did you pack enough underwear?" Annalise asked.

"Of course." Millie nodded and made her way back to the house. "Doesn't everyone pack more underwear than they need? Be right back."

"I'm coming with," Annalise said, peeling herself off the sticky chair.

"I'm sorry," Farzi said, holding her hand palm out and facing her friends, as if to stop the conversation in its tracks. "This is a thing?"

"Yes," Kat answered, still giggling. "You always take extra when you go away. Just in case you shit yourself for the first time in fifty years. Or pee from laughing so hard."

THIRTY-SEVEN

Millie changed clothes, and they brought over a clean Adirondack, though the fire and the laughter started dying out. Kat sensed a shift in the mood. Everyone was watching the last of the flames eating away at the charred wood.

"Should I throw another log on?" Annalise asked.

"Maybe one more," Kat answered at the same time as Farzi said, "I don't think so."

Millie was the tiebreaker. She threw a small log into the pit. "A compromise," she said. "Not a long burn, but enough to keep us out here a bit longer. I'm not ready to go inside."

Kat focused on the fresh log, wondering how long it would smoke before it caught. Her mind was at ease, the cannabis clearing it of any worry. If she could, she would never leave this place, staying exactly where she was with her friends until they all shriveled up and died.

"Millie," she said quietly, "thank you for inviting us to come here this weekend. I think I really needed this."

"I did too," Millie murmured. "Darren never allowed me to go anywhere alone. I can't fully explain how it feels to not have to be afraid." She sighed. "My daughter would love it here."

"Have you tried to find her?" Annalise asked.

"I searched her name on the internet, but nothing came up. She could have changed her name, gotten married … She's a Jane Doe. Name and location unknown."

Kat knew that if someone didn't want to be found, it would be hard, but not impossible. She fought the impulse to offer to help, knowing that it would lead to a conversation she'd rather avoid.

"I'm really sorry, Millie," was all she could say.

"I will never stop missing Kalan," Farzi said, wiping ash off her pant leg. "I still have very dark days when I can't paint, or sleep, or eat. I don't think a mother ever stops grieving."

"Grief never goes away," Kat said quietly. "The hole gets smaller, but the sadness is always there."

"I tried to conceal my grief by changing how I looked," Annalise blurted out. "Every time something hard happened, I called my plastic surgeon. It's not even about making me look or feel better. It's just about changing something."

"That's a terrible way to try to live," Millie sympathized. "I know, because I did it too."

"You had plastic surgery?" Annalise gasped.

"No … no …" Millie protested, "I tried to make myself fit into the person I thought I needed to be. For Darren, and for the church. I changed everything about who I was to make everyone else happy. And you know what? It didn't work. At all."

"I hope you've now reached a place where you don't feel you need to change anything," Farzi said. "I think we are fine exactly as we are."

Annalise looked down at her chest, a grin pulling at her lips. "You have to admit, though, these are pretty spectacular."

"Have you ever hurt someone with those while applying lashes?" Kat asked.

Annalise giggled. "It only happened one time, my first week back in the salon with the new boobs. But now I spend most of my time in the office."

"Do you miss working with customers?" Farzi asked.

"Yeah, I do, sometimes. I used to know all the best Portland gossip."

Farzi leaned closer to Annalise. "What's the best you ever heard?"

"You can't ask that!" Millie said. "What if she breaks some beauty code by telling us?"

"Then I guess I'll have to kill you." Annalise laughed. "Kat, you'll help me, right?"

Kat froze, a nacho hovering in front of her open mouth. "Why me?"

Annalise shrugged. "I think you know how to keep a secret. These two"—she wagged her finger at Millie and Farzi —"would give up everything with the slightest pressure."

"Really?" Kat tilted her head. "You've lived across the street from Millie for years and you didn't even know her husband was beating her. Either you're not very observant— which I know is not the case—or Millie *is* really good at hiding things."

"That's not something a woman broadcasts. I don't know how everyone at church knew." Millie threw another small log onto the fire. "Anyway, I've replaced those backstabbers with much better people."

"I'd say we've moved into the deep sharing stage of the high," said Annalise. "Also known as coming down. Can we drink now? I have a gorgeous dulce de leche cream liqueur that goes amazing with hot chocolate."

"I'll have one of those," Farzi said. "Let's go make them."

"I'll stay out here and watch the fire," volunteered Kat. Their voices faded as the three went inside. Kat sat back in her chair, looking up to the sky. The clouds must have rolled in, because she could not see a single star. Not even the quarter moon was strong enough to penetrate. This was the way of the winter sky in the Pacific Northwest. The months ahead would be wet and cold.

Gazing into the darkness in front of her, Kat listened to the ocean lap the shore. It seemed to be getting louder, but she wasn't sure if she imagined it or if a storm was moving in. She licked the salt from her lips, letting the serenity and calm wash over and through her.

Not telling Millie she had killed Darren was the only right choice, she decided. She had been trained to stay silent. Kat was doing more than protecting her friend from heartache; she was strengthening their friendship. It was frightening and wondrous all at the same time.

"You look like you're having an orgasm." Annalise's voice broke through her meditation.

"In some ways, this is better. All pleasure and no cleanup." Kat winked.

Annalise handed Kat a boozy hot chocolate and sat down, throwing her hair over the back of the Adirondack. Kat watched her watching the sky. Millie took a careful sip of her drink, the steam obscuring her face for a moment.

Farzi stood at the edge of the deck, staring into the darkness. "I can't remember the last time I felt so peaceful," she said. Her back was still to her friends. "It's safe here with all of you."

"I feel the same way, and I'm so thankful." Millie had both hands wrapped around the mug as she looked at the fire. "I laugh more now."

"I sometimes go down a dark hole, wondering what is wrong with me." Annalise sighed. "But when I'm with you ladies, I don't feel I have to apologize for my success or my choices."

Kat pushed herself into the back of her chair, as if trying to melt into it. She didn't want to play this game.

"I had the chance to leave Darren six months after we got married, but I chose to stay," Millie murmured.

Annalise reached over to squeeze Millie's hand. "Don't beat yourself up for that. You made the right choice for you at that time."

Millie shook her head back and forth. "No, I didn't. When the first slap happened, it caught me so off guard and it was so uncharacteristic for Darren, I forgave him. He cried, brought me a cold compress, then covered my face in little kisses that made me giggle. I told myself I loved him and had to accept his imperfections, just as he accepted mine. He said and did all the right things. I was such a stupid cow."

"Predators are very good at figuring out who they can manipulate," Kat pointed out. "I don't mean this in a bad way, but you were an easy target."

Millie nodded. "Anyway, I am not that person anymore, and I have you all to thank for it. God does indeed work in mysterious ways. I love that we're all so different, and I've really enjoyed your friendship."

"Did that sound like a breakup speech to anyone else?" Annalise asked. "Millie, are you dumping us?"

Millie tried to stifle a yawn. "Not at all, but I would like to go to bed. I'm suddenly really tired."

"Me too," Kat said, seizing the opportunity to avoid confessing any of her own secrets. She stood and stretched her arms over her head. "I'm going inside."

Farzi stirred the ashes to ensure the fire was out. Annalise picked up the now-empty cookie sheet. They filed into the house and shuffled to their bedrooms.

Kat tossed and turned for a while, uncomfortable in the stiff pajamas she had bought just for the weekend. Her mind wouldn't quit. She had successfully evaded revealing anything, so why wasn't she resting easy?

Because you've deliberately put yourself into a situation you can't control.

She thought she knew these women, but knowing how they take their coffee didn't mean she could get inside their heads. Following a mark to determine the patterns of their life was a simple task. Being part of a friend group came with an unpredictability that made Kat uncomfortable. She hadn't anticipated *liking* these women, much less feeling deeply part of something. She had thought she preferred solo projects over group work.

As her lids grew heavy and she drifted to sleep, she silently wished for a dream that would reveal how she could avoid confessing her sins and losing everything she had gained.

THIRTY-EIGHT

K at woke gradually, slowly becoming aware that she was not in her own bed. She burrowed under the covers, holding on to the warmth. Even with her eyes still closed, the light filtered through the window, penetrating her eyelids.

She heard a symphony of sounds from the kitchen. Beans hitting the metal bowl of a grinder. Water running. Millie muttering under her breath. She pulled the covers over her head, hoping for a few more minutes of sleep, but her bladder had other plans.

"*Pizdets*," she swore, throwing off the comforter.

When she was done in the bathroom, she sat in the armchair in front of the bedroom's window. Light gray clouds were visible at the tops of the tall pines, the sun fighting to break through. Kat needed it to be a beautiful day. If she had to be trapped inside for the whole day, she would lose her mind. Or fully confess and fuck up her friendships.

"Mmm, coffee …" Annalise's mumbled voice drifted from the kitchen.

Kat slid open the bedroom window, letting the chilly November air waft inside. She closed her eyes and took a few deep breaths. No air freshener could accurately capture the morning dewy scent of mossy pine in a forest. She let her mind wander back to the one summer she spent in Siberia, training with the KGB.

In some ways, she really missed the fellowship of her comrades, the discipline, and the unfailing reliance on following orders. Knowing what was expected of her gave her a sense of security. Mother Russia had no tolerance for outliers, for soldiers who complained or asked questions. And even though she was one of the most highly regarded and sought-after assassins, she knew her place. She was ultimately disposable. She knew that at any moment, she could be the one on the other end of the gun's barrel. She lived under the oppressive communist regime for half her professional life. Fear of elimination was a professional hazard.

But the thought of facing the firing squad of Annalise, Farzi, and Millie almost made her want to make a run for it. Siberia might even be nicer now with climate change.

You are not a coward, Katya, she told herself. *You are a master of invisibility and diversion. If you don't want your friends to know the truth, they won't.*

She threw a sweatshirt over her wrinkled pajama top and opened the door.

"Good morning!" she chirped. "That coffee smells good. Who made it?"

"Good morning," Annalise sang back. "Millie was up before god, I think, so she brewed it."

"I *was* up in time to see god's work," said Millie. "That sunrise over the trees was a show of all his glory."

Kat held back a groan. "No offense, but it's too early for worship. Let me have a coffee first and then you can praise god all you like."

"Millie, I for one fully support you in your godliness, praise Allah." Farzi yawned as she shuffled into the kitchen. She put her hands on her hips, arching backward, then forward. "That bed was just a little uncomfortable, but the view of the sunrise was worth it."

"I like how you both sprinkle your gods around like salad toppings," Annalise said, pulling her fingers through her rumpled hair. "Not always necessary, but certainly adds flavor."

"Okay, enough of this chatter," Kat ordered. "We should take advantage of the lovely morning. Let's get out on the beach before the weather changes."

After coffee, they met on the deck and made their way to the shore. Once she passed the grassy dunes leading to the beach, Kat stopped short. The tide was out, making the beach appear impossibly expansive. There was only one other person on the sand, about a mile away, with a dog who was running wild. Mist speckled her face, but Kat couldn't be sure if it was from the air or the ocean. She watched the waves spill over onto each other, using all their energy out on the sea, so that by the time they hit the shore, they were barely strong enough to wet the sand. The clouds looked heavy with rain, which was probably why the seaside was deserted.

"We're kind of in the middle here," Annalise said, swiveling her head to look down to both ends of the beach. "Which way should we go?"

"I want to go there." Farzi pointed to the mountain at the north end of the shore. "Can we hike that?"

Millie nodded. "I read that the Neahkahnie Mountain Trail is less than a mile and a half and an easy elevation. But at this time of year, it's probably really muddy."

"Let's go, anyway," Farzi said.

Kat looked at Farzi's socked and sandaled feet. "Did you bring hiking boots or sneakers?"

"I forgot to. I live most of my life in sandals, with and without socks. I'm fine."

"Well then, let's go," announced Annalise, heading north toward the mountain.

They walked without speaking for a while. Kat let the sounds of the ocean and the gulls determine her rhythm. She moved across the firmly packed sand with ease, her shoes barely leaving a mark. The air smelled briny, a mix of salt and slightly rotting fish. Kat smiled to herself. She had been to every single one of the oceans and they all had their own personality. The Pacific carried industry and power. The Atlantic made her wonder at the explorers who braved the rough waters stumbling onto new lands. On the breezes of the Indian Ocean, she detected spice and vibrant life. The most surprising was the Arctic Ocean. Winter lacked any odor, but in summer, certain areas of the tundra were thick with the scent of freshly turned earth and rotting compost.

"Penny for your thoughts," Farzi said, appearing at Kat's side.

"I was just thinking about oceans and how much I love them."

"Me too. I felt the pull of the ocean despite having lived most of my life in a landlocked country. Same as you, I suppose."

"Even when I was a child, I wanted to be anywhere else. It's no surprise I put myself into a career that involved travel."

Annalise called out from behind them. "What are you two whispering about up there?"

"We are plotting global domination," Kat said over her shoulder. She leaned closer to Farzi, lowering her voice. "Much easier when you have money, no?"

"You two still owe us a big reveal," Annalise said, catching up to them.

Kat's stomach clenched and she was relieved there was no breakfast threatening to rise up her throat.

Farzi draped an arm over Kat's shoulders. "We have decided to withdraw from the game of crones. You know all my secrets already."

Kat wrapped her own arm around Farzi's waist and snuck

a look at her friend's face. Every muscle was relaxed. She was telling the truth.

"Fine, but Kat"—Annalise waved her hand dismissively—"you haven't told us anything. How bad is what you're hiding? Don't you trust us?"

Kat shrugged one shoulder. "I'm flattered you think I am that interesting. Consulting for international firms was not stimulating, not even for me."

"How did you get into that? Was this something you studied in school?"

Kat kept her eyes on the mountain looming ahead of them. She sighed. She was going to have to give them something, a story close enough to the truth that wouldn't invite more questions.

"My parents sent me to boarding school in Russia," she explained, turning her head to look at the horizon over the ocean. "The kind where you threw away and forgot about your children. My father wanted to be rid of me, but my mother fought to have me stay in Uzbekistan. It was a good school. We were free to allow our personalities to develop, but we were also prepared for living an independent life. We were taught how to work, had extensive art and literature lessons, and intense physical education. We had the best medical care, better than most. We lived by the Soviet Moral Code, principle number one being 'Devotion to the cause of Communism.' The Soviet government kept a close eye on the students, plucking the best of us for work inside the politburo."

"Was it horrible?" Farzi asked.

Kat lifted her nose, inhaling the briny air. "Not at all. I had a wonderful education. The other students and the teachers became my family. Most of us went on to university, all paid for by the government. We had good jobs waiting for us when we graduated. People think Russia was a horrible place, where starving Soviets stood in bread lines and meat lines for hours in the harshest winters. Yes, lines were a part of life, but they were more social event than suffering. I remember standing in a grocery line with my mother when I was four years old. I waited patiently for my friends to arrive, and then we took off, playing games in the street while our mothers gossiped."

"Did your father ever come visit you at school?" Annalise asked.

"Never. I tried to find him when I graduated, but when I went home to Uzbekistan, a new family had moved into the house I grew up in." Kat chuckled darkly. "I guess that was the long answer to your question."

The wind kicked up as they walked the beach, their hair whipping in all directions. Rough waves rushed the shore. Farzi yelped as the frigid water splashed over her feet.

"We should head back," Farzi said. "There is definitely a storm coming."

Millie looked to the sky, pouting. "I really wanted to try to tackle that trail. Sometimes I do not like living in the Pacific Northwest."

"We can try again tomorrow," Kat said. "And if not tomorrow, maybe we can plan to come back another time." She kept her eyes on the sand.

"OOOH, I LOVE THAT IDEA," Annalise gushed. "We should make it an annual retreat."

Kat blinked away the sting in her eyes. There was a future to look forward to, and she could envision them coming out year after year, tackling the trail up Neahkahnie Mountain.

THIRTY-NINE

As they moved toward the cabin, Annalise pulled out her phone, herding them all to the ocean's edge. "Let's take some selfies before we head back." Kat waited awkwardly off to the side, not knowing where or how to stand.

"Kat, what are you doing? Get in here," said Annalise. "Don't act like you don't like selfies."

Kat pasted a smile on her face and reluctantly joined the group. The last group photo she had posed for was back in 1981, her graduating day at the academy. She stepped up beside Farzi, working her mouth into a grin.

"Okay, ready? One, two, three," counted Annalise. "Let me take a few more, just in case."

Annalise moved her arm up and down, left and right, snapping photos from all the angles. Kat's face hurt from locking her smile in place.

"These are really good. I'm texting them all to you now. Can I post them to socials?"

Kat had only recently joined Facebook and honestly didn't see much use for it. "Sure, go ahead," she told Annalise. Farzi and Millie nodded in agreement.

"We need to go," Kat announced, tilting her head to the ocean. "The clouds are coming faster."

They started walking back in the direction of the cabin. The beach was completely abandoned and shrouded in fog. They couldn't see the ocean and Neahkahnie Mountain was obscured. It was magical.

The beach was getting smaller with the incoming tide. Kat stopped to pull off her socks and sneakers. The sand was cold beneath her feet, the grains sticking between her toes.

"That's a great idea," Farzi said. Using Kat's shoulder for balance, she took off her socks and sandals. "Oof, that's cold. But I feel so connected to Mother Earth. You guys should try this."

Without hesitation, Annalise and Millie kicked off their shoes. "Ahh, nature's exfoliation." Annalise sighed as they continued walking.

"I'd have to walk for a hundred miles to rub the cracked skin off my feet. They are so scaly, I could pop balloons with my heels." Millie laughed. "I really should start going for pedicures."

"Careful, Millie," Kat said. "If Annalise hears you, she will plan a posh pedicure party for us. A hundred and twenty dollars for nail clipping and polish."

Annalise held her phone up in the air. "Already on it!"

Kat looked down at her feet, her toes covered in wet sand. Before she retired, getting a pedicure was a necessity of the job. Not just to keep up appearances, but also as a form of self-care. Kat enjoyed not being bothered by anyone for an hour, and listening to the aestheticians gossip was like eavesdropping on a soap opera. On more than one occasion, she had to stifle her laughter as the woman shaving the dead skin off her feet chattered on in Vietnamese, telling a story she thought Kat could not understand.

"Okay, Kat, time to spill your beans." Annalise cut into her thoughts.

Tension twisted in her shoulders. Lying for the job was an ephemeral necessity, but lying to her friends was different. She glanced at Millie. Her friend looked completely relaxed and content, so far removed from the woman she had once watched from the woods. Kat wanted more time to think. She needed to weigh her options. She saw the expectant looks on her friends' faces and blurted out the first words that came to mind. "I'm really embarrassed," she said. "I'm not ready to share."

"How bad can it be?" Annalise asked. "Were you a coke addict in the '80s?"

"A kleptomaniac?" Millie guessed.

"Did you pose naked while in college to pay tuition?" mused Farzi. "Were you in porn movies?"

Kat made no effort to hide her smile. "I wish it were that simple."

"Now I really need to know," Annalise implored. "It must be really juicy."

They were not far off from the cabin, and Kat could see the yellow Adirondack chairs peeking over the dunes in the distance. She lifted her face to the sky, feeling the first few drops of rain. *Please let it pour,* she begged, *then we can run to the cabin and forget about this conversation.* But the rain did not come.

As they neared the cabin, Kat realized if she wanted more than to just exist on the periphery of friendship, she would have to be honest with them. She could not carry the burden of guilt, no matter how skilled she was at hiding her emotions. Kat knew better than any of them how secrets catch up to you in the most devastating ways.

Kat slowed down to let her friends get ahead of her. What she wanted to say, she needed to say to their backs.

"I was an assassin," she declared.

Kat stopped and waited. She held her breath. She clasped her hands behind her back. She made a point of holding her head high so there was no mistaking her truth.

Annalise, who was at the head of the pack, turned around, but kept walking backward. "What a load of crap." She smirked. "Try again."

"I kind of believe her." Farzi grinned. "Did you see how she slayed those nachos last night?"

"Very funny, but I'm telling the truth," Kat protested. "I was paid to kill."

"Killing it like a boss." Annalise lifted her palm for a high five. "Women rule the world and all that."

Kat watched the space between them grow. She shook her head. "You're not listening to me. Why do you think I went to so many countries but never saw the sights? And speak so many languages? Don't you wonder why I never have any stories from my past to share? Why you are the only friends I have? I was trained to execute people, not embrace them."

Annalise, Farzi, and Millie finally stood still, eyeing her with scrutiny. Kat looked each one of them in the eye, her face a mask.

"You murdered people?" Millie whispered. "How? Wait, I don't need to know that. Huh."

"Huh," Farzi echoed.

Kat uncrossed her arms and relaxed her shoulders. It was out now. All she could do was wait, something she was exceptionally good at doing.

Millie broke the silence. "Do you ... do you still do this?"

Kat shook her head. "I retired three years ago."

One after another, they fired questions at her.

"How long did you do this?"

"How did you get into it?"

"What's the most you ever got paid?"

"Did you ever let anyone live?"

"What's your preferred method?"

Kat let them talk over one another, answering only the safe questions, keeping the grim details to herself. Their curiosity was intriguing, none of them seeming to care that she was an assassin.

"So … uh … like," Annalise stuttered, "have you killed anyone we may have heard of? Anyone famous?" She was bouncing on her toes, eager for gossip.

"Annalise, you can't ask her that!" Millie exclaimed.

Kat took a deep breath in through her nose, trying to still the hammering of her heart. She could feel her blood rushing through her veins. *This is what it must be like when my marks face death.*

"I will take that information to my grave."

"I bet you're taking a lot of stuff to your grave," said Farzi.

"I can just imagine some of the things you've had to do." Annalise was looking down, digging her toes into the wet sand. When she raised her head up, her eyes were filled with concern. "Do you have PTSD from any of it? Like, would you wake up and stab any of us to death in the middle of the night, thinking we were an enemy?"

Kat shook her head. "It doesn't work like that. I have not been in any war."

"What kind of person do you have to be to do this?" Millie wondered. "I know you're not overly emotional, but don't you have any remorse?"

"Not until recently," she began. Kat took a deep breath, trying to calm the churning in her stomach. She was done hiding behind the wall of deceit. "I have to tell you something, and it's horrible." She wiped at the tears about to fall from the corners of her eyes. The tide was snapping frigid water at Kat's feet.

"Millie." She took a deep breath in through her nose. "I killed Darren. I'm the one who made you a widow."

In what seemed like slow motion, Annalise and Farzi turned their heads to look at Millie. The woman's face sagged with sadness and contorted with confusion.

"No, that's not true." Millie was shaking her head. "He had a heart attack."

"No, Millie. We both know he didn't."

"What the fuck?" Annalise whispered. "Millie? What's going on?"

Kat saw everything wash over Millie's face: the panic of being caught, the defiance of denial, and finally, the pain of a new betrayal.

Millie bit down on her bottom lip, then squeezed her eyes shut. "Darren killed himself. The police and the paramedics said he put a gun in his mouth. He committed the ultimate sin." She looked at Kat, forcing her eyes wide. "Why would they say that if it wasn't true?"

Kat swallowed. "I was told to make it look like that, and I'm very good at my job."

Millie shook her head. Kat saw her face change again, now twisted with anger. "You've known the whole time we've been friends?"

"No. I only realized it when we had brunch at your house."

"And you didn't say anything?" Millie squeaked. "You sat in my home, breaking bread, and you didn't feel the need to … I don't know … bring it up? Or even better, leave and get the fuck out of my house?"

Kat withered under Millie's hot glare. Her thumb found a torn cuticle on her index finger and she picked at the skin.

"So when I was telling you how my church betrayed me, you were betraying me too." It wasn't a question. "Lying to me." Her tears fell freely now. "Trying to be my friend to ease your guilt?" This time, it was a question.

"I don't feel guilty about killing him, Millie. He was an abusive piece of shit. But I am sorry I didn't tell you sooner. I didn't want to mess things up. I've never been good at making or keeping friends." She was about to explain how her work made that impossible when Farzi cut in.

"And you're still not good at it," she said. "I think you should go now."

Annalise and Farzi bookended Millie, holding her up so she wouldn't fall onto the cold, wet sand. Annalise glared at Kat; Farzi jutted out her chin, pressing her lips together.

Kat nodded, lips pursed, keeping all her words trapped in her throat. She watched her friends move away from her, both Farzi and Annalise rubbing Millie's back. There was nothing Kat could say or do to change what she had done. The clouds above her head darkened even more, and the rain poured down in fat, hard drops, too late to save her. She walked toward the cabin, the familiarity of isolation creeping back into her bones.

FORTY

Getting back to Portland without a car was not an easy task. Kat walked ten minutes into town, the weight of her overnight duffel digging into her shoulder. She stopped in at the coffee shop, relieved to see they served alcohol.

"A coffee with Bailey's," she ordered, "but light on the coffee."

"I beg your pardon?" The girl at the cash register blinked.

"I got you, friend," said the barista at the espresso machine. "Some days are like that." He winked. Kat tried to smile, but her face was too settled into misery.

"Do you know if there is a bus to Portland?" she asked, taking the oversized mug from the barista.

Pushing his long blond bangs away from his eyes, the barista turned to look at the clock mounted on the wall behind him. "Not for another couple of hours. You have to take the bus from here up to Cannon Beach, and then a different bus from Cannon to Portland. You might want to grab a sandwich here for the journey, just in case there's no time to get something in Cannon." He leaned across the counter, holding a hand to the side of his mouth. "Their food is shit, anyway, if you ask me," he whispered.

"Is it possible to get a taxi to take me to Portland?"

"Sure." He nodded. "But that will cost like $200 minimum."

"Thanks," Kat said. She would pay $1,000 to get home faster, where she could pour a generous cognac to keep her company. "Do you have their number?"

He pointed to the back end of the bar. "On the bulletin board near the washroom."

Kat examined the board, regret stabbing at her as she read the notices for social clubs, gatherings, and artist-of-the-month events. She shook her head, disgusted with herself for letting her guard down. If she had never followed the bread-crumbs from the grocery store's bulletin board, she wouldn't have fooled herself into thinking she was capable of friendship.

Once a lone wolf, always a lone wolf.

Less than thirty minutes later, Kat sat in the back of the cab, watching the skeletons of leafless trees and bushes go by. The driver didn't flinch when she told him of her destination. She would compensate him well with a generous tip. He didn't attempt to make any small talk as he drove the Sunset Highway from the coast to the city, and she would add even more to the tip for that.

She replayed the beach conversation over in her mind. Should she have fought harder for forgiveness? Did they think she didn't care because she didn't defend herself? No matter how many ways things could have gone, nothing would change the fact that she put the bullet in Darren's head. Even if Millie forgave her for the lie of omission, Kat would always feel the need to apologize. Millie would only see the betrayal. Kat knew Millie—and Annalise and Farzi—would never fully trust her. Kat may not be an expert in friendship, but even she knew that was shaky ground.

She fucked up.

As the highway widened, then narrowed, then widened again, Kat found herself replaying Darren's death. There wasn't a single blemish on her career, except for the mess she made of Darren's execution. She had left a gaping hole in her process by not making sure she knew all the players in the game. Kat moved forward with the job, even though she hadn't identified the woman shuffling to the front door. If she had done her job properly, she would have bowed out the moment she met Millie at speed dating.

Her house looked smaller when the taxi stopped at the curb in front. She tapped her credit card on the terminal hanging over the back of the passenger seat and doubled the fare as a tip. She climbed out of the cab without a word to the driver.

"Thank you so much, ma'am," the cabbie called through the open passenger window. "You are very generous. God bless you and your family. You are a gift to this world."

Kat winced as he drove away. *You are the only one who thinks so.*

She'd only been gone one night, and already everything looked different when she walked in her front door. The clouds had followed her back to the city, and the dusky light coming through her picture window turned everything gray. With a sigh, she went to the kitchen, dropped three ice cubes into a tumbler, and poured herself a double shot. The cognac's mildly sweet butterscotch flavor hit the back of her tongue and she sipped, feeling the heat traveling down her throat.

"I missed you," she whispered to the glass. The bottle was a vintage XO, a retirement gift to herself. She last had some the night before speed dating, a celebration for deciding to do something different.

"Look how that turned out," she muttered.

Kat walked into her closet, turning on the light. She

looked at all the gowns hanging there, handling each one, spending a few moments with their memories. The gown she wore when she assassinated the president of an African nation. The dress with the stiletto dagger sheath built in from the hip, with a discreet slit from which she pulled it out. She fingered the black chiffon cape of the gown she wore when she poisoned the Italian designer who had made the dress.

Kat stood still, taking stock of all the luxury in the closet. That was all she had left of the life she had chosen. She could have been an administrator, disappearing in system paperwork. She could have walked away when the Soviet Union collapsed. She had been offered a position in foreign affairs— her language skills made her highly desirable to President Yeltsin—but she decided to stay the course. She had the contacts, the skills, and the itch to continue working as an independent assassin. The money was good and the lifestyle was the only one that felt comfortable.

Only now, with nothing to show for her efforts but a fat bank account, did Kat have regrets. She had lied to herself by pretending to believe it was okay to execute bad people. She had learned all she needed to about the underworld and what makes nefarious people do terrible things. But what did she really know? Nothing. She didn't understand ordinary people. Now that she had walked among them, it was painfully obvious to her that she was not built to be a friend. Making any kind of connection with anyone had proven impossible.

The ice cubes clinked in the glass when she brought it to her mouth and gulped the rest. Tossing the glass onto the carpet, she yanked the dresses one by one off their velvet hangers, not caring when the silk or tulle or organza or lace tore. She didn't stop until every gown was on the floor, a sea of fabric, sequins, and appliqué. She marched back into the kitchen to get a box of black garbage bags, pausing only to drink cognac straight from the bottle. She filled eleven bags with some of the biggest names in fashion, couture that cost a fortune.

She was sweating when she hauled the last bag to the black bin in her garage. She vacuumed the debris from the closet. As an afterthought, she gathered the hangers and threw those in the bin too.

Cognac bottle in hand, she flopped down on the sofa, not sure what to do with herself. The silence mocked her. *As if you could ever really have friends,* she heard it whisper. Kat stared at the empty wall in her dining room. She had planned to buy or commission a painting from Farzi to hang there.

As Kat worked her way to the bottom of the cognac, she replayed all the good times she'd had over the last eight months. She searched her brain for moments when she could have come clean and maybe saved the friendship. She imagined herself telling Millie what she had done when the woman stood in her closet trying to find a gown. She rewrote many of their conversations so that her friends forgave her when she confessed to killing Darren. She created an alternate universe where she never went to speed dating, moved to Mexico, and made headlines as a tourist who was murdered.

Kat didn't even try to fight the nausea when it came. She ran to the bathroom and threw up violently until she dry heaved, deserving every painful twist in her stomach, every acidic burn in her throat as the cognac found its way back out. She had one last thought before she passed out on the bathroom floor, her head tilted backward on the edge of the tub, her mouth open.

You can end it all and never feel pain again.

FORTY-ONE

K at felt like she was suffocating. She tried to take a deep breath, but she couldn't pull enough air into her lungs. Something was stuffed into her mouth; when she tried to breathe through her nose, a foul smell choked her.

When she finally forced her eyes open, she was cloaked in darkness, with no idea of where she was. Slowly, the layers of memory peeled back one at a time. She had drank all her cognac. She was in her house. She had been at the ocean yesterday. Her friends hated her.

She tried to take a deep breath again. As her eyes adjusted and focused, she realized she was under her covers, the top sheet wrapped over her head. She pushed the cotton away from her mouth and took a deep breath. She could smell the remnants of vomit pluming from her sour breath.

Sitting up with a groan, her headache made itself known with blunt force. This was going to be a doozy of a hangover. The last time she felt this rough was during training, when she and her comrades were forced to push the limits of their alcohol tolerance. Over the course of six days, they drank heavily, mixing alcohol, drinking the finest liquor and the cheapest swill, over and over again until they could get to the bottom of a bottle of vodka without getting drunk or sick. The point was to train their bodies to adjust to any level and kind of drinking. While all the recruits were throwing up, getting belligerent, and passing out, the agency lectured them about how important it could be to drink more than your mark. "It can mean the difference between their demise and yours," she'd heard her trainer say before she blacked out.

Kat padded into the shower, stepping into the frigid water. Turning up the heat, she let the steam envelop her, burning the skin on her scalp. She winced, but quickly checked herself. Overcoming pain was part of her training too.

In the kitchen, she opened the fridge, reaching in blindly to the back of the top shelf. She pulled out the jar of dill pickles, opening the lid with one twist. Bringing the rim to her lips, she took a single deep breath, let it out, and tipped her head back. She counted—one, two, three, four, five—with each gulp. Kat closed her eyes as her stomach protested. She needed the salt to stay in her body and restore the balance of electrolytes.

She chased the pickle juice with a glass of water and two pain relievers. After putting fresh water in the kettle to boil, Kat glanced at the clock on the stove. The sun wouldn't be up for another hour. She wondered if Millie was already up too, making coffee for their friends.

Millie's friends, she corrected herself. *You are no longer part of that circle.*

Kat sat at her kitchen table, sipping her instant coffee and looking out into her yard. Once the hangover burned off, she would get out there and prune. The garden was wildly overgrown and neglected. She realized she hadn't trimmed the lilac bushes last spring once they were done blooming. *You were too busy socializing,* she berated herself, *and now you have nothing to be proud of.*

Kat spent the next forty minutes cutting the overgrown

bushes and deadheading the flowers in the sodden and wilted garden. Her headache was still present but was now more of a nuisance than an obstruction. The garden still looked like a wild wasteland, but she stopped anyway. She was going to have a lot of time to fill.

She tried to read a book but found herself rereading the same paragraph over and over. She streamed a program to her tablet, but the moving images were bringing her headache back. Abandoning the freshly reboiled kettle, she crawled into bed again.

Kat curled up on her side, staring at the wall. Her phone lay silent on her night table. She scrolled Facebook, creeping Farzi's profile, and looking for new photos on Annalise's, specifically the selfie they took before Kat ruined everything. When Kat went to Millie's profile, nothing showed at all. She had been blocked. She deleted the app from her phone, but couldn't bring herself to delete the photos in her albums. Despite feeling the loss, she wanted to keep the proof that, for a short while, she did exist and was part of something wonderful.

Her final thought from last night drifted back to her. Never in her long and brutal career had she ever considered taking her own life. Solitude had been her sanctuary, but now it overwhelmed her. *Serves you right for trying to be someone you're not.*

The phone trilling near her head startled her from a dream in which she was traveling abroad with Annalise, Farzi, and Millie. She sat up quickly, eagerly grabbing the phone. Her heart sank when Unknown Number flashed on the screen.

"Hello," she said, wary of talking to a telemarketer.

"*Privyet, yagatka.* It's been a long time."

FORTY-TWO

The blood in Kat's veins went ice cold. "How did you find me?"

"Yagatka, please don't insult me. I never lost you."

Only one person ever called her by her nickname, "little berry." The man who recruited her, who taught her to be a killer, and who laughed in her face when she colored her hair by herself and it turned out strawberry red instead of the dark burgundy she was hoping for.

"What do you want, Vasily?"

"We need you for a job."

"I'm retired."

"That's a nice bedtime story."

"I'm no longer working, Vas. My answer will be no."

"We know you don't need money, yagatka, but you can't tell me you are happy being idle. You had fun playing with your friends. But you don't take a $400 taxi ride if things are good. I'm not going to convince you to come back to work, but maybe a job here and there would be a nice way to pass the time."

Kat held the phone to her ear, trying to control her

breathing. She had always expected the KGB—now the GRU —to be watching her since she went solo more than three decades after the collapse of the Soviet Union. Vasily was a master at getting inside her head. He knew she would consider taking on an occasional job.

"When?" she asked.

"In three days."

"And if I say no?"

"Then we will part ways for good. In Miami."

It was those two words that put all the pieces into place. She might not have been careful about concealing her new life, but she knew a snare when she saw one. The GRU was trying to lure her to her own death. Miami was the organization's choice location for dumping dead weight. It was a busy city, loud all the time, and it was an easy drive to the swampy Everglades.

"Why now?" she asked.

Vasily paused. She heard a hum on the line. Of course the call was being recorded.

"Presidential orders."

She knew the president by reputation. He had trained in the same institute but was quickly labeled a mediocre agent. He was hotheaded, motivated by jealousy, and had no tolerance for anyone he deemed a rebel or an enemy of his Russia. He was tying up loose ends.

Assassins don't retire, they just become difficult-to-kill targets.

"No, thank you, Vasily. My eyes are not so good anymore," she said. "But I can see the stove well enough that I won't burn the house down."

There was silence on the other end.

"Very well," Vasily finally said. "You were my best, Katya. Be well."

Kat put the phone down on her chest. Vasily understood her promise. Her secrets, and those of the KGB, would be buried with her ashes. If the president insisted on persistence, so be it. But she knew Vasily would report that she had been dealt with, and that would be enough.

Kat tried hard to put the call with Vasily out of her mind. The following day, she finished cleaning up the dead plants in her backyard, despite the nagging feeling that she was now a GRU mark. Why prune a garden she might never see bloom again?

Maybe she *should* return to work. There was nothing else on the horizon for her. The thought of starting to find friends once again exhausted her. Her life was simpler without all the hassles and complications of relationships. Love them and leave them had always worked for her, scratched her itch without all the *feelings*. It had taken her a year to find Farzi, Annalise, and Millie and months for her to loosen the grip of distrust. She would soon be sixty-five, and she was too old and too tired for new things.

After two days of filling her time with small projects in the house, she finally unpacked the weekend bag she'd left sitting by the front door. She dumped everything on her bed, putting away the clothes she never had the chance to wear. As she pulled out the cider-stained shirt, she smiled at the memory before her heart broke. But it was the extra pair of underwear that did her in. She grasped at her chest, and then the tears started to fall.

Kat sank down onto her bed, dropping her face into her hands. She had not let herself feel anything for decades, disconnecting herself from people. All the pain rushed at her as she sat next to the remnants of the disrupted weekend, trying to pull herself together. Her mind swam with all the things she noticed about her friends that she knew nobody else saw. How Annalise ate with gusto, not even finishing chewing her last bite before taking the next. That Farzi had a slight tremor in her left hand, just enough to make putting on mascara difficult but not impacting her painting at all. How

Millie tore open a packet of sugar, the tiny rips a deliberate attempt to stifle even the slightest rustle.

Watching the nuances of humanity came so naturally to her, she hadn't noticed that it was the smallest of habits that wormed their way into her heart. With their help, she had crawled out of the swamp of unfeeling, cleaned herself off, and let herself be happy. Now, her emotional bottle uncorked, she let everything flow. Her anger, her pain, her grief, her fear, her shame. She let the tears loose, feeling the loss with every sob, and screamed into the empty room.

FORTY-THREE

K at did not know how to be this person. In every act of every day, she felt the absence of her friends. She reached out to Seth and Nick, looking for companionship. Nick was seeing someone, but Seth was available. She met him for dinner, wearing the same boots she wore to date night. They spent the night together, both of them getting the kink out of their systems. After submitting to all her demands and satisfying all his, Seth oozed apathy. Kat was unsurprised and relieved when he made no move to set up another date. She no longer wanted that kind of intimacy in her life.

After spending too many days in the house, Kat downloaded a hiking app, put on her hiking boots and insulated rain jacket, and drove to the head of the closest trail. It would be quiet, as it always was midweek, and especially in winter when the gravel trails were damp. Her lungs and her legs worked hard as she climbed stairs to lookouts, pushed through overgrown trees, and navigated through muddy patches. She wandered onto the side trails, going deeper into the woods before circling back to the main loop.

The app had said the trail was a three-mile loop that should take just over an hour, but she roamed for close to four hours. When she found her way back to the parking lot, hers was still the only car. Her jacket was soaked, but she was toasty warm, thanks to the lining and the workout.

Her legs turned to jelly as soon as she sat in the driver's seat. Her quad muscles throbbed and she knew without a doubt she would wake in the middle of the night with spasms tearing at her calves. She unzipped her jacket, the heat off her body fogging the windshield. She had been working her body so hard, she hadn't noticed the December air chilled as she hiked. Her face was flushed, giving her a ruddy and healthy look. No one would know she was an empty shell.

As she drove home, her whole body came alive. The skin on her face tingled. Her muscles tightened. Her heart pumped a steady rhythm, and her mind was now calm and clear. For the entire duration of the hike, she had thought of nothing but exploring the surrounding forest. As she examined the strange structures of fungus and inhaled the distinct scent of mosses, all her tension unspooled.

As soon as she was back home, she opened the app, planning the next hike and the one after that. Without thinking, she reached for her phone and pulled up Farzi's number from her favorites, about to call her and invite her out for a hike. She caught herself before she tapped on her contact. Kat hadn't just burned that bridge, she'd packed it with dynamite and pressed the detonator.

She hadn't talked to or heard from anyone for nearly a month. She found herself crafting apologies in her head, not just to Millie but to the others as well. She would apologize first for deceiving them, then for being the one who killed Darren. She considered sending an email, but that felt too impersonal. Writing a letter to each of them would be too easy for them to ignore. And while sending a note might lift the burden of guilt for a few days, she knew she would end up feeling anxious waiting for a response that would probably never come.

Would they even come to the table if she invited them out to lunch? She spent one dark and dim mid-December afternoon drafting an apology to read to them over fondue at the Melting Pot. She imagined them sitting down with drinks and talking it out. She would invite them to have their say, to let her know what was on their minds. Kat would keep her mouth shut and her ears open, something she was very good at. But what if they had their say and left, or said nothing at all, or didn't even show up? People were habitual in their actions, but completely unpredictable in their emotions.

There was no good outcome from any approach, and too much time had passed, anyway. They had gone on with their lives and she had to carry on with hers. But she wasn't ready to start all over again. She was just too damned tired to try to meet new people.

Kat spent the rest of December walking alone in the woods. She replaced her push dagger—her weapon of choice and a comfort for her—with a hunting knife, carrying that alongside bear spray. She zigzagged across the state, following the recommendations of her hiking app. She was traveling again, this time only by car, with an overnight bag always at the ready. She hiked in central Oregon to see the spectacular views of the snow-covered Cascades, spending the night in a dingy hotel. The next day, she toured the nearby caves and was caught by surprise when the tour guide pulled out a bottle of prosecco from his backpack and filled little plastic flutes for a New Year's toast. She hadn't even realized it was January 1.

By the end of the month, her mind was calm and her body was strong. She resumed her weekly Wednesday visits to her local coffee shop. Kat got herself a library card and started reading again. She forced her way through the classics, failing to see what made them so popular. She toyed with the idea of learning how to play golf, but after simultaneously pulling a muscle in her shoulder and twisting her ankle at an indoor simulator, she decided it was not the sport for her.

When the weather turned too cold and wet for hiking, Kat went indoors for her exercise, swimming laps at the fitness center.

One afternoon, as she swiped her card at the pool, a voice from behind startled her.

"Katya, is that you?"

Kat turned. A vaguely familiar woman in her late forties was smiling at her.

"It's me, Seren? We met at a yoga class? A couple of years ago?"

"Okay, yes. I remember. Seren. Short for Serendipity."

"See? We were meant to meet. Again. How *are* you? How long have you been coming here? Are you still going to yoga?"

Kat shook her head. "I swim. When did you get that?" Kat pointed to the bottom of her own nose.

"This septum piercing? About eight months ago. It's supposed to help me communicate with the divine and my higher self."

Kat fought the urge to roll her eyes, lifting her lips into a smile. She always thought these piercings made people look as stylish as a cow about to be led to pasture. "Does it work?"

"I'm not sure, but I feel sexier than ever." She winked. "Hey, do you want to grab lunch sometime?"

Kat paused. The last time she saw Seren, she was tempted to push the cotton-headed woman off a cliff. "That would be nice." She smiled.

"Give me your phone," Seren said as they walked together to the changing room. "I'll add my number."

Kat unlocked the screen, then handed over her phone.

"New phone?" Seren asked but continued chattering before Kat could answer. "I never can figure out how to migrate my contacts over either. It should be easy, right? I do it one by one too. It takes me hours. Okay"—she handed back Kat's phone—"now call me so I can save your number."

Without bringing the phone to her ear, Kat pressed the

call button. Seren took the vibrating phone out of the side pocket of her yoga pants.

"Great!" Seren hit the ignore button. "I'll call you later and we'll make a plan."

Kat watched Seren bounce out of the changing room. She opened an empty locker and stared into the blank space. Maybe going out with Seren, who only seemed to see the good in people, was exactly what she needed.

FORTY-FOUR

Kat felt sorely out of place at Plant Soul Café. She sat stiffly in one of two velvet green armchairs, the only seats available when she walked in. Immediately, she became aware of the gap between her age and the rest of the clientele. For the first time in her life, her pale, unmarked skin made her stand out among the tattooed bodies around her. She stared at the varied piercings of the customers sitting at the round tables, wondering how high the pain tolerance needed to be to pierce an eyebrow, tongue, or cheek. She could see into the open kitchen, where two more young people worked, their tattoos snaking out from underneath their aprons, down their arms, and up their necks.

Two hammock chairs hung in front of a whitewashed brick wall. Kat could not imagine how anyone could manage sitting in those while drinking a hot beverage. She squinted to make out the entrées, acutely annoyed that the place seemed designed to make her feel unwelcome.

Just as Kat pulled out her phone to recheck what time she and Seren had agreed to meet, the wind chime above the front door sang its tune.

"Oh, we're both early!" Seren exclaimed, leaning over to

hug Kat. "Do you want to sit here or in the hammocks? It's totally freeing to let your legs dangle while you eat."

Kat raised an eyebrow. "I do not have the coordination required to make that a reasonable choice."

Seren shrugged a single shoulder. "Okay. We can stay here, but we'd still have to use our laps as tables. What are you going to order?"

"I'm not sure. Have you been here before?"

"I'm here at least once a month." She waved to the woman behind the counter. "Hey, Kim."

The woman smiled. "Do you want the usual, Seren?"

"Please." She nodded. She turned to Kat. "Can I order for you? I know all their best dishes."

Kat glanced over the menu. She couldn't identify half the things, and for the others, she had very low expectations. In her limited experience, vegan restaurants were not typically known for culinary prowess.

"Go right ahead," she told Seren.

"Are you allergic to anything?" Seren asked. Kat shook her head.

Kat moved to a table that opened while Seren paid for their lunch. She looked at the food coming out of the kitchen, unsurprised by salads and plates of beet hummus.

"I thought this was a vegan place," Kat said, watching an omelet go by.

"It is," Seren said. "That is a munglet."

"A what?"

"A yellow mung bean omelet. Three times the protein of an egg, you know."

Kat watched as the patron cut into the not-omelet bursting with grilled vegetables and what Kat presumed was vegan meat. It looked deceivingly delicious.

"Would you like to try a sample of our emo rosemary cauliflower soup?" One of the cooks from the kitchen was now standing at the table, holding out a tray of espresso cups filled with a pale liquid.

"Emo?" Seren laughed. "Will it make *me* cry or did it make *you* cry?"

"Both." He grinned. "But seriously"—he leaned closer, lowering his voice to a whisper—"we ran out of *L*s and *N*s for the menu board."

Kat was still trying to figure out what they were talking about as Seren took two cups.

"Cheers," Seren said, raising her sample.

Kat sniffed the soup before taking a small sip. She tasted the rosemary, then the cauliflower, then citrus. "Yeah, I know, wow," Seren said.

"Oh!" Kat cried. "Lemon! Without the *L* and *N*, I get it now."

Seren laughed, a loud and shrill burst that made Kat recoil. Other patrons turned to look, perplexed, as Kat was, as to how such a large noise could come from such a small woman.

"I always knew you would make me laugh," Seren said.

"How did you know that?"

"My intuition is always spot-on. I learned how to open my third eye and expand my clairvoyance. When we first met, my higher consciousness told me we would meet again when the time was right for both of us."

Kat didn't even try to stop herself from rolling her eyes. "I don't believe in any of that."

"I knew you would say that. You'll come around. Haven't you ever had something happen that you can't explain? Like you're thinking about how it would be nice to have a vegan restaurant in the neighborhood and then, boom"—she held up her arms, palms out—"one hangs their sign."

"You noticed it because you were looking for it. That's how our brains are wired. If you think you haven't seen many yellow cars on the highway, that's all you'll start seeing."

"Exactly!" Seren exclaimed. "Because you've opened your third eye. Your subconscious does all the work and allows you to get to a higher level of perception and intuition."

As Seren chatted on enthusiastically about vinyasa yoga, Kat tried to visualize spending time with her, but she was too pragmatic to be friends with someone whose feet were not firmly planted on the ground. They would never see eye to eye on anything important. But maybe that was okay and a good place to start building a friendship? Perhaps she had been too harsh in her judgment when she first met Seren. Friendship requires you to overlook and embrace the things that are different about your friends, that much she had figured out.

The arrival of their lunch spared Kat from having to argue about how unreliable intuition could be. Seren had ordered a falafel salad for herself and what looked like a burger for Kat.

"What is this?" Kat asked as the cook put the plate in front of her.

"Our black bean and mushroom burger, topped with our homemade garlic sauce, lettuce, tomato, and mung bean shoots. The bun is our own vegan bread recipe. Enjoy!"

Kat examined the sandwich, raising an eyebrow. "They sure do work hard to make it look like real meat."

"Trust me," Seren said, stirring up her salad, "that is a life-changing not-burger. You'll never want to eat a real one ever again."

"Doubtful." Kat frowned.

"So?" Seren prompted as Kat took her first bite.

Kat had to admit, the vegan patty was very tasty.

"It's good," she said. "Not dry like most veggie burgers. But it's not meat and my brain knows it."

"Then retrain your brain."

"I don't think it's that simple."

"Sure it is." Seren stabbed at her salad. "You just have to change your mindset and be open to new experiences."

A bitterness brewed inside Kat's chest, causing her to gnash her teeth. It was being open that resulted in her sitting in a café with a woman twenty years younger than her in an attempt to not be alone. Being open made her vulnerable and weak. She opened her home and her heart and ended up miserable and lonely, just as she was before.

They finished their lunch, Seren chatting endlessly about chakras, crystals, and energy healing. Kat let her prattle on, too tired to point out that passing your hands over someone's sternum could not relieve them of anything other than money.

"Why don't you come to my studio for a Reiki session?" Seren offered. "I can feel the heaviness coming off you, particularly in your feet. It's like you're stuck in mud or concrete and unable to move. Can I release that for you?"

Kat smiled politely. "Thank you, but no. I'm not ready for that yet. I'm not a big believer in spiritual healing."

"Spirituality is an act of faith. You have to believe in something you cannot see, and I know that's hard for a lot of people. I have never seen my heart, but I know I have one. I'm alive. I feel it thumping in my chest. I trust my third eye to keep my intuition sharp in the same way I trust my heart to show me love."

Kat gazed at Seren, wondering if it was worth her time to explain how intuition was flawed. Measured and calculated knowledge was the only way to be sure of anything. She would never let a *feeling* govern her choices again. Her job had required precision and attention to detail. Every move had been planned carefully so she could execute a kill with precision and accuracy. Look what happened when she let that slide. *To be disillusioned is a gift.*

"Do you meditate or spend time in nature?"

Kat felt a stab of regret. "I hike as much as I can."

"Why?"

"I like being outdoors. I like the smells, the sounds of my boots crunching ground. I can lose myself in the woods."

"So you feel like you separate from your normal self? If hiking brings you to a higher plane, then you are already spiritually healing."

"I never thought of it that way."

Seren smiled. "See? You have taken the first step to enlightenment."

Kat looked around. This place, this woman, and this food were so foreign to her. How did a friendless, cold-blooded assassin find herself in an incense-infused café eating mung bean shoots and talking about spirituality? Farzi would be peeing her pants laughing. Millie would be praising Jesus for the salads. Annalise would be swinging salaciously in one of the hammocks. Kat realized she wasn't in the wrong place, she was just with the wrong person.

"Seren, thanks for inviting me to lunch," she said, throwing her napkin over her plate. "You *have* opened my eyes. I know what I need to do."

FORTY-FIVE

Kat decided to leave her car in the parking lot and walk the three miles back home. Not only would the movement of her legs feel good, she would also have time to think. She needed to figure out how to win her friends back.

The sky above her was a typical February gray, threatening rain at any moment. Over the next hour she came up with, then discarded, idea after idea. By the time she got home, her body and brain were both invigorated. Her blood was pumping, her leg muscles were awake, and her face tingled from the cold. She made herself a cup of green tea, sitting down at her kitchen table to map out her scheme. She would do what came naturally to her. She would surveil and plan the perfect moment of contact, just like she did with a mark.

On Monday morning, Kat sat in her car in the darkness before dawn, watching the fronts of both Annalise's and Millie's houses. She parked away from the lamps, on the street running perpendicular to the cul-de-sac. A familiar thrill ran through her veins: the first day on a new job. Typically, she only had the basic details about a mark, such as names, where they worked, where they lived, marital and family status. The rest was up to her to discover. She decided to start with Annalise.

Even though she'd known Annalise for almost a year, Kat didn't know if her friend went to her office every day or even every morning. She would sit and wait, then follow Annalise. Kat took a few deep breaths to calm the nausea building in her stomach. Stationary surveillance was simple, but this time she was watching a friend, and that felt wrong. She thought about aborting her mission and finding another way but came up empty.

She sat in her car for two hours before there was any movement on the cul-de-sac. A man and two teenagers emerged from the house at the U end. The man wheeled two duffel bags to the back hatch of his SUV; the teens shuffled to the car with backpacks and hockey sticks. This family was off to early-morning practice.

Another fifteen minutes passed with little activity. It was barely past seven o'clock in the morning. The sky was dark blue, dense with clouds. The sun was starting to rise, painting a thin blush line at the horizon. Kat saw lights coming on inside three other homes, including Annalise's. Moments later, Annalise's garage door began to rise. Kat paid little attention to the sporty Audi backing out. She was looking at her friend, perched on the stairs leading from the house into the garage, waving and blowing a kiss to her husband. Kat rubbed the left side of her chest, trying to soothe the pain that flared there.

Annalise was smiling, but even from where she sat, in the dark of her car, Kat could see this was not a smile that reached her eyes. Despite the foundation, Annalise looked tired and worn. Annalise watched her husband leave and then Kat caught it. It was only the briefest flicker, a quick look across the cul-de-sac at Millie's house. But Kat saw the sadness and loss and longing. No matter how much makeup one wears, or how wide the smile, grief plants itself in your whole being. Annalise's shoulders rounded and she sighed before pushing the button to close the door to the garage. Something had happened to her friends over the last few months.

Kat sank back into her seat, still massaging her chest. She looked over her shoulder at Millie's dark house. The BMW was not in the driveway. Perhaps Millie had moved it into the garage to protect it from the dusting of snow that fell overnight. Kat scanned the front, wondering if Millie had moved. She looked for the usual signs of a lifeless house: an overflowing mailbox, burnt-out exterior lights, flyers and newspapers piled at the front door. Movement at the side of the garage caught her eye. A raccoon climbed out of the green compost bin, a wrinkled apple core in its jaws.

She's there and at least she is eating.

The sun was now up, warming the inside of the car, but not easing the chill. Her nose and fingers were cold, and the damp was working into her bones. Kat sat and waited for another hour for Annalise to emerge. The garage door opened, and Annalise, in her Cadillac SUV, backed out and drove off. Coasting with the morning traffic, Kat followed Annalise to her flagship store, the biggest Blink on the coast. Kat parked across the street, watching as her friend drove into the parking lot, then walked into the storefront. Annalise had a brief conversation before disappearing into an elevator at the back of the salon. She could see the second floor through the glass front, but Annalise never emerged.

After waiting twenty minutes, Kat decided to make a move. But when she went to get out of her car, her right hamstring cramped and her back seized. She had been sitting behind the wheel for almost four hours. Her body was no longer used to this kind of surveillance. Blowing a breath through her lips, Kat pivoted in the front seat, wincing through the pain. Her left ankle gave out when her foot hit the street, and she smacked her elbow on the window as she tried to catch herself.

"For fuck's sake …" She waited a moment, then grabbed the edge of the door frame, using it as leverage to pull her body out of the car. Her hands on the back of her hips, she hobbled to the sidewalk, using the hood as support.

"Ma'am, are you okay?" A young man stopped in front of her, his arms extended in an offer of support.

"I'm fine." Kat waved him off.

"Are you sure? You look a little … unstable."

It's like the young man saying the words made it so. She felt a wobble in her knees. She looked down at the curb, which now looked unmanageable. In the split second before she decided to reach out, she envisioned herself tripping on the curb's lip and breaking her hip.

"Thank you," she said, allowing him to support her elbow and walk her to the safety and flatness of the sidewalk. "I must be more tired than I thought."

"I get it." He smiled. "My great-grandma has trouble sometimes too."

"I'm fine," she muttered, more to herself than the young man. She straightened her back, walking toward the cross-walk, holding herself as erect as she could. She could feel the young man's eyes watching.

"Let me help," he said, appearing by her side.

"I swear to god"—she scowled—"if you've come to help me cross the street like I'm an ancient, I will push you into oncoming traffic."

He retreated, putting his arms in the air.

The interior of Blink was more than Kat expected. While not the first store Annalise had opened, this salon was the largest in the chain. Annalise told them this was lucky store number seven and she'd signed a lease so good, she took over all three floors of the commercial building for Blink's head office.

Kat could see Annalise's glamorous touches everywhere. The wall just to the right of the front door was home to a floor-to-ceiling painting of Audrey Hepburn in *Breakfast at Tiffany's*. Behind the reception desk, scripted letters spelled out *Hello, Gorgeous*. Flat massage beds lined both sides of the space, separated by screens covered in three-dimensional silk flowers. Chandeliers hung from the ceiling, delicate and feminine, not garish and exaggerated. An elegant black metal staircase divided the space in two and led to the second floor. Kat smiled as she read the words printed on the front of the stairs, one word per step:

A

GOOD

SET

OF

LASHES

CAN

FIX

ANYTHING

...

EXCEPT

A

MUGSHOT.

On the final step, the quote was attributed to Tinsley Mortimer. Kat had no idea who that was, but knowing Annalise, she guessed it was some socialite or fashion icon.

"How can I help you?" a voice said to her left, startling her.

A woman with multicolored locs and impossibly long lashes smiled at Kat. "Do you have an appointment?"

"No," Kat answered, still sweeping her eyes over the salon.

"Would you like to make one?"

"No." Kat's eyes found familiar dark globes mounted on the ceiling. She tilted her head and frowned. She had been so distracted by all the luxury and Annalise's touches that she had failed to notice the cameras.

"Would you like a tour?"

"No."

The receptionist seemed unbothered by Kat's one-word answers. "Do you need a brochure? For services? For franchise information?"

"Yes, franchise. Thank you."

"Sure. I'll be right back."

Kat watched her walk to the elevator, taking long strides in her high heels. She smiled at Kat just before the doors closed.

Kat's analytical brain kicked in. She knew the likelihood of anyone actually watching the cameras was probably nil, unless there was a reason to check. The receptionist was likely heading to the offices to gather a franchise package. And that would alert Annalise who, without question, would check the cameras to see who was asking.

What the hell was she thinking coming here?

This wasn't a typical job where she was a random stranger. Kat was not prepared to see Annalise. She didn't have a script, nor had she planned her next move. Kat had made a sloppy and careless mistake. She glanced at the camera, then strode out of the salon, crossing the street to get back to her car. She started it up, screeching away from the curb and around the corner, out of sight.

She pulled into a parking lot, turning off the ignition. Kat loosened her grip on the steering wheel and took a few deep breaths through her nose. Her hands shook and adrenaline flooded her veins. Never in all her years as an assassin had she ever felt fear and panic like this.

"What is wrong with me?" she said out loud.

She closed her eyes, rested her head against the headrest, and focused on calming her body. Once her breath and her hands steadied, she was able to think clearly again. Planning the assassination of a high-level political figure was nothing compared to mending fences with your girlfriends. Her mind worked overtime as she drove home, trying to find a better way to get her friends back.

She still had no plan when she got to her house. She knew nothing about perpetuating friendship and rebuilding trust. These were not skills in her wheelhouse. Surveillance, subterfuge, deception, and evasion were where she found comfort and could flourish. None of those areas of expertise could serve her now.

Kat made herself a fresh cup of coffee, ignoring the rumbling in her empty stomach. Maybe a hike was what she needed, even though the forecast called for heavy rain at the higher elevations. On her way to the bedroom to change into her hiking gear, the empty wall in the dining room caught her eye. She stopped, examining the blank space for a second before it became crystal clear what she needed to do.

When she emerged from her closet, she was dressed in a fitted cashmere sweater, wide-leg dress pants, and heeled boots. She stood in front of the full-length mirror in her bedroom, examining herself from head to toe. She nodded firmly, once. From the top drawer of her highboy dresser, Kat pulled out oversized square-frame sunglasses. The masquerade was complete, and she was ready for the job ahead.

FORTY-SIX

The front window of the Water Street Gallery was a spectacular display of creativity. In the narrow space, an oversized golden birdcage stuffed with moss stood next to a striped settee. The serene scene was framed by plants and ivy draped from the ceiling. Behind the settee, a blue wall was home to a series of small floral paintings of different sizes and shapes. Kat stood in front of the window, taking in the chaos that somehow managed to be beautiful. She didn't know where to look and at the same time just wanted to get lost in the display.

She strode into the gallery like she owned the place: head up, examining the artwork. A bald man in a mock turtleneck sweater was moving a series of pedestals, grouping them together. He paused to acknowledge Kat when she walked in. He looked her over and made a decision about who she might be.

"Good afternoon." He smiled. "What brought you in here today?"

Kat barely glanced at him. "The art, obviously. Oh, and the gorgeous window display."

"I'm glad it caught your eye. Were you interested in any of those pieces?"

Kat shook her head. "Not really. I need something bigger."

Again, he swept his eyes over her, lingering for a moment on the Hermès Birkin hanging off her forearm.

"Let me get someone to help you. Koyo," he called over his shoulder.

A woman with silver hair woven into long braids emerged from the doorway at the back of the gallery, carrying a canvas almost as high as she was tall.

"I'll be right with you," she said. "Omari, can you please help me mount this?"

The man rushed over, pulling on white gloves he pulled out of his trousers pocket. He took hold of the bottom of the frame and the two of them lifted the painting onto barely visible hooks on the white wall.

"Welcome to my gallery." The woman smiled. "My name is Koyo. How can I help you today?"

Behind her sunglasses, Kat examined the woman. Her lips were painted a rich plum, perfectly complementing her dark skin. She spoke with a musical accent, a combination of British English with Arabic notes. *South Sudan, most likely,* Kat thought. Koyo dressed fashionably and functionally in a belted white shirt that reached her thighs, worn over black leather pants. *No, not leather,* Kat thought, *vegan leather. Likely polyurethane.*

"I'm looking for a painting for my dining room." Kat pulled off her sunglasses and looked around the gallery.

"Wonderful! Do you need to choose by size or color or theme?"

"By size, I think. The wall is white and the dining room table is a natural walnut."

"Oh, that's perfect." The woman brought her hands up in front of her chest, clapping them quietly. "We can go wild with color. How long and high is the wall?"

Kat looked up to the ceiling to give the illusion that she didn't know the exact dimensions. "I'm not sure about height. Standard, I guess, but I have twelve feet of length."

Koyo smiled widely. "Then we have many options. Please follow me. We are setting up a new exhibit in the front here, but the second salon has a wide assortment that is hung."

Koyo's heels clicked on the concrete floor, but she walked with a light step. The woman had presence, but she didn't overpower the space. She had the perfect disposition for someone accustomed to selling millions of dollars' worth of art: confident, but obsequious.

In the second salon, canvases of all sizes, shapes, and colors were mounted or leaning on the walls. Kat's eyes zeroed in on an abstract landscape. Clusters of rusts and greens crowded the front of the painting, leading the eyes to blues and whites of water in the center. At the farthest focal point, silver and white peaks loomed over the whole scene. Without needing to peer at the signature, Kat knew it was Farzi's work. She had seen that same scene in real life that weekend at the beach house as they walked toward Neahkahnie Mountain.

"Do you have any more like this?" Kat asked, pointing to Farzi's painting.

"Would you like to see more abstract landscapes or more from the artist?"

"Either. Both." Kat chuckled. In order for her plan to work, she needed to play her part perfectly. Art collector, pragmatic, not eclectic, open to persuasion despite having already decided to buy the Neahkahnie abstract.

"Let's start with more abstracts. We have a few artists whom we've recently acquired."

Kat followed Koyo to the back of the gallery. With a quiet grunt, Koyo leaned into the edge of a wall. Kat kept her face impassive as the wall pivoted, creating a passageway and revealing a storeroom slash gallery. Every inch of wall space was covered with paintings. Koyo walked over to a metal flip rack that stretched from floor to ceiling.

"Feel free to browse through these if nothing on the walls catches your interest. I'll be up front with Omari."

Kat examined the paintings on the walls. There were several of Farzi's canvases, but there were more artists than she could count. Kat gazed at a forest landscape, wondering if it was one she had hiked. She locked eyes with a portrait of a very sad woman. She studied a watercolor of the Portland skyline, with Mount Hood dominating in the background. Kat roamed the space, counting time in her head, walking back to the front of the gallery after thirty-one minutes.

"I will stick with my first instinct. I'd like that abstract." Kat pointed to Farzi's painting with her chin. "There is one condition, though. I'd like the artist to deliver the painting."

Koyo forced a smile. "That's an unusual request. May I ask why?"

"Two reasons. I don't trust delivery people, and I'd like to meet the creator."

"I can assure you, our delivery service is diligent and careful. We've been using them for decades and never had a single issue."

Kat shrugged. "It's a trust issue for me. I had a very unfortunate—and expensive—experience with an art shipper. I was assured by them, too, that they provided the highest level of service."

Koyo clasped her hands just below her belt. *She is faltering,* Kat thought, *but trying to stay confident.* "I'm not even sure I could convince the artist to deliver this herself."

"Does she want to sell her painting?" Kat sniffed. Her pulse picked up speed. She was enjoying the power play. God, how she had missed this.

"Surely she understands how this works. And I'm confident you don't want to lose your commission." Kat gestured around the space. "It's nice knowing your rent is covered for the year. And I have many blank walls." Koyo took a short breath and adjusted the belt at her waist. "I'd like to close this sale today."

"Yes, of course. There's a coffee shop a few doors down where you can wait while I sort everything out."

Kat tilted her head. "There's also another gallery down the street. If you let me walk out that door, there's a good chance I won't come back."

"Please allow me to get you a coffee." Omari stepped in. "Or some champagne, if you prefer, while Koyo contacts Ms. Noor."

Kat sighed loudly, knowing both Koyo and Omari would read this as bored exasperation and do whatever they could to keep her happy. A satisfied customer is a repeat customer.

"I would like a cappuccino, if you don't mind." Kat considered requesting one from a café across town, just for the fun of it, but keeping things tight and brief was always preferable. Omari nodded, taking his coat off a hook near the front door.

"Actually," Kat said, "I've changed my mind. I'd like a decaf flat white. And two pistachio macarons, if they have them."

"And if not?" Omari asked.

Kat tilted her head and paused, savoring the power. "A salted caramel tart will do. If they don't have either of those things, then just the coffee, please."

"My pleasure," Omari said as he walked out.

Koyo looked up from her phone. "Can I fill you in on the artist while we wait for her to reply?"

Kat listened as Koyo gushed about Farzi. "I could feel the magic in her work," Koyo said. "From the minute I saw my first Noor piece, I knew I had to build an exhibit."

Kat paid attention, enjoying the narrative inconsistencies between the story Koyo had constructed to sell art and what Farzi had shared over the past year.

Omari returned with three coffees, and they sipped and chatted about art. When Koyo's phone rang and she retreated to her office holding it to her ear, Kat knew Farzi was at the other end. She didn't have to hear the conversation to know Farzi would be reluctant and hesitant. She would ask questions, but in the end, she would fully trust Koyo's instincts about this new collector with the odd demands. Koyo would promise to send Omari to accompany her, remind her there was real potential for multiple sales, that it increases her value as an artist when collectors can meet her, see her, smell her, and shake the very hand that creates. For a serious art collector, that handshake is like shaking god's hand.

Koyo returned, a smile spread across her face. "When would be a good time to deliver?"

FORTY-SEVEN

"You are a sneaky bitch."

Farzi stood on the front stoop of Kat's home, the lines on her forehead framed by the fabric of her hijab.

"I saw the address, but the name on the invoice threw me off. I thought maybe you moved or I remembered your address wrong. But you knew that would happen, didn't you?"

Kat didn't answer. When she had planned this, she hadn't anticipated Farzi being so hostile.

"You're wearing hijab again?"

Farzi ignored the question. "We're ready to bring the painting in. I'll shake your hand and smile nicely so Omari can report back to Koyo that I fulfilled my duty."

Kat stepped back, opening the door wider. Omari waved from the back of the cube van, its doors spread open. Farzi joined him, climbing inside the cargo space.

Kat stood in silence, watching the two of them carefully lift the bubble-wrapped painting out. Omari carried the front end and Farzi supported the back, walking slowly to the house.

"Hello, Ms. Crane. It's nice to see you again." Omari smiled. "Where would you like this?"

"In the dining room, please."

"Would you like us to hang it as well?"

"That would be very helpful." His extended presence would give her time to figure out what was going through Farzi's mind.

Omari went back to the van to get the tools he needed. Farzi stood with the framed painting leaning against her legs. She watched Omari through the window in Kat's living room.

"Please don't be mad," Kat said. "I didn't know how else to talk to you."

"Deception comes naturally to you, I suppose," Farzi spat.

"Yes." Kat looked down at her feet. "But apologies do not. I am truly sorry."

Farzi whipped around to face Kat, the fabric at the back of her hijab fluttering at her shoulders. "For what? For being who you are? For lying to all of us? For tricking me into coming here? For not being genuine? For being a murderer?"

Farzi's anger seemed so fresh, too raw to be just directed at Kat. She saw fury blazing in Farzi's golden-brown eyes.

"Not murder, assassination."

"There's no difference," Farzi snapped.

"Not to the person who dies, no," Kat admitted. "But one is business, while the other is chaos."

"How do you sleep at night, knowing you've taken so many lives?"

Kat crossed her arms. "I sleep just fine. I will not apologize for doing my job, and doing it well. I never took a job that wasn't warranted. They were all monsters."

Farzi snorted. "That's a convenient way to justify it."

"Why are you wearing hijab again, Farzi? What are you hiding from?"

Omari knocked on the open door. "Is it okay to come in?"

Kat nodded. She left Farzi and Omari in the dining room and went into the kitchen to put on the kettle. "Would anyone like coffee or tea? Water?" she called out.

"A tea would be lovely," Omari answered. Kat heard Farzi huff and she smiled to herself. Omari was the perfect buffer. Farzi had to stay to keep Koyo happy.

The painting was hung by the time the tea was ready. Kat carried a tray with mugs, the teapot, milk, and sugar into the dining room. She pulled an additional chair to the long side so they could all sit and examine the painting.

"It's perfect," Kat said. "You are very talented, Ms. Noor."

"Thank you," Farzi muttered, not touching the tea Kat had placed in front of her.

"Why don't you share the inspiration for this work?" Omari urged.

Kat took a sip of tea to hide her grin. She wasn't sure if Omari was genuinely oblivious to the tension or if he had been instructed to do what was necessary to build a relationship with a potential long-term collector.

"Yes." Kat nodded. "I'd like to know what was meaningful for you about this landscape."

Farzi's jaw clenched. She looked up at the painting, taking a few shallow breaths before she answered. "Coming from landlocked Kabul, I've always been fascinated by oceans and mountains that aren't dusty brown most of the year."

"I see," Kat said, "but we all know art is an essence, not just an admiration for topography."

"Wow," Omari exclaimed. "Ms. Crane, you truly appreciate not just the art, but the intention. I'm curious now too, Farzana."

Farzi was close up to the painting now, inspecting every nook and cranny. She lifted her hand, fluttering her fingers over the oil as if brushing off dust only she could see. She sighed, turning to face Kat.

"This place is special for me." She met Kat's eyes, the gold in her irises glowing. "The light was beautifully shrouded in the fog while still keeping things bright. The edges dividing the mountain from the ocean are always blurred to the naked eye, even on the clearest days. You never know if you are seeing the truth of nature or a trick of deception. That's what I wanted to capture in the abstract. I wanted to blur the sharpness of the angles, soften the rawness and power."

Omari brought a hand to his chest. "This is why I love working with artists. The spirit of creativity runs deep."

"It sounds like you are maybe masking some pain," Kat said.

Farzi turned back to the painting, her shoulders tense. "Painting *is* a release for me. When I am done, I feel relief, but I am also deeply connected to the canvas. What was it about this painting that spoke to *you*, Ms. Crane?" Farzi tilted her head, a slight smile playing on her lips.

Kat rose, pushing away from the dining room table. She walked to where Farzi stood, coming up beside her. "It's comforting for me. I can see it's a mountain, but it's not one hundred percent clear. I can still interpret it how I want. I can see the cragged peaks if I want to, but I can also feel the soothing curves of the ocean. Your painting reminds me that landscapes change, but it can take a long time to see the difference."

Kat turned her head to look at Farzi. Her friend was nodding and fluttering her fingers on her lips. Kat hoped she understood she was trying to say she wanted Farzi back in her life.

"Can I offer you some bread and dip? In my culture, it's customary to serve obi non and suzma when you invite new people into your home."

"I have to get back to the gallery," Omari said. "Farzana, if you'd like to stay, I can send an Uber to come pick you up when you are ready."

When Farzi locked eyes with her, Kat no longer saw anger

there. Something released in Kat's chest, a knot of anticipation and fear finally loosening.

"No need, Omari," Farzi said, and Kat could feel her insides coiling up again. "I can walk home from here." Farzi extended her hand to grasp Kat's. "It's a pleasure to meet you, Ms. Crane. I'd very much like to break bread with you."

FORTY-EIGHT

K at blinked away the tears that threatened to fall, grateful that Omari thought her emotional reaction was triggered by the art and not the artist. Once he had gone, Kat went to the kitchen, returning to the dining room with the bread she had baked the night before, the dip she had spent two days making, and a tray of assorted olives. Kat popped a green olive into her mouth as she passed the loaf across the table to Farzi.

"You could have called," Farzi said, crossing her arms in front of her chest.

"I thought you might hang up on me. I thought I would wait a while ... and then too much time passed."

"And you felt it would have been weird, so you concocted this crazy scheme instead?" She gestured with her chin to the painting. "You didn't have to spend so much money to get me here."

Kat shrugged. "I genuinely like the painting, Farzi. Even ... before ... I had planned on paying you for a painting to fill that space."

"Thank you, then." Farzi let her eyes drop to the obi non but kept her arms in front of her chest.

"Oh, for fuck's sake." Kat sighed. She leaned forward and tore off a hunk of bread. "Just eat some. I promise it's fine. I'm not trying to kill you." Kat held the piece out to Farzi.

Farzi met her eyes for a moment before yanking the bread from Kat's hand. She dragged the bread through the yogurt dip, closing her eyes after she took a bite. "This is so much better than the store-bought stuff," she moaned. "But that doesn't mean I've forgiven you yet."

"Farzi, I wish I could go back and change things, but I needed time to figure out how to tell you all what I had done. It's not something you bring up in casual conversation."

Farzi nodded, swallowed a sip of tea, and took her time choosing an olive. Kat waited, not knowing what to do or say.

"So, how have you been?" Farzi finally asked.

"I'm okay. I've taken up hiking. I'm catching up on reading. I go to the coffee shop every Wednesday." Her face reddened. Hearing her life as a list of routine checkboxes was embarrassing.

"Sounds nice," Farzi said. "Maybe I can go hiking with you sometime."

"I'd like that. More tea?" Kat asked. Farzi nodded. "I miss you," Kat blurted out as she poured. "I miss all of you."

Farzi stroked the scarf of her hijab at her neck. "I miss you too. I never felt good about not talking to you. I tried, Kat, I really tried to bring us all back together. Millie was inconsolable, as I'm sure you can understand."

Kat leaned back into her chair, hugging her mug of tea to her chest. "I do," she muttered. "I regret saying anything, but I don't at the same time. It was killing me inside."

Farzi nodded as she dipped another piece of obi non into the suzma. The fragrant dill filled the space between them at the table.

"How is Millie doing now?" Kat asked.

"I have no idea." Farzi shrugged.

Kat swept her eyes over Farzi's torso and then sat up so

fast, she nearly dropped her tea. How did she miss the rounded shoulders, the distant gaze, and the lilt missing from her voice?

"What happened between all of you?" she asked.

Farzi pulled her hand back from the dish of olives. "What makes you say that?"

"Your sadness is written on every part of you, Farzi. Your accent is harsher. And you are wearing hijab again. So you either met a new man and are reclaiming your Muslimhood, or you are trying to shield your grief with a head covering."

Farzi dropped her head even lower and covered her face with her hands. Kat waited patiently for her friend to speak.

"Something changed in Millie after you left. She cried every time we got together. She hardly said anything about anything and was particularly explosive when Annalise and I tried to talk about you. She barely laughed or smiled. Then she stopped coming out. Ignored our texts and calls. We managed to lure her out for dinner to celebrate Annalise's fifty-third birthday, and that's when things went … really bad."

Farzi plucked a napkin from the holder, wiping the tears from her face. She unwrapped her scarf from her neck, then pushed the hijab back off her head.

"Millie was back to her judgy, not-drinking ways," Farzi started, "but Annalise and I thought she was still in shock. She barely said a word and was so removed from the conversation. Annalise asked her so many times if she was okay. Millie just kept saying 'I'm fine.' I was the one who snapped."

Kat widened her eyes. "What happened?"

"I told her off. I said if she didn't want to be there, she shouldn't have come. She was ruining what was supposed to be a celebration of our friend. Annalise said it was okay, that she was happy to be out with her friends, but it pissed me off."

"Did Millie come around?"

Farzi ran her fingers through her auburn hair, shaking it

loose. It spilled over her shoulders. "No. She *exploded*. She went on a rant about how she should never have left the church, how we were basically the devil in disguise. She called Annalise an attention-hungry tramp who was fake from head to toe."

"Shit. What did Annalise say?"

"Nothing. She didn't have a chance, because Millie turned on me. Said I was an adulterous abomination who should have stayed in my country and been stoned to death."

Kat gasped. "Holy fuck, Farzi. Was she having a mental breakdown?"

"I don't know. Even if she was, I think this is truly how she feels. She even took a few shots at you."

Kat put down the piece of bread she had just ripped off the loaf. "Tell me."

"She said you made the choice to not be a decent human being, that it made her sick to her stomach that she … are you sure you want to hear this?"

"Farzi, you know who I am. I'm not fragile. They are just words."

"She said she was for sure going to hell for welcoming a killer into her life. According to Millie, you are a demon who is incapable of compassion." Farzi looked down at her lap. "I'm sorry to be the one to tell you this."

Kat chewed the flesh off another olive and rolled the olive pit around in her mouth, letting it clack against her teeth. This was not the Millie she knew. Her friend was quiet in her admonishments. Her faith was shattered, true, but Millie was kind to the core. She lashed out in less hurtful ways, crossing the cul-de-sac to make a new friend as an act of spite. She didn't throw stones or toss insults or rage. This had to be something else.

Kat tucked the olive pit into her cheek. "She's deflecting," she said. "I'd bet my life that something else is going on. Is she seeing anyone? Someone who might be abusive?"

"I don't know." Farzi shrugged. "I have never seen her so … so … enraged."

Kat brought a napkin to her mouth to catch the pit. "What does Annalise think?"

"That Millie feels betrayed for a second time and she's chosen to cut everyone out of her life. Annalise knocked on her door, sent flowers … nothing worked." Farzi tore off a hunk of obi non. "Maybe we should talk to Annalise. Figure out a way to reach out to Millie together."

Kat shook her head. "The three of us approaching Millie will seem like an attack. She'll feel cornered."

"Good point. So, what do we do?"

Kat looked at the painting now dominating her dining room wall. "I have an idea."

FORTY-NINE

Once again, Kat sat in her car at the cross street of Annalise and Millie's cul-de-sac. She had been watching and following Millie for four days. The woman was getting a lot of deliveries—groceries and takeout. Judging by the fast-food chain paper bags dropped on the doorstep, Millie was comfort eating. The grocery delivery bins filled with bagged salads, a few apples, frozen entrées, and potato chips told a sad story of a woman uninterested in cooking or caring.

When Millie left the house on the second day of surveillance, Kat followed. Millie drove the BMW to church—a new one—and Kat slipped in just as Millie went into the confession booth.

Less than ten minutes later, Millie emerged. Kat expected her to kneel in a pew and pray, but the woman rushed out, head down, unaware of Kat hiding in the shadows of the colonnades in the side aisle. Kat listened for the sounds of a car door opening and closing, then slipped out the door just as Millie drove away from the parking lot.

Kat casually walked to her car parked on the opposite side of the church. She could still see Millie a block away, waiting at a stoplight. Kat followed Millie back to the cul-de-sac. Once the BMW was parked in the garage, Millie disappeared into the house.

Kat did not see her again—or any movement inside the house—until the fourth day, when Millie opened the front door to retrieve a food order. At the same time, Annalise emerged from her house and raised her hand to wave. Millie didn't wave back.

As soon as Millie was tucked back in her house, Kat was out of her car. She strode to Annalise's house, fuming at a slight that wasn't even aimed at her. After ringing the doorbell, she looked over her shoulder, checking if Millie was watching. The curtains did not move.

"Took you long enough," Annalise snarked when she opened the front door. "Come in."

Kat followed Annalise through the entryway and took in the space. Just past a set of stairs was the kitchen, an expansive room with dark gray cabinets with brass hardware, white quartz countertops, and pot lights. It was very masculine, a sharp contrast to the feminine touches at the salon.

"This is Matteo's domain," Annalise said. "Big stove, big fridge, big oven … he's the chef here."

"You know what they say about men with big appliances," Kat joked.

Annalise smiled widely. "All true. Can I get you something to drink?"

"A coffee would be great. Annalise, why aren't you and Millie talking?"

Annalise had her back to Kat, fishing in a cupboard for beans and mugs. She shook her head.

"I know Farzi told you what happened. I don't know what's going on with Millie."

"Do you think she can ever forgive me? I mean, not for killing Darren, but for not telling her?"

The coffee maker came to life, whirring the beans into grinds. "Maybe? Not likely? I don't know. She's cut us all off."

"I don't know how to navigate this, Annalise."

"I know. Maybe if you had led a *normal* life, you'd know how to kiss and make up with your friends. Then again, we wouldn't be having this conversation."

"I need your help, but I don't know with what, or how ..."

Annalise placed a steaming mug next to Kat, who was leaning against the island. "Need some enhancer?" She held up a bottle of Bailey's.

Kat nodded. "Just a splash."

Annalise poured a heavy shot. "Would you be okay leaving it to me to approach her? I think Millie'd be more open to talking to me than you."

"Farzi said you tried, but Millie won't talk to you either. I mean, she didn't even acknowledge you when you waved."

Annalise paused with her mug at her lips. "Excuse me? Have you been *watching* us?"

Kat felt heat in her cheeks. "Well, uh, um ... yes. It's what I do. I'm sorry? I guess that's not going to help the situation ... But, look, I have a certain skill set—it's where I'm comfortable."

"Why didn't you just knock on Millie's door?"

"I don't like confrontation."

Annalise turned and leaned over the sink, snorting and sputtering her coffee.

"I fucking missed you." She laughed, wiping her mouth with a pure white linen tea towel. "And by the way, next time you come to my salon, you better say hello. Slinking away like a common criminal is beneath you."

Kat's face relaxed and her jaw loosened. She wanted to hug Annalise, but amiable skin-on-skin contact still felt weird to her.

Kat nodded once. "Okay. I will trust you know what to do. And Annalise? I missed you too."

FIFTY

"This is not going to work." Farzi stood next to Kat, rubbing her gloved hands together, trying to keep warm.

"Yes it will."

Kat leaned back against the brick wall, immediately feeling the cold through her jacket. It was a welcome sensation, having had a few hot flashes this morning, even at ten years postmenopausal.

"How can you be so confident?"

Kat unzipped her collar, allowing cool air to flood into her parka. "You know what I used to do for a living. I made myself an expert in human nature."

"Human nature is unpredictable, I think."

Kat smiled. "It's not, actually. The unpredictability comes from using the wrong lens to interpret behavior."

"I don't even know what that means."

"It means I can't use the same tactics for everyone."

"You manipulated me to come to your house, but you asked Annalise for help. Am I supposed to feel good about that?"

"Koyo was the one who manipulated you. Annalise offered

to help. You would only agree to direct contact with a buyer if the request came through someone you trust implicitly. Annalise thrives on being a leader because she's accustomed to being valued only for her looks."

"So you played on our strengths and weaknesses."

"No. I see you both for who you are."

Farzi furrowed her brow. "What about Millie?"

"I called and left her a message."

"What did you say?" Farzi burrowed further into her coat to avoid the wind. Kat stepped in front of her, acting as a shield.

"I said I'm not very good at being vulnerable, but I wanted to say that having her in my life changed me for the better. I said I'm not a terrible person, but I would have killed Darren eventually, anyway, for hurting my friend. We all make mistakes, and if nothing else, I want the chance to apologize again for mine. That I may not believe in god, but he blessed me by bringing you all into my life."

"Are you sure she'll come? Maybe she didn't listen to the message."

"She listened. As for showing up, I can only hope." She tipped her chin forward. "Here comes Annalise."

Farzi turned around. Annalise was half walking, half running toward them, her long parka preventing her from fully moving. Her blond hair was tucked into an angora hat. She got to Farzi first, wrapping her arms around her.

"Fuck, it's cold," she moaned into Farzi's hair. "You smell like hope and sunshine, Farzi, and that's warming me up."

Annalise pulled away and took a few steps toward Kat. "I don't give a shit if you're not a hugger, I'm coming in." Annalise pulled Kat's arms apart and threw herself against Kat's chest.

"Oof," Kat huffed. "Take it easy on my girls."

Annalise pulled back and looked at Kat's bosom. "Please, they're not even up there anymore."

Kat raised her eyebrows. Annalise did the same, then waggled them. "I know a good surgeon who can fix that."

"No, thank you. I've just learned how not to pinch them when I roll over in bed."

Annalise pulled her hat down over her ears. Her eyes sparkled. "I can't wait to tell you what I did." Annalise looked up at the awning above the front doors. "What is this place? The Wreck Room? What is that?"

"You'll see." Kat smiled.

They stood on the sidewalk, the three of them bouncing on their toes, holding their arms close to their torsos to keep warm.

"So ... is Millie coming?" Farzi asked.

Annalise nodded. "Yup. One hundred percent. I ordered a package and snuck it over to Millie's stoop in the middle of the night. She had no choice but to cross the cul-de-sac again and bring it over."

"That's a bit of a risk. She could have brought the package over in the middle of the night like you did," Farzi said.

"I know, which is why I did this on Wednesday night. She goes to confession every Tuesday and Thursday morning, so …"

"She'd be feeling clean and wanting to keep doing the right thing," Kat finished. "So clever, Annalise. I'm impressed. How did you figure that out?"

"You're not the only one capable of surveillance." Annalise grinned. "Also, I've been doing some reading about subterfuge and deception. I care about my friends' interests."

"Is this an ambush?" Millie was suddenly standing behind them, her cheeks blistered red from the cold.

Kat answered "yes" at the same time as Annalise blurted out "no".

"So, once again, you're being deceitful. Your voicemail really convinced me that you were interested in being a genuine friend. Once a liar, always a liar, I guess." She pointed her chin at Annalise. "I'm not surprised that you are part of this," she said. "But I had a higher opinion of you, Farzi. Looks like you've all managed to pull the wool over my eyes. Have a nice life, ladies. I'm not interested in whatever this is." Millie tucked her neck deeper into her coat and turned to walk away.

"Millie! Wait!" Kat called after her. Millie strode down the sidewalk, but Kat caught up to her. "Please stop. I want to talk to you."

When Millie didn't slow down, Kat continued pursuing her.

"You can keep running, Millie, but I'll keep chasing you," she said to Millie's back. "You're my friend, one of the first ones I ever had. I'm learning how to be a better friend to you. I need your guidance … I need everyone's help here. We have some things to work out. Please."

When Millie stopped suddenly, Kat almost crashed into her. Her friend whipped around, tears forming in her eyes.

"It must be nice to go through life with zero guilt," Millie spat. "To do as you please. To snuff out a life without considering the impact on that person's family. Was it luck that let you walk away with zero consequences? Or are you just so inhumane and unfeeling?"

Kat stared at Millie, searching for the kind woman she knew. "I had to be," she said. "Not just for the sake of the job, but for the sake of my sanity. I had to learn to not dwell on what I was doing. I walked through every day with the knowledge that it could be my last. You know better than most, Millie, what a struggle it can be to get through another day without dying."

Millie tried to blink away her tears, but they were frozen on her lashes. "I'm so mad at you, Kat," she fumed, her hands fisted. "For what you did and that you lied, and that you never felt any of us would accept who you are. How could you betray me like that when you knew I already suffered that at the hands of people I thought had my back? I don't need you in my life, Kat. I can carry on without any of you."

Kat put her hands into her pockets. "I know I violated your trust. I made a mistake, Millie. I may be a social idiot, but I'm a human being. I want to belong. I want to have something to look forward to. I want us to be friends, and I'll make the amends necessary.

"But you are full of shit if you think you don't need us. It's because of us that you have the confidence to live again. You would never have gone to speed dating without Annalise. You would have skipped the gala without my gown. Farzi gave you the balls to chase the things you want for yourself. It's not just a one-way street, Millie. I've learned from you too. We all have learned from each other. I see that now."

Millie used the back of her glove to wipe at her tears. "Tell me one thing you learned from me," she challenged.

Kat took a short, cold breath in through her nose. She locked eyes with Millie, steeling herself for what she needed and wanted to say.

"You showed me that with the right people around, I can be happy."

Millie's eyes watered again. She breathed in through her nose as she looked up to the sky. Millie brought her gloved hands to her face, covering her eyes and cheeks. Kat waited, wanting to speak, but not knowing what more she could say.

Millie nodded. "Fine."

"Fine?" Kat echoed. "Are you talking to me or ..." She pointed up.

"Both of you, I suppose."

"Will you come back and do this thing with us?"

"Yes, I will. You owe me a drink."

Kat smiled. "I'll buy you the whole damn ... darn bar."

"Thank fucking Christ," Annalise blurted out when she

saw Kat and Millie approaching. "Oops, sorry, Millie. It slipped out. Can we go inside now?"

Millie chuckled. "Once a heathen, always a heathen, I guess."

"Come. Let's go in." Kat held open the door, filing in after her friends.

FIFTY-ONE

Kat stumbled on the Wreck Room months ago the same way she'd found speed dating—a brightly colored poster on the grocery store community board.

Feeling angry? Unleash. De-stress. Break shit.

She visited the website on the poster and read the news story about the therapeutic benefits of smashing light bulbs, computer screens, printers, and ceramics. She'd been about to send the link to Annalise, Millie, and Farzi, momentarily forgetting they had parted ways.

Now they hovered at the front desk, together, listening to the instructions. Kat dug around in her purse, fishing for the reading glasses she'd finally relented to wearing.

"Those are new," Millie said. "When did you start wearing glasses?"

"I've needed them for years, but I didn't want to admit it." Kat shrugged a shoulder. "I'm old and I need them to read. It's no big deal."

"They look nice," Farzi said. "Maybe I can craft a chain for you—"

"Absolutely not," Kat interrupted. "That is one step too close to senior citizen for me."

"Not if you treat your glasses like an accessory," Annalise said. "We should go shopping for a bunch of different frames, so you have choices."

Kat shook her head. "I'm not that invested. I only need them to read." She picked up the waiver and fluttered it. "I was too proud to wear glasses, but I am not so stupid to sign something I can't see."

Once they all signed their waivers, they changed into coveralls. Outside their rage room, they put on their chest and neck protectors, covered their faces with safety masks, and donned helmets.

"I feel like I'm on the bomb squad," Annalise said through the plexiglass shield covering her face.

Inside the room, an assortment of items were spread out against the far side. There was a table and some pedestals they could use to bring items up to their height. On their right, propped against the wall, were their weapons: hammers, baseball bats, sledgehammers, and golf clubs.

"We just go," Kat said, picking up a bat. She walked to the far wall and placed a green glass vase on a steel pedestal. She swung the bat, releasing a howl as she made contact. The vase flew off the pedestal, hitting the wall and shattering into shards.

"That was for my father, who condemned me to a loveless life."

Annalise snatched a golf club from the corner, striding purposefully to a glass coffee carafe. She looked back to her friends, a fiendish smile on her lips. "This is for every man who felt entitled to my body." She lifted the club over her head, bringing it down with all her strength onto the glass.

"My turn," Farzi said, holding her hand out for the club. She placed a lamp on the pedestal and pulverized it with an overhead swing. "Screw you, Taliban bastards." The lamp cracked and fell to the floor. Farzi paused, then lifted the gold club over her shoulder, bringing it down over and over again until the ceramic was a pile of dust. She wiped sweat from her brow and turned to her friends. Kat's mouth hung open.

"What?" Farzi said.

"You smashed that lamp like it was a skull."

Farzi nodded once. "To me, it was." She held the club out to Millie, who shook her head.

"It's okay if you're not ready yet," Annalise assured her. "I can go again."

"I'm ready," Millie said, "but I want to use the sledgeham-mer." She dragged the steel-headed tool across the room. With a grunt, she lifted it above her head.

"This is for the shitty music you blared to muffle my screams," she hissed. Millie brought the sledgehammer down on a stereo system, ducking back as the volume dial flew off toward her. The silver knob hit her chest with a muted plunk, then clattered to the floor.

For the next twenty-five minutes, they took turns smashing, cracking, stomping, and throwing, not only objects, but their pain and rage.

"You don't have the right to touch me!" Annalise screamed as she clobbered a cookie jar.

"I never wanted to get married in the first place!" Farzi yelled before cracking a mirror.

"Screw you for making me feel unworthy when it was you all along," hissed Millie, throwing plates at the wall.

"Why were my dreams unimportant?" grunted Kat, smashing in the door of a microwave.

They stopped with five minutes left in their session. They leaned against the walls, all of them panting and sweating. Shards of glass and ceramic were stuck to the fibers of their protective suits. Debris speckled the strands of their hair poking out from their helmets. Dust and splintered wood coated their hiking boots.

"We look like we've dipped ourselves in glitter." Annalise laughed. "Come from a raging rave."

"That felt so good," Farzi said, smiling behind her scratched face shield.

"I think that was good for us, yes," Kat stated.

Millie took the baseball bat from Kat's hands and started beating up a printer she had lifted to the table. They watched her, silently, as she swung over her head, and then from left to right.

"I'm a sinner. I'm garbage. I'm a terrible person," she screamed.

"Millie!" Annalise called out. "You are none of those things!"

Millie whipped around, pointing the bat at Kat. "I'm as bad as you," she hissed, then turned to smash the printer some more. "I may not have pulled the trigger, but I put in the order." She lunged forward, throwing all her body weight behind the bat. The remains of the printer blew apart. Millie watched as an ink cartridge hit the wall, leaving a magenta splat.

"Millie, what did you just say?" Kat kept her voice low and steady.

Millie sighed, her whole body going slack. She kept her back to her friends.

"I made the call, Kat," she said flatly. "I'm the one who hired you to kill Darren."

Farzi pushed up her face guard. Annalise sucked in her breath. Millie took off her helmet and turned to Kat.

"*I'm* the monster. Not only for what I did, but for how I treated you too. I'm a hypocrite. I paid for my husband to die and then shit all over the person who took the job."

Kat could not take her eyes off Millie. The woman was shaking—from exertion, from fear, from guilt—it wasn't clear. Despite her years of watching, assessing, planning, the disguises, the aliases, and the espionage, Kat had not seen this coming. Never in a million years would she have pinged the shuffling housewife as someone who ordered a hit. Now that she knew Millie, Kat could see how strong her friend really was.

Kat glanced over at Farzi and Annalise. They were both still, their eyes locked on the mess at the far wall. Millie was looking at her, her eyes pleading.

"I don't understand …," Farzi mumbled. "Isn't murder a sin?"

Millie shrugged. "Yes, but he needed to die. My church wasn't helping. The police never did anything. So I paid someone. I never imagined I'd ever meet the assassin face-to-face, let alone become friends with her."

"Do you … do you want your money back?" Kat stuttered, keeping her eyes locked on Millie's. *I'd give every penny I have to make this right.*

"Heavens, no," Millie protested. "You were paid for the work I asked you to do. Friends need to support their friends' businesses."

Kat pressed her lips together, but the snort of laughter escaped anyway. Annalise lifted her head and turned. As soon as they locked eyes, Kat was done. She erupted in a fit of giggles, joined by her friends.

Outside the Wreck Room, Millie opened her arms. "Can we just hug it out and get on with life?"

Kat took a few tentative steps forward. Millie met her halfway, pulling Kat into her embrace. Annalise and Farzi closed the circle, squeezing the air out of Kat's lungs.

"Right now, I think we all need a drink," said Farzi.

"I know a place"—Millie grinned—"with the best strawberry shortcake shots."

As they walked two by two, arm in arm down the sidewalk, Kat matched her steps to those of her friends.

ACKNOWLEDGMENTS

Even though writing is a solitary activity, there were many people who had a hand in helping me get this book to the finish line.

My beta readers Corlie Garanito, Joyce Burke, and Lisa May LeBlanc gave me invaluable feedback and a boost when I wasn't sure if this story had any teeth. Thank you for your honesty and friendship.

Thank you, Zoey Duncan. You continue to astound me with your brilliant skill as a developmental editor. I am glad these women were able to give you insight into what lies ahead for you.

New to my book family is Jennifer Sommersby. Not only is Jennifer a sharp copy editor, she is also a fantastic writer. Please read the Planet Lara series she penned as Eliza Gordon. They are truly a delight. Thank you, Jennifer, for your particular pedantry.

Thanks to proofreader Catherine Szabo, who always gets my books ready for the final step.

I owe a debt of gratitude to Lisa Perotta, who had Jeff and I over for dinner and had me laughing so hard I was crying. Lisa is the inspiration for the cannabis basket mix-up. And by inspiration, I mean it really did happen to her. Cowboy on, my friend.

And naturally, the acknowledgements must close with my deepest gratitude to my family. My husband Jeff reads everything I write, multiple times, and never stops telling me to keep going. Every writer should have such a supportive partner. To my eldest son, Mason, who did not hold back when offering his thoughtful and helpful criticism: thanks for being kind and trying very hard not to hurt my feelings. To Westin, my younger son, who read this story and offered very little feedback: it's good enough that you finished reading the book.

Manufactured by Amazon.ca
Bolton, ON

43871352R00189